*"Capricorn. You run the risk
of making a fool of yourself today."*

So begins *America Today's daily horoscope*
for three un

"Be careful aro
of the opposite sex.
pass you by if you d
may bring luck—
many guises and isn't always easy to recognize."

Can investor Derek Palmer
keep the secret of his success from Melissa?
Sceptic Michael Gordon puts little faith
in astrology...until an ice storm
strands him with housemate Keely.
And Sonoma's Spence Reid gets
an unexpected surprise with the appearance
of former ugly duckling Francesca!

Find out what happens
to these three Capricorn heroes when it's

WRITTEN
IN THE
STARS

by three of your favorite Harlequin authors

Judith Arnold
Kate Hoffmann
Gina Wilkins

Plus a bonus *astrological love guide*
follows these stories to help you chart
your own course for romance in 2002!

Judith Arnold is the bestselling author of more than sixty-five romance novels, and has fans worldwide. A winner of numerous awards, including *Romantic Times Magazine's* Best Series Romance Novel of the Year, Judith makes her home in Massachusetts with her husband and two sons. Juggling a full-time writing career with motherhood is challenging but rewarding. Judith's husband has always been an active father. While the three men are at the theater watching alien invasions, she's at her computer, working on love and happy endings in her latest book.

Kate Hoffmann began reading romances in 1979 when she picked up a copy of Kathleen Woodiwiss's *Ashes in the Wind*. It inspired her to try her hand at her own historical romance. But when she gave that up to write a short, humorous contemporary novel, she found her métier. She finished the manuscript in four months, placed first in the 1993 national Harlequin Temptation contest and quickly found a happy home with the line. This talented award winner has gone on to write over twenty more novels. A former teacher, Kate has also worked in retailing and advertising. She now devotes herself to writing full-time and resides in Wisconsin.

Gina Wilkins is the proud author of more than fifty books for Harlequin and Silhouette Books. She is a three-time recipient of the Maggie Award for Excellence, sponsored by the Georgia Romance Writers, has won several *Romantic Times* awards, and frequently appears on Waldenbooks, B. Dalton and *USA Today* bestseller lists. Gina particularly enjoys speaking at schools, where she emphasizes literacy, goal-setting and motivation. A lifelong resident of central Arkansas, she credits her successful career in romance to her long, happy marriage and her three "extraordinary" children.

JUDITH ARNOLD
KATE HOFFMANN
GINA WILKINS

WRITTEN
IN THE
STARS

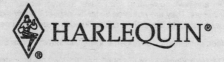
HARLEQUIN®

TORONTO • NEW YORK • LONDON
AMSTERDAM • PARIS • SYDNEY • HAMBURG
STOCKHOLM • ATHENS • TOKYO • MILAN • MADRID
PRAGUE • WARSAW • BUDAPEST • AUCKLAND

Special thanks and acknowledgment are given to Susan Kelly for her contribution to WRITTEN IN THE STARS

ISBN 0-373-83476-4

WRITTEN IN THE STARS

Copyright © 2001 by Harlequin Books S.A.

The publisher acknowledges the copyright holders of the individual works as follows:

IN THE STARS
Copyright © 2001 by Barbara Keiler

SHOOTING STARS
Copyright © 2001 by Peggy A. Hoffmann

STAR CROSSED
Copyright © 2001 by Gina Wilkins

This edition published by arrangement with Harlequin Books S.A.

® and TM are trademarks of the publisher. Trademarks indicated with ® are registered in the United States Patent and Trademark Office, the Canadian Trade Marks Office and in other countries.

Visit us at www.eHarlequin.com

Printed in U.S.A.

CONTENTS

Dear Reader,

When I conceived the story for "In the Stars"—
about a business "wizard" who uses his daily horoscope
to guide his stock market investments—I thought the
idea was whimsical and humorous. I've since learned
that quite a few stockbrokers rely on astrology to
determine their buys and sells. Apparently, my hero,
Derek Palmer, isn't quite as crazy as I'd imagined!

Well, he isn't exactly sane, either. He commutes to work
on roller skates, endures a feud with a neighborhood
squirrel and falls madly in love with the one woman
to whom he can never reveal his business strategy. Life
isn't easy when the world thinks you're a wizard.

I had great fun writing this story, setting it in beautiful,
wintery New York City. And I especially loved watching
as Derek and Melissa Giordano, the object of his
affection, learn to place their trust in the stars, and
in love. I hope you have fun reading it!

Judith

Judith Arnold

IN THE STARS

Judith Arnold

CHAPTER ONE

*Capricorn. You run the risk of making a
fool of yourself today. Be careful around
animals and members of the opposite sex.
An unexpected opportunity will pass you by
if you don't act on it. Someone in a hat may
bring luck—but remember, luck comes in
many guises and isn't always easy to recognize.*

DEREK PALMER took a sip of scalding coffee,
winced, and studied the horoscope closely.
Eleven words in the first sentence, and one of
them was "risk." Interesting.

He typed "eleven—risk" into his Palm Pilot,
reread the horoscope, then typed "fool, sex, opportunity, hat, luck." "Animals," "members"
and "guises" were nouns, but they were plural.
His system worked only with singular nouns.

"My system," he muttered, then shook his
head. "Yeah, right." He had no system, and if
his partners ever found out—worse, if the firm's
clients ever found out—his reputation would be

worth about as much as a fistful of slush on a warm day.

But the thing was, the horoscopes worked. And until they stopped working, Derek wasn't going to stop using them.

He took another slug of coffee. It had cooled down enough to not blister his tongue, and his surroundings became clearer as the caffeine soaked into his body. He was seated in the dining nook of his tiny kitchen, surrounded by white appliances, maple cabinets, a checkerboard floor. A window overlooked the vest-pocket garden behind the brownstone. In the spring, his first-floor neighbor would plant flowers down there, seed a few square inches with grass, and try to bring a hint of suburbia to the Upper West Side. Derek didn't know why she bothered, since the building stood only half a block away from Central Park. If he needed a greenery fix, that was where he headed.

He needed a greenery fix right now, but even Central Park wouldn't offer much green in mid-January. Flurries danced through the gray air— not sticking, not blanketing the ground in beautiful white drifts, but simply speckling the air.

He popped the rest of his English muffin into his mouth while he skimmed the front-page headlines. Then he flipped the newspaper open to the horoscope once more. When he got to his office, he would read the *New York Times* and the *Wall*

Street Journal—newspapers full of detailed, literate descriptions of the day's events but lacking horoscope columns. The editors probably assumed that anyone intelligent enough to read the *Times* or the *Journal* was too high-brow for daily astrological forecasts.

Derek didn't exactly consider himself a high-brow intellectual, but he had a few impressive diplomas from Ivy League universities. He'd stumbled onto horoscope-based investing as a joke, trying it on paper a few times, using various codes and strategies. When those paper-based investments kept performing better than the real one he recommended, he'd figured the daily horoscope published in *America Today* was as accurate a predictor of stock performances and trends as all the erudite journals and insider forecasts he studied.

Whatever worked and earned his clients a good return on their investments—whatever kept the partnership flourishing and the profits flowing in. If astrology did the trick, why not? His partners thought he was a genius—in fact, they'd dubbed him the Wizard, a nickname now known well beyond the confines of their firm. Nobody needed to know Derek based his investment advice on the daily newspaper horoscope. As long as his investment advice was making everyone a lot of money, his "system" didn't matter.

He finished his coffee, folded the newspaper,

and rinsed his mug in the deep-basin sink. After a quick detour to the bathroom to brush his teeth, he stuffed his loafers and briefcase into his backpack. He then donned his lined leather jacket, clamped on his in-line skates and strapped on his helmet. Perhaps it would be easier to walk downstairs in his socks and put his in-line skates on once he'd reached the sidewalk. But he'd grown quite adept at navigating the stairs on in-line skates.

He couldn't in-line skate to work every day, but on days when he could—such as today, when he had no pressing appointments, no formal obligations requiring a dress coat or a tailored blazer—he enjoyed coasting downtown on the blades. The exercise exhilarated him, and given the chronic bumper-to-bumper traffic of rush-hour Manhattan, he moved faster on his in-line skates than most people did in cars or buses. In-line skating was also more efficient than subway-riding, which was always a zoolike experience during the morning crush, especially at the Columbus Circle station where he changed trains.

The few flurries wouldn't slow him down; they weren't sticking to the pavement. The air was raw but not subfreezing, and the exercise would keep him warm.

He'd nearly made it to the corner of Central Park West when Herman accosted him. Herman was a cantankerous squirrel who liked to perch

himself on one of Derek's windowsills and bang
his acorns against the panes. Derek had thought
squirrels hibernated in the winter, but either he
was mistaken or New York City squirrels were a
breed apart. They scampered around the neighborhood, teetering on the branches of leafless
trees or planting themselves on the sidewalk in a
shameless play for breadcrumbs.

Other people might assume that the squirrel
Derek had named Herman was actually an entire
army of squirrels so nearly identical in appearance he couldn't possibly tell them apart. But he
knew Herman. Herman's fur was a bit more silver than that of the other squirrels, and he had a
malevolent glint in his beady black eyes. He always stared at Derek menacingly. Derek wasn't
sure why Herman hated him, except for the fact
that Herman was stuck on the icy ledges of Derek's windowsills while Derek was warm and
comfortable inside. Or perhaps it was because
Derek, unlike most of his neighbors, wasn't a
sucker. He didn't keep Herman supplied in stale
bread crusts.

Ordinarily, Derek would ignore Herman. But
today Herman sprang at him from the ornate
wrought-iron railing of a neighboring brownstone. He dropped to the sidewalk directly in
front of Derek, his fluffy silver tail vicious in its
gracefulness and his eyes gleaming with malice.

Derek might despise Herman, but he wasn't

going to run over the furry beast if he could avoid it. He kicked one foot back onto the in-line skate's brake, but Herman swung around and darted to the railing, forcing Derek to jerk his other foot off the pavement. He spun for a moment, then went down in an undignified sprawl.

He could have sworn he heard Herman snicker.

The doorman of the corner apartment building hurried outside to see if he could help Derek. No help needed; Derek knew how to fall without injuring himself. One knee of his khakis was dirty, and beneath it his skin felt a little tender. A bruise would be darkening that knee by tonight. But he was otherwise all right. His backpack was intact, and so was his body.

He contemplated returning to his apartment to change his trousers. A quick glance at his watch nixed that idea. It was already nine-fifteen, and he was expected at his office at nine-thirty. As it was, he was going to be late.

As he stood, the doorman swatted ineffectually at his trousers. "Those things are dangerous," the guy clucked, gesturing at his in-line skates.

"The only thing dangerous about them is when squirrels from hell get in your way," Derek argued, glaring at the railing where Herman had been lurking. Herman was no fool, though; he'd pranced off before Derek could chase after him. "Thanks for the help. I'm fine, really." He nod-

ded at a few other pedestrians who had stopped
to gawk. Then he centered his backpack between
his shoulder blades and took off, proof that he
really was okay.

Except for his left knee, which was a little
achy. He'd put some ice on it at the office. At
least he hadn't torn his slacks.

By the time he'd reached the heavy traffic of
Fifty-seventh Street, his knee had stiffened. The
sidewalk wasn't quite as packed as it would have
been ten minutes ago, but it was still pretty
crowded. On the stretches where the pedestrian
flow knotted up, he coasted out into the street
and glided alongside the parked cars. Skating in
traffic wasn't the safest activity, but he figured
that if he could survive a run-in with Herman, he
could survive the crazy cabbies of midtown without serious injury.

At last he reached the boxy glass building on
Avenue of the Americas that housed the suite of
offices occupied by Dayton, Palmer & Schwartz.
He skidded across the lobby to the elevator bank,
pressed the up button, tugged off his helmet and
shook his hair to free it from the helmet's mold-
ing shape. The elevator doors in front of him slid
open, and he coasted inside.

A woman with a cardboard tray jammed with
take-out coffee joined him in the car. The air
filled with the aroma of gourmet brew. His left
knee twinged, and he unclipped his left in-line

skate and wiggled his foot out of the boot. The woman with the coffee gave him a censorious look and got out on the fourth floor.

"My leg hurts, all right?" he growled at her once the doors shut and he knew she couldn't hear him. He lowered his foot to the floor and the knee felt a little better. Bending to remove his other in-line skate, he nearly lost his balance as the elevator jerked to a halt at the eighth floor.

Sighing, he straightened and propelled himself out of the elevator on one in-line skate, using his left foot to push himself along as if he were riding a scooter. "Derek, where have you been?" shrieked Gloria, the secretary/receptionist as he half walked and half rolled into the office, his arms embracing his helmet and his left in-line skate.

"I'm not that late," he insisted, flashing her a smile as he step-skated past her desk.

"Yes, but—"

"Let me take my jacket off, and then you can yes-but me," he called over his shoulder, hobbling and coasting down the short hall that led to his and his partners's offices.

Abby Schwartz flung open her door. "Derek, you—"

"Yeah, yeah." He rolled past her.

"There's someone—"

"Derek," Stan Dayton bellowed, yanking open his door. "You've got to—"

"Hey, do you mind?" He spun around on his skate and glowered at his partners. "I know I'm late. I got attacked by a squirrel, all right? Give me a minute to catch my breath." Before either of them could speak, he pivoted back to his office—and saw the woman standing in his doorway.

The first thing he noticed was her hair, tumbling past her shoulders in a barely tamed cascade of thick black waves. The hair framed a heart-shaped face—large eyes, a flat nose, full, soft lips and a chin that came to a cute little point, like an elf's. Her slender throat was flattered by a thin gold chain with a pearl pendant that nestled in the hollow between her collarbones. She wore a burgundy wool suit with a knee-length skirt, and simple black high heels.

Very, very nice.

But she was standing in his office, and he was standing in the hallway, with one skate on and one off, grime streaked across his trousers and his hair mussed from his helmet, which he held in front of him like a shield. Beneath his scruffy leather jacket, his tie hung loose. He was in no condition to meet a new client.

She stared, her lips pressed together and her brown eyes narrowing as she assessed him. It wouldn't take a Mensa genius to figure out that his first impression of her was a hell of a lot better than her first impression of him.

"Um...hello," he said, trying to infuse his voice with cheer.

She peered past him at Abby and Stan, whose hovering presence he could feel behind him in the hallway. She turned back to him for a final once-over, then frowned.

"Surely this can't be the Wizard," she said.

HE WAS not what she'd expected.

If he'd swept into his office wearing a black robe and a sorcerer's hat with arcane runes adorning it, she might have been less surprised. Given what she'd heard about the investment genius Derek Palmer, aka the Wizard, she'd been counting on someone at least a bit cleaner.

He had one in-line skate on and one in-line skate off. His hair, a thatch of pale brown as straight as straw, stuck out from his head in odd tufts. His trousers were in desperate need of laundering.

She'd come to Dayton, Palmer & Schwartz because of the Wizard's reputation. New York City boasted plenty of other investment firms—bigger firms, older firms, household-name firms. But she wanted to dazzle her new boss, to make enormous profits for his charitable trust, to prove he'd been wise to take a chance on her—and the buzz in certain circles was that Dayton, Palmer & Schwartz was an exciting firm to work with because they had the Wizard managing their major stock fund.

She'd had high hopes when she'd arrived at their office at 9:00 a.m. The two partners she'd spoken to, Stanley Dayton and Abigail Schwartz, had seemed sharp and smart. They'd described their backgrounds—apparently all three partners had met working for one of the huge investment firms on Wall Street, and they'd quit to establish their own firm three years ago. They'd presented her with quarterly statements going back to their founding. They'd been poised and professional, and she'd thought this would be an excellent firm to entrust with some of the foundation's money.

"I would like to meet Mr. Palmer," she'd said when the other two partners had finished selling her on their services. "I understand he's the one who formulates the investment strategies, and I'd like to talk to him."

"Of course," Abigail Schwartz had said. "He's usually in by now. I guess he got held up, but he should be here any minute, if you'd like to wait."

"His office is right down the hall," Stanley Dayton had added, then offered to escort her there so she could wait for him.

Nothing in the office revealed much about the kind of person he was: two computers, a bunch of locked drawers on his sleek white desk, a print of a Mondigliani nude on one wall and neutral beige carpet on the floor. A navy-blue blazer hung on a peg attached to the back of his door. He probably liked to dress casually in the office, and then toss on the jacket if he had an unscheduled meeting.

So she'd expected that he wouldn't be wearing a jacket when he arrived. She hadn't expected that he wouldn't be wearing shoes.

He swung a heavy-looking backpack from his shoulders, unbuckled the strap and extracted two cordovan loafers from its depths. After stepping into the left loafer, he removed his other in-line skate and shoved that foot into the right loafer, his gaze never leaving hers.

Even with shoes on, he wasn't the most reassuring sight. There was something enigmatic about his face, a harshness in his jaw and a softness in his hazel eyes. The corners of his mouth quirked into an ironic smile. His nose was long and straight, and even though his leather bomber jacket didn't seem particularly suitable for the office, it had a raffish sort of charm.

"A squirrel?" she questioned him.

He tossed his in-line skates and helmet into a corner of his office, then unzipped his jacket. "The demon rodent from hell," he said, extending his right hand. "I'm Derek Palmer, and you're...?"

"Melissa Giordano." His tie was crooked, his collar unbuttoned. She had to wonder how a man who arrived at work ten minutes after his partners said he would arrive—and forty minutes after most normal businesses opened their doors— looking like a refugee from a roller-derby competition, could be trusted to manage anyone's investments, let alone Ronald Towers's. "I tell you what, Ms. Giordano," he was saying. "I need to get an ice pack on my knee, and then you can tell me why you're in my office."

"She's there because I told her she could be there," Stanley Dayton interceded. He filled the doorway, a bit huskier than the Wizard and clad in an impeccably tailored gray suit that lent him an aura of confidence and competence.

But he wasn't the man who managed the fund she wanted to invest in.

"I didn't say I minded her being in my office," Derek stated, fidgeting with the knot of his tie and walking with a slight limp toward the chair behind his desk. "I just said I wanted to know why she was here. I'm sorry, Ms. Giordano," he added with an ingratiating smile. "I'm in pain. I need an ice pack, and then we can talk."

"Perhaps it would be better if I left," she said, turning toward the door.

Stanley Dayton remained where he was, blocking her escape. "Okay, so he's eccentric." He gestured vaguely in Derek's direction. "But trust me, when it comes to investments, well, you saw the quarterlies. He's brilliant.''

"He's in pain," she pointed out, feeling rather uncomfortable about having come here at all. "He was attacked by a demon squirrel."

"From hell," Derek elaborated. Glancing over her shoulder, she watched him lift the handset of the phone on his desk. "Gloria, could you please get me an ice pack? I totaled my knee. And why don't you get some coffee for Ms. Giordano? I don't know why these partners of mine didn't offer her a cup."

"I don't want any coffee," Melissa informed him. Those partners of his had offered her coffee, tea, hot chocolate and orange juice in an effort to keep her occupied while they awaited their tardy colleague.

He met her gaze and nodded, then said into the phone, "Forget the coffee. Just bring ice... I don't know where. Maybe the coffee shop downstairs?" He hung up, propped his left leg on his desktop and gave her another ingratiating smile. "So, what can I do for you?"

Not much, she thought. She'd wanted to meet him because she'd wanted to see, with her own eyes, the man who had performed such magic with his stock choices over the past two years. She'd wanted to acquaint herself with the man who might manage a portfolio for her boss's charitable trust. Ronald Towers might micromanage his real estate business, but he gave his foundation staff free reign. He explained that the better they managed the trust, the more money they'd have to donate to worthwhile programs.

Handing a significant chunk of the Towers Foundation over to Dayton, Palmer & Schwartz no longer seemed terribly sound—at least, not if Derek Palmer was the one who would decide how best to invest it. The man couldn't even get himself to his office in one piece. Was she really going to entrust him with the foundation's money?

Ignoring him, she addressed Stanley. "Thank you so much for your time. I'll be meeting with some other investment firms before I make any decisions. I'll get back to you." She took a determined step toward the door, and Stanley reluctantly fell back, allowing her to pass. She didn't miss the bitter frown he sent Derek before he followed her down the hall.

"You know, geniuses are sometimes a little eccentric," he said. "The bottom line is, Derek is a genius."

Abigail Schwartz joined them halfway down the hall. "You've seen the quarterly statements. The bottom line is, look at what he's accomplished, investment-wise. No one else is going to get you such a high return."

Possibly. But eccentric was one thing. Eccentric, unkempt, cranky and late were four things.

True, he was in pain—due to a scuffle with a squirrel, the thought of which made her want to laugh and shudder simultaneously—but still, she needed to work with someone solid and respectable and…well, *normal.*

Maybe Derek Palmer was normal most of the time. Maybe he performed stock market miracles. Maybe he could offer a higher return on the Towers Foundation's investment than anyone else.

And maybe he had the most beautiful eyes she'd ever seen on a man.

But Ronald Towers was taking a huge chance on her, which made her feel as if she'd better not take any chances with his money. She certainly didn't think she ought to take a chance on a man who could go one-on-one with a squirrel—and lose.

CHAPTER TWO

MELISSA DIDN'T KNOW why she was so angry.

She was still seething when she arrived back at her office, in the unfortunately named Towers Tower on Fifth Avenue. The elegant complex, owned by her boss, still daunted her on occasion. Right now she was too irked to be overwhelmed by the opulence of the building with its exclusive stores, overpriced apartments and offices housing Ronald Towers's extensive business pursuits.

Until just one month ago she'd worked in a dreary office in the accounting department at City Hall. After earning her M.B.A. two years ago, she'd been thrilled to find a job in the city, not too far from her parents in Queens. And if the work at City Hall had been less than thrilling, at least it had been steady and secure. It had paid her enough that she could share a pathetically minuscule one-bedroom apartment with her college friend JoAnn, who had a much more exciting, if less well-paying job as an assistant to a shoe designer. The arrangement was simple. Melissa was in charge of stocking the kitchen with the occasional quart of premium ice cream or gourmet roast coffee, and JoAnn was in charge of securing invitations to interesting parties.

It wasn't a bad life for a twenty-six-year-old single woman. But Melissa's twenty-seventh birthday was inching up on her, which inspired her to picture herself at age thirty. She hadn't cared for the picture of herself a few years from now, crunching numbers in her windowless cubicle at City Hall.

So when she'd heard that Ronald Towers, the legendary real estate mogul, was hiring, she'd sent in an application.

She'd hoped he would hire her for an accounting position. But he'd surprised her by offering her a position with his charitable trust. "I've set up this foundation to do good works," he'd explained. "I've made billions in real estate, as you know—" Towers had a robust ego and loved flaunting his wealth "—and if I don't give some back, people will hate me, and that would be intolerable. So I've established the Towers Foundation and endowed it with fifty million dollars. I've got a staff that manages the foundation for me, but the others on the staff are all in their forties or older. We need some young blood there. And your experience working for the city government won't hurt, either. What do you say?"

After recovering from the shock of his unexpected offer, Melissa had said yes.

She'd always believed in careful planning, in mapping out her professional course, in visualizing her future—and no visualization had ever included her working for a charitable trust. But the opportunity had seemed worth the risk. So had the salary, which was almost double what she'd been earning at City Hall.

The rewarding part of the job was scouting for worthy causes to support, evaluating applications and fantasizing about all the good fifty million dollars could accomplish. The anxiety-producing part of the job was managing those fifty million dollars so they wouldn't evaporate. The foundation grants came not from the principle but from the interest and dividends on the fifty million dollars. If the foundation could increase those earnings, they could increase their charitable expenditures.

As soon as she'd arrived at her new office in the Towers Tower on Fifth Avenue, she'd received her first assignment: to analyze the foundation's investments and to look for ways to increase its earnings. It was that assignment that had taken her to Dayton, Palmer & Schwartz.

The Wizard. What a joke! Derek Palmer was a crackpot. How on earth could clients trust him with their investments?

She had no idea how he'd managed to make so much money for his clients. But five minutes in his presence convinced her his success had to be a result of luck rather than genius.

"How'd it go?" Tom called over to her. He was one of the older staffers, who never talked down to her or treated her like the novice she was. "Is Dayton, Palmer & Schwartz everything the rumors say it is?"

She pulled off her coat and hooked it on the tree in the corner of their shared office. Her half of the room was twice the size of the cubicle she'd inhabited at City Hall. From its windows she could see the baroque spires of St. Patrick's Cathedral just up the street. "Two of the partners were great. The third one was weird."

"You don't have to deal with all three of them, do you?" While Tom was more flamboyantly dressed than Derek Palmer—in a pink dress shirt, colorful tie and beige suspenders—she couldn't help but notice that every item of his clothing was clean and crisp.

"The weird one is the one who'd be managing the money."

"The Wizard?" Because he was bald, Tom's forehead seemed endless, and his eyebrows had plenty of room to arch in surprise. "The way I hear it, his stock fund is outperforming all the biggies. If I had some spare cash to play with, I'd hand it over to him to invest."

She slumped into her chair and sighed. "I can't begin to imagine why he's got such a hot reputation. I wasted fifteen minutes waiting for him to show up. He claimed he was late because he'd been attacked by a squirrel.''

"No!'' Tom looked appalled. "Did they catch the squirrel and test it for rabies?''

That brought Melissa up short. Had Derek Palmer been bitten by the demon rodent from hell?

She didn't think so. He hadn't been bleeding. Just dirty. "I wouldn't be surprised if he'd invented the entire story. It was a little more original than 'the dog ate my homework,' but just as unbelievable. I'm telling you, Tom—the guy seems like a nut.''

"You really didn't like him, huh.''

Melissa sighed again, trying to contain the annoyance that threatened to overwhelm her. Why should she be so put off by Derek Palmer? His partners had a right to be furious with him, since his bizarre entrance had convinced Melissa to cross their firm off her list. But other than consuming an hour of her morning, why should her trip to their office and the few minutes she'd spent in Derek's company leave her so agitated?

Because of his eyes. Because of the lean length of his left leg propped up on his desk, and the golden highlights in his hair, and his crooked smile that made no apologies, even as he said he was sorry for having arrived late. But mostly... his eyes.

Since settling in New York City two years ago,

she'd dated a fair number of men. Some had been pleasant, one or two had shimmered with possibilities, most had been losers. But none had ever managed to unsettle her so thoroughly without even doing a thing.

Maybe what rankled was the fact that she'd expected...a wizard. She'd expected Derek Palmer to glow with intelligence, to be focused and frighteningly astute. She'd expected to be so astonished by his brilliance that she'd have to exercise extreme willpower to not write out a huge check and hand it to him on the spot.

When she'd pictured their meeting—and she had, many times—her vision hadn't included dirty khakis and a fiberglass helmet with silly racing stripes painted along the sides.

"He's just not the one for us," she said, aware of the deep disappointment that weighed down her words.

Tom scrutinized her, as if trying to discern a reason for her decision—or for her mood. Apparently unable to, he shrugged. "Well, we've got a meeting with the regional director of Meals-on-Wheels in a few minutes," he reminded her. "Forget about the Wizard. If he's a nut, we sure don't want to let him get near Towers's money."

DEREK ARRIVED at the Towers Tower at a quarter to five. If Abby and Stan had had their way, he would have been here much earlier. But he'd had a full day of work to finish before going home to change into clean clothes so that he could chase after Melissa Giordano to beg her to reconsider investing money with Dayton, Palmer & Schwartz.

All right, so he hadn't exactly charmed her that morning. He'd been in pain, to say nothing of dealing with the humiliation of having been bested by Herman. Was that any reason for Abby and Stan to harangue him for the rest of the day about what a coup it would be to win the Towers Foundation account?

It was their job to woo and wow the clients. His job was to monitor the investments. Even so, he'd telephoned Melissa Giordano's office four times. Each time, he was told she was away from her desk. Which was why he'd come in person to see her and make amends.

Between attempts to reach her by phone, he'd spent the day on the computer, manipulating vast sums of money. Working with eleven percent of his total funds, he'd invested some in a technology stock called SolTex. It was a volatile stock, but he'd keep a close eye on it. He'd generated a nice day's profit on a six-hour investment in HiWatt Industries, another technology company. And he'd bought into Folderol, an entertainment start-up.

He'd used eleven percent of the money because his horoscope had had eleven words in the first sentence. SolTex played off "sex," HiWatt played off "hat" and Folderol played off "fool." Nothing else on the boards had resonated in terms of his horoscope, but he felt good about those three investments, and even better when he researched the stocks through the on-line services he subscribed to.

Not bad for a day's work. But the way Abby and Stan had been carrying on about his having let Melissa Giordano slip through his fingers...a person might have thought he'd accomplished nothing worthwhile.

He'd in-line skated home at a quarter to four, taken a quick shower, scowled at the purple bruise that puffed his left knee, and donned a fresh pair of trousers, a shirt just back from the cleaner's, and his most subdued necktie. For the final touch, he'd traded his bomber jacket for his wool dress coat. He surveyed the street for signs of Herman before he exited his brownstone and hailed a cab to take him to the elegant Towers Tower on Fifth Avenue. The business card Melissa had left with Abby had stated that her office was located there.

Melissa hadn't seemed like a Towers Tower type. Sure, she'd been polished and well-groomed, but there was an accessibility about her face, an openness in her gaze, that seemed at odds with the pretentious Towers Tower.

Of course, she did work for Towers and thus

wouldn't get to choose where her office was located. But entering the gaudy lobby with its steep, multistory escalators, its marble floors and elaborate plantings and chi-chi boutiques, Derek wondered if this was really Melissa Giordano's kind of place.

A guard in livery stood at a podium near the elevator bank. Derek presented Melissa's business card to him, and he gave Derek permission to go up to the fifth floor, where Towers Foundation was located. Even the floor of the elevator was marble. A person would probably be arrested for wearing skates into this building.

At the fifth floor, he exited into a carpeted lobby furnished with fancy leather couches, Tiffany-style lamps and a couple of Winslow Homer seascapes that, for all Derek knew, could be originals. The place resembled a society matron's living room more than the reception area for a charitable foundation. He spotted the receptionist's desk, camouflaged by a few exotic-looking potted plants, and approached. "I'd like to see Melissa Giordano, please. My name is Derek Palmer."

The receptionist, a young woman who wouldn't have had much difficulty moonlighting as a cover girl for a fashion magazine, pressed a button on her telephone console and spoke softly to someone on the other end of the line. Then she disconnected. "Ms. Giordano is out, but if you'd like to speak to her colleague, Mr. Trumbull, you may go in.''

Derek didn't want to speak to Mr. Trumbull. He wanted to speak to the woman with the fabulous hair and the equally fabulous legs, the dark, judgmental gaze and the cute little chin. But he'd come here to win the Towers Foundation account, and he probably had a better chance of achieving that with Melissa's colleague than with her. Swallowing his disappointment, he thanked the receptionist and followed her down a hallway to a door, which she knocked on before opening for him.

Inside the office stood a thin man in a loud pink shirt, a tweedy Irish walking hat, and a welcoming smile. "Hi, I'm Tom Trumbull," he said, extending his right hand.

Derek shook it. "Derek Palmer," he introduced himself.

"I understand you're known as the Wizard."

One of these days, reality was going to catch up with Derek's reputation. Word was going to get out that his wizardry was based on random nouns and numbers plucked from his horoscope in a daily newspaper. Sometimes he simply wanted to shout, "No, I'm *not* the Wizard! I'm just a guy who's had a fantastic run of luck."

He wasn't going to shout now, not when Abby and Stan were breathing down his neck to bring Melissa Giordano's business to their firm. He shook Tom's hand and managed a modest smile. "'Wizard' is a bit of an exaggeration. I gather Melissa has left for the day?"

Tom pushed away from his desk and lifted the lined trench coat lying on a nearby chair. "She took off around an hour ago for a dental appointment. She was going to head straight home after that."

"Damn." Derek gazed past Tom at Melissa's abandoned desk. A small leafy plant sat in a painted ceramic pot on one corner, and on another a framed photograph of an older couple. Her parents, maybe?

"Is it a big problem?" Tom asked.

Derek offered another sheepish smile. "I got off on the wrong foot with her today. Literally," he added under his breath, remembering his socked foot and stiff knee. "I'd really like to change that. For the sake of your funds, of course. If I could convince her to do business with us, you'd get a very nice return on your investment."

"Now, that sounds like the Wizard," Tom commented, digging a knit scarf from the sleeve of his coat and wrapping it around his neck.

"I'd really like to talk to her today, before her lousy first impression of me solidifies." Derek eyed Tom hopefully. "I don't suppose you'd know where her dentist is located? Maybe I could catch up to her there."

Tom returned Derek's measuring gaze. He pulled his hat a little lower, then slid his arms through the sleeves of his coat. "I don't know where her dentist is," he said.

Derek let out a sigh of frustration. Of course, he'd probably make an even worse impression on her if he sprang himself at her while her mouth was packed in gauze and numb from Novocain.

Tom touched his hat again, adjusting the narrow rim above his eyes. "This is about more than investments, isn't it?" he guessed.

Derek opened his mouth to deny the hunch, then thought better of it. A little honesty might win him some points with the man. "I'd like to talk to her," he admitted.

One final assessing gaze, and Tom relented. "All right. I'll give you her home address. But don't tell her where you got it." He twirled his Rolodex file, pulled a square of notepaper from a pad on his desk, and jotted down a street address. "I shouldn't be doing this—but I like the idea that even though you're the Wizard, you don't rely on magic to get what you need."

Derek wondered if it was going to take magic to get Melissa to hear him out. He tucked the square of paper into his shirt pocket and shook Tom's hand again. "Thanks. I'll…well…just *thanks*."

The grin Tom gave him implied that he knew Derek was thinking about more than just investments—and that was why he'd shared Melissa's address with him. A little discreet matchmaking, maybe?

Derek wished his only interest in Melissa was to invest her funds. But while he could fool everyone else, he never, ever, tried to fool himself. He knew as well as Tom did that if he saw Melissa again, investments would not be the only thing on his mind.

MELISSA'S TEETH were minty smooth. Her mouth tingled. Most people hated going to the dentist, but she had healthy teeth and she loved the way they felt after a professional polishing.

Even a successful dental checkup couldn't cheer her as she ducked out of the biting, flurry-filled air into the vestibule of her apartment building. She gave herself a few seconds to thaw out, then turned to unlock the mailbox she and JoAnn shared.

Taped to her box was a business-size envelope containing a thick, rectangular slab of something. Her name was inked boldly across the front of the envelope.

Being a paranoid New Yorker, she frowned and fell back a step, then peered around her. The vestibule looked the way it always did—plain, unglamorous, with pale green walls and a locked glass inner door. She inched closer to her mailbox and touched the envelope. The rectangular object inside was wrapped in some sort of paper that rattled.

It felt like a chocolate bar.

Taking a deep breath, she untaped the envelope and lifted the flap. Not just a chocolate bar—it was a generous-size sample of imported dark chocolate enclosed in delicate gold foil. It shared the envelope with a sheet of paper, which she pulled out and unfolded.

Melissa,
Please give me another chance. You won't be disappointed. Trust me—it's in the stars.
                                        Derek Palmer

If she hadn't known better, she would have thought it was a love note, or at the very least, a message from a man hoping for more than her business. Chocolate—Godiva chocolate, no less—was more romantic than the sorts of gifts most business people gave to attract new clients.

It's in the stars. What was in the stars? There weren't even any stars visible this evening. Purple-gray clouds filled the dark evening sky.

She crossed to the outer door and nudged it open. Derek Palmer was standing under the nearest lamppost, no more than ten feet down the sidewalk. Only he wasn't the same Derek she'd met that morning. He wore a dress coat with the collar turned up, and shoes instead of skates. His bare head was speckled with melting snowflakes that glinted in the light of the streetlamp.

When she didn't retreat into the vestibule, he pushed away from the lamppost and sauntered toward her in a slightly lopsided gait. She'd noticed his eyes that morning, but not his smile— probably because he hadn't been smiling. Who could smile after being ignominiously defeated by a squirrel?

But he had a lovely smile. Not too big and clearly hesitant, it warmed his face and lit his eyes. When he was only a couple of feet from her, he limped to a halt. "If you tell me you're allergic to chocolate, I'm going to open a vein," he said.

"I'm not allergic to chocolate."

His smile grew a little wider. "If you don't let me buy you a cup of coffee and listen while I tell you how great Dayton, Palmer & Schwartz is, my partners are going to open one of my veins for me."

"You really do live a life of danger, don't you," she teased.

"Skates, squirrels and partners. There's danger everywhere I look."

She laughed, and the instant she did, she knew she'd have to have a cup of coffee with him. "Let me take my mail upstairs and drop off my briefcase," she said, gesturing toward the thick leather portfolio hanging by a strap from her

shoulder, "and then we can go get some coffee."
It would be easier to invite him up, but she *was*
a paranoid New Yorker. And anyway, it wouldn't
make sense for her to host a drink of coffee when
he, not she, was the one trying to make amends.

"You will come back, won't you?" he asked,
his smile tinged with a mixture of optimism and
worry.

"I promise." She considered the risks, then
pushed the outer door wider. "Why don't you
wait in here? It looks like the snow is coming
down harder."

He joined her in the vestibule, and the room
suddenly seemed to shrink in size. She hadn't
realized how tall he was—in his office that morning, he'd stood crookedly in his single skate. But
wearing two normal shoes, he loomed a good six
inches above her five-foot-six-inch frame, and he
smelled of soap and citrus. His cheeks were
ruddy from the cold, his eyelashes spiked where
snowflakes had melted on them.

She turned away, embarrassed to realize she'd
been ogling him. A twist of her key unlocked the
mailbox, and she pulled out the letters inside. A
few bills, some credit card solicitations—nothing
remotely as exciting as the letter that had been
taped to the outside of the box.

"I'll be right back," she said before unlocking
the inner door. With his hands buried in the pockets of his navy-blue coat, he nodded.

She ought to take her time and make him wait—but she was too eager to return to him. Much too eager. The elevator's predictable sluggishness stoked her impatience. When it finally squeaked to a stop on her floor, she bolted out of the car and raced down the hall to her apartment. "Jo?" she called as she entered, even though she knew her roommate wasn't home. If she had been, she would have brought the mail upstairs herself.

Melissa dumped her bag on the wooden chest that doubled as a coffee table and linen storage, then rushed down the hall to the bathroom to check her hair and makeup. The flurries had made her hair even curlier; she attacked it vigorously with her brush but noticed no difference. She freshened her lipstick and told herself that looking her best was important only because she was a professional. Coffee with Derek Palmer was a professional engagement, and nothing— not his eyes, not his smile, not even a gourmet chocolate bar—was going to change the nature of this meeting from professional to anything else.

But as she hurried back downstairs to meet him, she couldn't convince herself that professional was all she wanted it to be.

CHAPTER THREE

THE EATERY at the corner of her block was too nice for just coffee. The bar alcove was bustling, and enticing aromas wafted out from the kitchen. Early diners were already drifting in and being seated at candle-lit tables covered with forest-green linen tablecloths.

The waiter led them to a booth and left them with menus. A quick perusal and Derek realized that he'd feel like a fool if he only ordered a cup of coffee in this place. "We could get something to eat," he suggested as Melissa folded her coat onto the banquette next to her. "Or a glass of wine." He didn't want her to think he was coming on to her, but he just couldn't see sitting at this cozy booth in an atmospheric restaurant at quarter to six and *not* ordering dinner or a drink.

She flashed him a look, then glanced at the unopened menu in front of her. "I guess I am a little hungry," she conceded. "Let me make a call." She pulled a cell phone from her purse and punched a few buttons. "I'm sorry about this," she mouthed before turning her attention to the phone. "Hi, Jo? Good—you're there. It's me. I

won't be home for dinner tonight, okay? It's just
a business dinner. I'll see you later." She disconnected and smiled apologetically. "I know
it's rude, using a cell phone at a restaurant table.
I'm really sorry."

The hell with rude—Derek was scrambling to
recover from the news that she'd had to check in
with someone named Joe. Who was he? Her husband? Her lover? Her significant other?

It shouldn't matter, but it did. Especially now,
when Derek was seated only the width of the
table away from her and the candlelight was
dancing over her face. Damn, it mattered.

Just a business dinner, she'd told Joe—empha-
sis on *just*. Derek had better stay focused on that,
win her account for his firm, and stop obsessing
about the fullness of her lips and the dark radi-
ance of her eyes.

He wished he hadn't suggested dinner at all.
But the waiter had returned to their table, and
Melissa ordered a grilled chicken Caesar salad
and a glass of Chardonnay. He was stuck.

He requested a bacon cheeseburger and a la-
ger. The waiter took their menus, abandoning
Derek to Melissa. Married Melissa? Two-timing
Melissa?

He couldn't restrain himself. "Who's Joe?" he
asked.

"My roommate." She stared into his face, as

if trying to read his mind. Then she chuckled. "JoAnn."

He was far too relieved—that Jo was a female, and that Melissa hadn't bolted from the table once she'd realized what he was actually asking. He beamed a smile at her as the waiter arrived with their drinks, and he lifted his glass and tapped it against hers before drinking. "Here's to wise investments," he said.

She sipped her wine, then lowered her glass. "Now tell me why you think my trusting you with the Towers Foundation's money is 'in the stars.'"

He'd written the note he'd taped to her mailbox hoping only to intrigue her. A few cryptic sentences and some high-quality chocolate—he'd figured that after opening the envelope, she wouldn't be able to deny him a hearing.

But he wasn't going to explain that his investment choices were dictated by the stars according to his astrological system of investing. While the stars did influence him at work, he'd never admit that to any of his clients.

"All I meant is that you're destined to invest with us, so you might as well not fight it."

"How did you find my house?" she asked.

No way would he betray Tom Trumbull. "I looked you up in the phone book," he lied.

She shook her head. "The phone is listed in JoAnn's name."

He took a slow drink of beer, buying time to come up with a new story. "I looked you up in the Towers company phone book. This employee directory thing. I went to your office—since you refused to take my phone calls all day," he said pointedly, "and I saw this directory thing on a desk and flipped through it."

"A directory 'thing'?"

"Yeah." Before she could question him further, he changed the subject. "So how did you get hooked up with Ronald Towers, anyway? Is he really as arrogant as he seems on TV?"

"He's a very generous man," she insisted. "He's a hard-nosed businessman, of course, but now that he's amassed a fortune, he wants to give some of it back."

"My partners mentioned that his foundation has an endowment in the tens of millions." He seemed to have succeeded in distracting her from the directory thing, and he relaxed into the upholstery. "How much of that do you want to invest with us?"

She laughed. "I'm not sure I want to invest any of it with you. You still have to convince me I should trust Mr. Towers's money with a man who can be defeated by a squirrel."

Their food arrived, interrupting their conversation. The basket of steak fries that came with Tom's burger was so huge, he nudged it to the center of the table and urged Melissa to help herself.

As they ate, he described Herman to her. "Herman's got a Satanic gleam in his eyes. And his tail—the fur is like little razor blades. If he flicked you with it, he'd probably draw blood. I don't know why he attacked me this morning. All I can say is, if I was as coldhearted as he is, I would have run him over. But I'm a good guy, so I tried to avoid him and wound up hurting myself instead."

She seemed to find his Herman saga quite amusing. Her laughter was low and throaty, and her eyes shimmered. She obviously knew he was exaggerating, but his tale was so entertaining she didn't seem to mind.

From Herman, the conversation turned to the subject of in-line skating. He told her about how he'd started in-line skating in middle school—how he'd hung out at skate parks and learned tricks; how his grades had dropped even faster than he did when he was flying down a half-pipe; how his parents had taken his in-line skates away and told him that if he didn't get straight A's on his report card, he'd never get them back. "So you see, it was because of my in-line skating that I became a top student," he explained.

"I haven't been on skates in years," she admitted. "And I've never tried in-line skates."

"Never? You've got to try them. They're great. What size shoe do you wear?"

"Why do you ask?"

"Just humor me. What size?"

"Seven and a half. I hope you're not planning to buy me in-line skates."

"You prefer chocolate, huh." He grinned. Of course he wouldn't dream of buying her in-line skates. But it never hurt to be prepared, to stock-pile information until such time as he needed it.

"I prefer chocolate," she confirmed, although her low-calorie dinner—and her slender figure—belied her claim.

"Do you like ice-skating? Bicycling? Skate-boarding?"

She laughed. "I never developed a passion for any of those things. When you were hanging out at skate parks, I was working at my father's store."

"What kind of store?"

"He and my uncle own a corner grocery in Sunnyside, Queens. I used to help out there on weekends. In fact, I still go out there on week-ends sometimes, to give them a hand with their bookkeeping."

"Really?" He tried to picture a teenage Me-lissa: her hair pulled into a wavy ponytail, per-haps, and her body clothed in snug-fitting pants and a flimsy little tank top, Teva sandals and a foxy ankle bracelet. Maybe she'd be humming a

Madonna song while she stocked shelves. All the boys in the neighborhood would loiter inside the store, praying for a moment of her attention. If he'd grown up in Sunnyside, Queens, he would have begged his parents daily to let him run down to the corner store for a quart of milk, just for the opportunity to flirt with Mr. Giordano's beautiful daughter.

She wouldn't have flirted back, though. She would have been earnest and serious, the way she was now. She would have told him skating up and down the aisles wasn't allowed. Working for her father, she wouldn't have had time for such frivolities as in-line skating at all. She was definitely the sort to think long and hard before trusting an investment broker who in-line skated to work—let alone based his buy-and-sell decisions on the horoscope column in *America Today*.

"Tell me more about your firm," she requested, as if she'd sensed the direction his thoughts had wandered.

"I met Abby and Stan on Wall Street," he said, nudging his empty plate away and settling back on the banquette with what was left of his beer. While he would rather have spent more time questioning her about herself, he was on a mission: to win the Towers Foundation account for the firm. Having persuaded her with chocolate and dinner and good conversation to prove that he wasn't a total loser, he now had to transform himself into an unmistakable winner in her eyes. "We were all hot shots working in back offices, figuring out investments for corporate retirement funds. We were moving around large sums of money, and we had tons of responsibility. Also horrible hours and obnoxious bosses. So we decided to get out and start our own brokerage firm. Abby's the organization person. She knows just what needs to be done, how to keep everything flowing smoothly, what to file when and with whom. Stan's our client guy. He oversees the marketing of our funds, keeps the customers happy, makes sure the lines of communications are open twenty-four/seven."

"And you're the investment genius."

He was hardly a genius, but he wasn't going to tell her that. "Well, there's a lot of give and take among us all. But I trust Abby and Stan to exploit their strengths, and they trust me with mine."

"The quarterly reports they showed me were pretty impressive."

"*Pretty* impressive?" He grinned to take the heat out of his boast. "They're astonishing."

"So astonishing I intend to check you out with the S.E.C. to make sure you aren't doing anything 'creative.'"

"You mean, like lying and cheating?" He held out his hands, palms forward, as if to demonstrate he had nothing to hide. "I don't blame you. You won't find anything bad at the Securities and Exchange Commission. We're one hundred percent legitimate.''

"Do you miss Wall Street?"

He shook his head. "A year after I left, the firm I used to work for tried to lure me back— for double the salary and all kinds of perks. But I like being my own boss. Because we're small, we've got flexibility. We risked our own money to set up the partnership, and everything we earn is ours.''

"Why are you located so far from Wall Street?"

"With computers, you don't have to be on the street anymore. We have a trader working for us down at the exchange, but we handle most of the investments by computer." He smiled slyly. "Besides, if we were down on Wall Street it would be too far away from my apartment for me to skate to work.''

"Where do you live?" she asked.

He was thrilled that she was curious enough to ask. "West Sixty-ninth Street. I'm on the second floor of a brownstone. It's a great neighborhood.''

"Is it a walk-up? Doesn't that hurt your knee?"

He shrugged stoically. "It's my own fault for banging myself up. Anyway, it's just a bruise.''

"I noticed you limping earlier.''

He fought against a smile, delighted that she'd been paying close enough attention to him to notice that he was favoring his swollen knee. He gazed across the table at her and thought about how nice it would be if she offered to massage his calf muscles, which kept developing cramps because of the way he'd altered his stride.

The hell with his leg. He'd like her to touch him everywhere. The moment he'd seen her in his office that morning, her beauty had registered on him despite his pain and aggravation. He'd responded instantly to her fresh-scrubbed face, her curly hair, her golden complexion and that adorable chin, which was much too pointy, but seemed utterly perfect when combined with the rest of her face.

Abby and Stan hadn't badgered him all day to go after her because she was good-looking, though. First things first: he had to get her to invest at least a chunk of Towers Foundation money with Dayton, Palmer & Schwartz.

"The important thing," he said, refocusing, "is that if you invest with us, we're going to make money for you. If the Towers Foundation wants to do good deeds, it needs to invest its principal wisely. You won't do better with another brokerage."

"As I said, I was impressed with your quarterly statements." She took a sip of wine. "I just wish I understood how you got those returns."

"I'm good at what I do," he said simply. It wasn't a lie.

"The prospectus Abby gave me said you were a graduate of the Yale School of Management."

He nodded. His professors had filled his brain with investment theories, most of which made a lot more sense than picking nouns out of an astrology column. He could just imagine what the faculty would say if they knew how much more success he'd had with his own silly scheme than with all the investment philosophies they'd taught him.

"Well," she said, dabbing her mouth with her napkin and setting it on the table, "I'm not going to give you the key to the foundation vault, Derek—but I *am* going to consider letting you invest some of our money and see how it does. Bear in mind that if you lose money, AIDS researchers won't be as well funded. The public schools will have a bit less money to spend on new textbooks and classroom computers. And fewer shut-ins will receive Meals-on-Wheels. The Towers Foundation isn't about getting rich. It's about subsidizing people and programs in need of financial support."

"I understand." Her warning touched him. He liked the idea of making money for his clients— but he liked the idea of making money that would be put to good use even more, adding something of value to the world. "I appreciate your giving me a second chance."

"You really did make a lousy first impression," she scolded.

"Blame Herman the squirrel."

She laughed. Derek smiled—not because he felt confident that she'd do business with him, but because her laughter sounded like music in the wind, sweet, gentle and subtly sexy. It suddenly occurred to him that more than wanting her business, more than wanting to earn high dividends for her fund so it could be spent on worthwhile causes, he wanted to make her laugh.

CHAPTER FOUR

"HE SHOULDN'T BE DOING all that lifting," Melissa murmured under her breath. She was seated on a stool behind the front counter of Giordano's, watching her father unload cartons of canned soup from a hand truck. A year after his heart attack, he still looked gaunt and fragile.

Her mother, in charge of the cash register, only sighed. "What can I do? I'm always yelling at him to take it easy. He ignores me."

"Uncle Eddie—"

"Uncle Eddie tells him to take it easy, too. The doctor tells him to take it easy. He promises to take it easy. Then he sees how much work there is to do, and he starts lifting heavy cartons."

"He and Uncle Eddie should hire someone," Melissa said. "Not just kids to fill in after school, but someone full-grown—and full-time."

"Sure. And then they'll have to pay him a full-grown, full-time salary. That salary's going to come out of Dad's pocket. You know that."

If anything, Melissa knew the finances of the store even better than her mother did. Ever since she'd earned her accounting degree, her father and uncle had relied on her to keep the store's books for them. She was happy to do it, and it made hiring an outside accountant unnecessary.

The store was profitable, but when divided in two, her father's and uncle's shares of the profits weren't going to make either of them rich. Her parents were still in debt from the medical bills that had piled up after her father's heart attack. He shouldn't be working so hard, but her mother was right: if he hired someone to replace him, his own earnings would drop.

If only Melissa made enough money to help her parents out, her father could cut back on his hours. With her new position at the Towers Foundation, with its higher salary, she was hoping she'd be able to help support her parents—especially if she did an excellent job and got a raise.

A couple of teenage boys swaggered into the store. Her mother peered up at one of the strategically positioned ceiling mirrors so she could keep an eye on them as they headed for the refrigerator case at the rear of the store. They each chose a bottle of soda and then sauntered back to the front of the store, their fleece-lined jackets and backward baseball caps looking stylishly grungy. One of them slapped a five-dollar bill onto the counter. Melissa's mother counted out their change, offered them a bag which they refused, and wished them a good day. They grunted pleasantly in reply.

Once they had departed, she glanced over her shoulder at Melissa. "So, what's with you? Why do you have that look in your eyes?"

"What look?" Melissa asked innocently.

"Like your mind is halfway around the world. You better not mess up those books," she added, jabbing her thumb in the direction of the computer print-outs Melissa had been reviewing.

Melissa didn't mind her mother's scolding. Despite her grim expression and sharp words, she was a loving woman. She worried about Melissa's father every minute of every day. That didn't always leave time for her to express herself gently.

"I wouldn't dream of messing up the books," she assured her mother.

"So what *would* you dream of?"

"Dad hiring more help."

"Besides that. You're dreaming of something, aren't you?"

Melissa fiddled with her pen. She wasn't about to admit to her mother that she was distracted by thoughts of the man she'd had dinner with last night.

"Something's up with you." Her mother persevered. "You look like you got bit by something."

A depraved squirrel, Melissa thought—and a giddy laugh escaped her.

Her dinner with Derek was supposed to have been about business. And it was. After talking to him—not the battered, half-crazed, one-skate Derek she'd met that morning, but the poised, funny, dangerously alluring Derek who'd shown up at her apartment at the end of the day—she'd resolved to ask the foundation's staff to consider Derek's firm as an investment option. Over their meal, Derek had convinced her that his wizardry at investing could reap a very nice return for the foundation. So, technically, their dinner had been a business outing.

But more than business had been going on between them last night. Every time he'd smiled, every time his gaze had intersected with hers...

In the stars, he'd written in his note. And each time she'd looked at him, she'd understood, without quite knowing why or what it meant, that whatever was occurring between them had been somehow preordained.

Melissa was a hardheaded woman, not a romantic. She didn't believe the stars had any control over mortals. But even so...last night, with Derek, she'd found herself believing.

The door swung open, letting in a gust of cold air. She turned to greet the customer and gasped.

"Hi," Derek said.

What was he doing here? He lived on the Upper West Side; why would he be shopping for groceries at her father's store in Sunnyside, Queens?

He clearly hadn't come to shop. Clad in jeans, sneakers and the leather aviator jacket he'd been wearing when he'd staggered into his office yesterday morning, he carried a bulky sports equipment bag on a strap over his shoulder. His hair was windblown and a wool knit scarf was wrapped rakishly around his neck.

Melissa could feel her mother's curiosity as if it were a concrete block pressing into her back. She carefully closed her file and stood. "Mom, this is Derek Palmer, a business associate of mine."

"You have to work today? Melissa, you should have told me. We wouldn't have had you come in to review the books if we'd known you had work to do."

"I don't have work to do." She kept her gaze on Derek, trying to figure out what he was up to. Something, she was sure. His cheeks were ruddy from the cold, and his smile brimmed with mischief. He didn't look like someone who'd stopped in to purchase a lottery ticket and a pack of spearmint gum. "How did you find this place?" she asked him. "And don't tell me you looked in a directory thingie." She still hadn't figured out how he'd located her apartment last night. No one at the Towers offices would have left a staff list lying around on a desk, available for snoops like Derek to browse through.

"I took the subway out to Sunnyside and prowled the neighborhood, asking people if they knew of a grocery store owned by someone named Giordano. The second person I asked told me about Giordano's.'' He waved toward the door, above which a sign reading Giordano's hung. ''Not exactly dazzling detective work. Any chance you could spare a few minutes?''

Before Melissa could speak, her mother said, ''Go, go! The books can wait.''

Melissa glanced over her shoulder at her mother, who was grinning so broadly the smile seemed to inhabit her eyes. She had never made any secret of her desire for Melissa to meet a decent man and settle down. Melissa had the ghastly feeling her mother had decided that Derek was a promising candidate.

Melissa was hardly convinced that he qualified as decent. ''Just a few minutes,'' she warned him, sliding the folder into a drawer beneath the counter.

''You'd better get your coat,'' Derek warned her, then sent her mother a smile charming enough to fill the poor woman's mind with images of white satin, gold bands and sacred vows. She handed Melissa her jacket and returned her eager grin to Derek.

''I'll be right back,'' Melissa told her mother, speaking loudly enough for Derek to hear.

''Take your time,'' her mother said, then deliberately turned her attention to a blue-haired elderly woman who'd entered the store. ''Mrs. Manetta, how are you? We just got a shipment of those ice-cream novelties you like so much.''

With a slight shake of her head, Melissa slipped on her jacket and circled the counter to join Derek by the door. He held it open for her, and she refused to glance back at her mother as she stepped outside into the cold January afternoon.

Yesterday's flurries had left no accumulation, and the sun made the day feel warmer than it actually was. Derek guided her around the corner to a side street lined with neat, modest row houses. Leafless trees stood along the curb; cars were parked in driveways barely long enough to accommodate them.

One block away was the house she'd grown up in; her parents still lived there. She knew this neighborhood better than she knew the street she currently lived on. It was a quiet working-class community, and even though her education had carried her to the world of Ronald Towers and his elite Fifth Avenue skyscraper, Melissa felt at home here.

Derek scouted the street, his gaze settling on a concrete step that connected the sidewalk to the front walk of one of the houses. Taking Melissa's arm, he ushered her to the step, sat, and unzipped his bag. Out tumbled two pairs of in-line skates, along with assorted pads and braces.

"Derek." She didn't know whether to laugh or to flee.

He spread the empty bag out on the step so she wouldn't get her khaki slacks dirty when she sat. "Come on. Just a spin around the block."

"Spin is right. I don't know how to skate on in-line skates."

"How do you know you don't know how?"

"I've never done it before."

"Before you worked for the Towers Foundation, you'd never worked for a foundation before. Then you did it and you discovered you could do it. Come on," he goaded, yanking off his sneakers and clamping on his in-line skates. "I rented these just for you."

At least he hadn't bought the molded turquoise plastic skates he held out to her. Still, she eyed them with misgivings.

"Trust me." He patted the flattened sports bag, and she reluctantly lowered herself to sit next to him. "It'll be fun."

"Whatever possessed you to do this?" she asked, lifting one of the skates and studying it warily.

"You told me your shoe size. I had the information, and I felt it was my moral duty to put it to good use." His own skates on, he stood and then hunkered down in front of her like Cinderella's prince, as if by slipping her foot into the in-line skate he would seal some romantic understanding between them. "We'll just go around the block," he promised. "You'll have fun. Nothing wrong with having fun, is there?"

"What if I get attacked by a squirrel?"

Derek laughed. "You think Herman's got any cousins in Queens? Come on, put on these skates so I can give you a thrill."

Just gazing into his face gave her a thrill, she thought, and hastily averted her eyes. She didn't want him to know that his mere existence thrilled her. Bad enough that he could track her down at her parents' store, spirit her away and convince her to remove her shoes. It would be far worse if he realized that she'd gone from thinking he was a nutcase to developing a rather massive crush on him.

A few minutes of teetering around on a pair of brightly colored in-line skates would probably cure her infatuation pretty quickly. She struggled to clip them on and Derek covered her hands with his, adjusting the clips for her. His hands were warm in spite of the cold day, strong and decisive. Once her feet were encased in the in-line skates, he stuffed her shoes into the sports bag, then took each of her hands in turn and fastened a wrist brace onto it. She tried to not respond to the feel of his fingers against her palms, her forearms and the backs of her hands. She tried to not imagine what it would be like to have his hands move up her arms and over her body.

"Okay," he said robustly. "Now the knees." He strapped pads around her knees, and more erotic ideas flashed through her mind, of his fingers touching her thighs and shins and the ticklish backs of her knees, not through her slacks, but skin to skin.

She turned her face from him to let the winter air cool her cheeks. But a wave of warmth swept through her as he stood, closed his hands securely around hers, and eased her to her feet.

Whatever unwelcome arousal had overtaken her earlier fled before an onslaught of pure dread. Her feet wobbled and slid under her, and if Derek hadn't slung an arm tightly around her waist and held her up, she would have gone sprawling across the pavement. She bit her lip to keep from shrieking.

"Easy does it," he murmured, his mouth much too close to her ear. "Don't panic. You're not going to fall."

"Wanna bet?"

"Sure. Let's wager dinner tonight."

"You mean, if I fall I won't have dinner with you?"

His smile was thoughtful, hopeful. "That's the bet. We've both got a lot riding on you maintaining your balance. Okay?"

"No, I'm not okay," she said with a nervous laugh. "But I guess I'm as ready as I'll ever be."

His arm still around her, he turned to face the sidewalk. "You told me you've skated before," he reminded her. "This is the same thing, only on a slightly narrower base. If you want to stop, just tilt your foot and hit the concrete with the brake." He demonstrated with his foot, angling it so the round plastic knob on the end of the skate pressed the sidewalk. "See?"

"Sure, I *see*," she muttered. "Doing is not the same as seeing."

"We'll take it nice and slow." He hoisted the strap of the sports bag over his shoulder, then released her and glided around to face her. She stood petrified, her hands sticking out from her sides for balance, her heart beating in double time.

"Nice and slow," he repeated, taking her hands in his. He started skating backward, and her only choices were to move forward or to let go of him. She didn't want to let go of him, so she skated. Slowly, but not nicely. She moved her legs stiffly, pushing one foot a few inches forward, then pushing the other foot a few inches forward. Derek looked so graceful, so comfortable, as he pulled her along the sidewalk. She felt like a klutz.

"Don't look down," he cautioned her. "That'll make you lose your balance. Look straight ahead."

Looking straight ahead meant looking at him, at his determined chin and his seductive eyes. It meant looking at his wide smile and thinking wicked thoughts about what his lips would feel like on hers.

Her heart accelerated from double time to triple time.

Why should she react this way to him? So far,

his greatest asset seemed to be his ability to change her mind—and that wasn't an asset she valued highly. She *liked* her mind. She liked the way she thought, the way she planned things out. She liked logic.

At least one thing about Derek was logical: his investment skill. Everything else he did was totally illogical, though: his in-line skating to work as if he were a goofy high schooler, his wooing of clients with cryptic notes and candy bars, his summer-hot smile and toasty hands on a frigid January afternoon. And his willingness to skate backward, just so he could help her skate forward.

It dawned on her that he was moving more rapidly, pulling her along at a quicker pace. "I thought you said we'd take it nice and slow," she said breathlessly, experiencing a fresh surge of fear when she noticed the speed of the sidewalk sliding beneath her wheels.

"Don't look down," he instructed, giving her hands a light tug.

She lifted her eyes to his again. "You're going too fast."

"Actually, the faster you go, the easier it is to maintain your balance. Like riding a bicycle."

"The faster I go, the harder I'll fall."

"Do you think I'm going to let you fall when so much is at stake?" He flashed a grin at her. "Just look at me and stand straight. There you go—see?"

She didn't exactly "see," but moving a little faster didn't seem as scary as she'd expected. The cold air felt refreshing as it washed over her cheeks. Above her, the winter sun lit the afternoon sky.

They skated past her parents' house, and she dared to wriggle one hand free of his so she could point it out. "I grew up there," she told him.

"Really?" He braked to a smooth stop, and she rolled into him—fortunately, not going fast enough to knock him down. He studied the cozy brick house and grinned. "I'm picturing you scooting down the driveway wearing those metal roller skates that needed a key to attach to your shoes."

"My mother had skates like that," Melissa told him. "My skates were bright plastic, with fat wheels."

"But they attached to your shoes, right?"

Smiling, she nodded. "You couldn't skate fast in them. I guess that was why I liked them."

"Don't think of it as skating," he suggested. "Think of it as flying." And with that, he flew away from her, all the way down to the corner, where he made another smooth stop and spun around to face her, his arms outstretched as he waited for her to join him.

She bit her lip, sucked in a deep breath, and started skating on her own. Her legs felt even more wobbly at first, the slightest motion of her foot or ankle propelling her farther than she'd anticipated, and she kept her arms out at her sides—like wings. He'd said she should think of it as flying. The wings of a flightless bird. A turkey, probably.

That thought made her laugh, and laughing made her relax. She allowed herself a little more speed and let her hips settle into balance. She even lowered her hands slightly, her arms still sticking out but no longer horizontal. The wind rejuvenated her, and Derek's welcoming stance at the end of the block encouraged her.

Yes, she could do this!

The only problem was, she couldn't stop. As she neared him, she tried to touch her brake to the sidewalk, but tilting her foot made her feel so unstable she straightened it again. If she could steer a little better, she'd aim for the grass strip that bordered the curb. The grass was dead, so she couldn't kill it by in-line skating onto it. But if she hit the grass she'd likely fall, and then she wouldn't be able to have dinner with Derek.

If she didn't fall, though, she was going to skate right into him.

She was gliding faster. Another attempt to press the brake against the pavement made her feel so lopsided, her arms popped back up to horizontal again. Derek loomed closer and closer, and she was going to crash into him. "I'm sorry!" she shouted as the distance narrowed between them. "I can't stop!"

She slammed into him—but they didn't go

down. He stood rock solid, absorbing the impact
of the collision and closing his arms around her
to keep her upright. Her feet skidded and scrambled underneath her, but he wouldn't let her fall.

He must really want to have dinner with her
tonight.

Either that, or he simply wanted an excuse to
hold her.

She gripped his jacket with her fisting hands
and struggled to catch her breath. Her body was
pressed to Derek's, hips against hips, chest
against chest, her head cushioned by his shoulder. She smelled his aftershave, a clean, tangy
fragrance. She felt his hands flattening at the
small of her back; he was leaning in toward her.

It took more courage to gaze up at him than it
had to strap on the in-line skates. The moment
her eyes met his, the words *I can't stop* took on
an entirely new meaning.

His mouth came down on hers, light but firm.
His lips touched, brushed, caressed. They nipped,
they tasted, they stroked, they claimed.

She couldn't stop—and she didn't want to.

If the ground felt shaky beneath her now, the
in-line skates had nothing to do with it. If her
heart raced, it wasn't from fear—or if it was, it
wasn't from the fear that she'd wind up with a
broken wrist. Kissing a man the way she was
kissing Derek, desiring a man as much as she
desired him, could leave a woman bruised and in
pain.

But while she might not trust her feet in in-line skates, she trusted her heart enough to let it fly.

His hands wandered up her back and into her hair, digging into the dense waves and holding her head steady. One of her feet skidded and he steadied her leg with his knee. Through the worn leather of his jacket, she felt the lean contours of his sides, the hard ridge of his lower ribs.

He skimmed his tongue along her lower lip and she sighed and opened to him. Derek was giving her a thrill, all right—a far more intense one than the in-line skates had led her to expect. His tongue surged against hers, dueled playfully and then overpowered her, filling her mouth with a possessive thrust that resonated throughout her body. He let his fingers whisper against the nape of her neck, then slid one hand forward to cup her cheek and angle her face so he could kiss her even more deeply.

She lost her awareness of the fact that they were standing on a public street corner in her parents' neighborhood, the block where she'd grown up. People who had known her all her life could peek out their windows and spy on her as she kissed a man.

If any of her parents' neighbors were observing her in this passionate clench with Derek Palmer, so be it. Derek was all that mattered—his hands warming her cheeks, his tongue flicking against her teeth and then reluctantly withdrawing, his breath emerging in a harsh sigh that left a trail of white vapor in the cold air.

"You didn't fall," he whispered.

"In other words—" her voice was low and uneven "—I have to have dinner with you."

"I'm afraid so." His words were solemn, but his eyes sparkled with humor.

"That'll teach me to try skating."

"I think we've both learned an important lesson," he declared. A smile curved his lips and teased a dimple into his cheek.

Melissa agreed that there had to be some lesson in all this—but damned if she knew what it was.

Damned if she cared.

CHAPTER FIVE

DEREK LEANED BACK into the pillow he'd
propped against the headboard and smiled.
Through the door of his bathroom, he heard water running in the sink. Melissa was brushing her
teeth, using her finger. Having a woman spend
the night at his apartment wasn't such a common
occurrence that he kept spare toothbrushes on
hand.

Fortunately, he kept condoms on hand. A good
supply.

From the moment he'd seen Melissa looming
in his office doorway Friday morning, he'd desired her. He'd told himself all he wanted was
her foundation's money, and maybe her respect,
instead of the look of horrified contempt she'd
given him when he'd hobbled into his office on
one skate.

But the truth was, he'd wanted *her*.

When he'd come home last night from their
dinner, he'd found the newspaper spread open on
his kitchen table, just the way he'd left it that
morning. He'd crossed the room to fold it and
add it to the recycling pile, but the horoscope had
caught his eye.

You run the risk of making a fool of yourself. He'd certainly done that, starting with the gainer he'd taken at the corner and continuing with his first encounter with Melissa. He'd run a risk of making a fool of himself that evening, too, when he'd left the chocolate and the note for her.

Be careful around animals and members of the opposite sex. One always had to be careful around psychopathic squirrels. If Derek had paid closer attention to that Capricorn write-up, he might have been better prepared for Herman's sabotage. As for being careful around members of the opposite sex, well, he hadn't been careful around Melissa when he'd met her, and she'd been grossly underwhelmed by him.

An unexpected opportunity will pass you by if you don't act on it. The opportunity to win the Towers Foundation as a client had come very close to passing him by. It was only because Abby and Stan had nagged him that he had acted on it and—he hoped—salvaged the account.

Someone in a hat may bring luck—but remember, luck comes in many guises and isn't always easy to recognize. What was the name of Melissa's colleague? Turnbull? No, Trumbull. Tom Trumbull. He'd worn a hat, and he'd given Derek Melissa's home address. How lucky could a guy get?

Pretty damned lucky. Every line of that horoscope had come true for him yesterday. He'd never before considered horoscopes as accurate

predictors of what might happen to *him.* He'd
only used them for guidance in his investments.

Maybe he ought to start paying more attention
to them in a personal context.

He heard the water turn off and his smile deepened, settling into his soul. Dinner with her tonight had been wonderful. He'd picked her up at
her apartment at seven. She'd introduced him to
her roommate; the ''Jo'' he'd feared as a rival
for her affection was a skinny, trendy woman
wearing bright red nail polish and high-heeled,
fake-lizard boots that she said were some man-
ufacturer's overstock. She'd been heading for a
party at a loft in TriBeCa, and she'd invited them
to join her, but fortunately Melissa had declined.

They'd eaten a comparatively sedate dinner at
an Italian restaurant in her neighborhood, where
she'd explained to him the nuances distinguish-
ing northern Italian from southern Italian cuisine.
''My ancestors were from Naples,'' she'd said,
''but I prefer northern Italian cooking.''

She'd told him about her parents, how they'd
both grown up in Sunnyside and been high
school sweethearts. They'd married as soon as
her father had returned home from Vietnam, and
he and his brother had opened the corner grocery
store, fending off competition from the super-
market chains by catering personally to their
neighbors and customers. She'd told him about
her father's heart attack, about how close she and
her mother had come to losing him, and how they

both worried so much about his health. "It isn't just the heavy lifting in the job. Physical exercise is good for him—although it has to be the right kind of physical exercise, and I'm not sure lugging heavy cartons of merchandise qualifies. But there's also a lot of stress in running a small grocery store. I really wish he'd cut back a little on his work. I know he would if he could afford to. I help my parents out as much as I can. If I do a good job for the Towers Foundation, maybe they'll increase my salary and I'll be able to help my folks out even more."

She'd asked him about his own family, which he considered much less interesting than hers. But she'd said the idea of growing up the son of a teacher and a pharmacist in a bucolic Philadelphia suburb sounded pretty exotic to her. He'd told her about his twin sisters, three years older than him and just about the best-behaved daughters his parents could have dreamed of, which in contrast made his boyhood mischief seem far naughtier than it actually was.

They'd drunk Chianti Classico and shared a dessert of tiramisu, and throughout the entire meal Derek had remembered the way her mouth had trembled and softened beneath his when he'd kissed her that afternoon. Her lips had been sweeter than the creamy Italian delicacy, more intoxicating than the hearty wine. Once he'd settled the bill, he'd decided to run the risk of making a fool of himself with her again. He'd asked her if she would come home with him.

He hadn't expected her to say yes. She clearly wasn't the casual-sex type. He could only assume she felt the same irresistible pull he did, the same implacable yearning. She must have understood, as he did, that what was developing between them had been designed by destiny, beyond their control.

Just as the stars ordained the horoscope, they seemed to ordain that Melissa and Derek belonged together.

He heard the bathroom door open and glanced toward his bedroom doorway. Melissa appeared in it, wearing a plaid flannel shirt of his. The tails fell to mid-thigh, and if she unrolled the sleeves they would drop well past her fingertips. The top two buttons were undone, and she was the sexiest woman he'd ever seen.

His body reacted instantly to her presence. She smiled shyly and padded to his bed, her bare feet silent against the area rug that covered the hardwood floor. "I love your sink," she said as she sat on the edge of the mattress. "A porcelain pedestal sink. And the faucets—they looked like jacks. You know those jacks little girls play with?"

He supposed his four-pronged faucets did look like jacks. What he loved was not his sink but her enthusiasm about it. He also loved the velvety texture of her skin, its tawny undertones, and the way her long, thick hair tumbled around her face, making her look utterly wanton. He loved the delicate slenderness of her wrists, the tapered length of her fingers, the sleek contours of her thighs beneath the edge of his shirt.

He reached for her and pulled her into his arms. "If I'd known you had a thing for sinks, I would have mentioned those faucets right off the bat," he said before brushing a kiss against the crown of her head.

Her smile grew even more bashful. "It's obvious you didn't need to use your sink to lure me here."

He kissed her again, pushing her hair back from her face so his lips could find her forehead. "I don't know how I managed to lure you here. But I'm sure glad I did."

"You don't know?" She leaned back and peered into his face, searching it. Her smile was gone; she looked serious, almost grave. "You don't know why I came here?"

"Luck?" he guessed.

"You." She traced the edge of his chin with her thumb. "I came here for you."

His heart bumped against his ribs. He couldn't recall a woman ever saying anything so romantic to him before, so *scary*. But even if he hadn't been prepared to acknowledge it, he'd known right from the start that this wasn't a fling, a passing amusement. It had the potential to be as serious as Melissa looked right now. Luck or no luck, stars or no stars, this thing—whatever it was—was real.

He kissed her, a deep, devouring kiss, his own way of telling her what she'd told him in words. As he kissed her, he moved his hands down the front of her borrowed shirt, opening the buttons, pushing back the fabric. Then he turned her in his arms, lifting her over his lap and next to him onto the mattress. Her breasts were beautiful, larger than he'd expected and pale, and so sensitive that he had only to sketch circles around them and her nipples swelled tight. He bowed to kiss one and then the other, and she made a sound in her throat, a breathy plea. He wondered if he could please her just by kissing her breasts.

Probably—but he didn't have that much willpower. As he ran his tongue over one taut nipple, her legs shifted restlessly, kicking against the sheets, and her hips surged. She made that noise again—and listening to her moan like that was probably enough to make *him* come.

She ran her hands down through his hair to his shoulders. Her fingers were cool, still slightly damp from her recent encounter with his pedestal sink, and they made his skin feel warmer than it was. She traced wavy lines across his back and he had to force himself to breathe regularly, to keep nibbling her breasts rather than to haul himself up and demand that she touch him where he truly wanted to be touched, where he was not just warm but white-hot.

This, too, was luck. He'd been with enough women to know that it wasn't always so good, so intense. Melissa's body was perfectly attuned to his. She didn't have to tell him where to touch her, or how. Whatever he did seemed to bring her pleasure. And watching her respond, feeling her respond, made him crazy to do more, to make the pleasure even greater for her.

He skimmed his hands along her thighs, and her fingers tensed against his sides. He pressed her legs apart and touched her, and she arched into his hand.

She was so wet, so ready. He slid one finger deep and she cried out, his name tumbling from her lips. He had to stop stroking her to reach for a condom, and he was surprised when she snatched it out of his hand and nudged him onto his back. She rolled the sheath onto him, her fumbling fingers turning him on far more than deftness might have. He gazed up into her face and saw a maelstrom of emotions in her eyes—desperation and delight, a longing as elemental as life itself.

He lifted her up over him and she settled her legs around his hips. Her hair spilled into his face, a gentle black shower of curls as she propped herself above him. He brought his hands to her hips, letting his thumbs wander down between her thighs and moving her against him. With a helpless gasp, she took him in, and then he was the helpless one, pinned on his back while she rode him.

He slid his hands up to her breasts and then back down to her hips. She made that noise again, the one that just about killed him, and he had to close his eyes and regroup to keep himself from finishing too soon. Once he'd regained control of himself, he opened his eyes in time to see her bite her lip and arch her throat, striving, reaching, needing.

He brought his hand between them, down to where he was inside her. His touch broke her rhythm. He touched her again and she moaned, one last deep release of breath as she let go.

Her body throbbed around him, fierce pulses that set him off. He closed his eyes once more, wanting only to feel, to feel her skin and her weight and her marvelous body wringing sensation from him.

Luck, he thought. Maybe luck, maybe lust. Maybe another four-letter word that started with an *L*. There had to be some profound, otherworldly reason sex with her was so incredible. It wasn't technique, it wasn't chemistry. It was something more, something he might not be able to define or explain. Something that simply had to be accepted on faith.

SHE WASN'T SURE how long she lay limp in his arms, her body smoldering like a fire that simply didn't want to burn itself out. If she hadn't heard the knocking, she probably would have remained exactly where she was forever.

But there it was again, a sharp tapping sound. "What's that?" she whispered.

"Hmm?" He sounded half asleep, but he stirred under her and brushed a sweat-damp strand of hair back from her cheek.

"I heard a noise. A knocking." She pushed herself up enough to see his face.

He was frowning. "I'm not expecting any company." He angled his body up slightly, glanced toward the door and then toward the floor. "And I don't think we made enough noise to disturb the neighbors. Although—" he gave her a wicked smile "—I suppose we could be a bit noisier if we put our minds to it."

He looked a little too drained to try anything noisy, at least for the next few minutes. She needed a bit more time to recuperate, too. A bit more time to just lie with him, his arms wrapped around her and his body cushioning hers. A bit more time to get her pulse back to normal and her mind clear.

Actually, her mind was pretty clear. It had been clear the entire evening. Even when she found herself doing something totally out of character—agreeing to spend the night with a man she'd met only a day ago—she'd been completely conscious of what she was doing. She'd chosen to make love with Derek not to satisfy

some reckless, heedless urge but for lucid, justi-
fiable reasons.

One was that he was so damned sexy. Not the
most sterling rationale, but the truth was, he
turned her on. His smile played on her emotions
in myriad ways. His eyes were expressive on
countless levels. His touch, no matter how in-
nocent, aroused her.

But there were other reasons, too. She'd never
been the sort of person who acted on impulse.
She liked to think things through and plan things
out. But he'd gotten her to rearrange her plan for
today—reviewing the books at the family grocery
store—and to do something whimsical: learning
how to in-line skate. And after he'd kissed her a
few times, she'd gotten pretty good at it. Good
enough that she hadn't fallen once.

Thank heavens for that. If she'd fallen, they
might not have had dinner together, and then she
wouldn't be in his bed right now, feeling his
chest rise and fall against her cheek as he
breathed, feeling the possessive weight of his leg
wrapped around hers.

She liked his playful streak, mostly because
she knew that behind his playfulness he was a
tough-minded man. He'd been daring enough to
leave the safety of a large Wall Street firm to set
up his own company with a couple of colleagues—and he was talented and diligent
enough to make that company a success. Melissa
didn't measure success by wealth. To her, suc-

cess was the ability to make a dream come true, through hard work, honesty and careful planning. By her standards, her father and Uncle Eddie were hugely successful, because they'd had a dream of owning their own neighborhood grocery, and they'd made it happen. It didn't matter that they earned a modest income. What mattered was that through their own efforts, they'd achieved their dream.

Derek was like that. He was the Wizard, the genius behind his company's success. Of course his partners contributed greatly to the firm: without strong customer service and meticulous organization, an independent brokerage such as theirs would never survive. But Derek was the one with an uncanny talent for investing, the one whose virtuosity at buying and selling stocks made his partners' efforts worthwhile.

She knew her own limits. She'd always been something of a plodder, accomplishing her goals through sheer tenacity. But she admired those dazzling people who were blessed with unfathomable intellectual gifts, who could comprehend ideas and discern trends most people never noticed or understood. More than admired—she was enthralled by them.

Derek was one of the blessed few. How could she not fall in love with him?

She heard a distinct tapping sound again. "Did you hear it?" she asked.

He sighed. "It's Herman."

"What?"

"Herman. The squirrel from hell."

She laughed at the absurdity of Derek's statement. Sure, he was the Wizard, a certified genius. But that was no guarantee against silliness. "How could a squirrel—"

The tapping sounded again and was actually more of a clicking. Without explanation, Derek groped for the flannel shirt he'd lent her earlier. It had gotten tangled up in the sheets, so he shook it out and helped her slide her arms into it. He grabbed his boxers from the night table and slid them on. With a jerk of his head, he signaled her to follow him to one of the windows.

When she was standing beside him, he tugged open the drape. A large, plump squirrel sat on the outside sill, an acorn in his front paws. For a second he stared through the window at Derek and Melissa, then banged his acorn against the glass. Tap-tap-tap.

"I don't believe it!"

"Believe it. This squirrel is my nemesis. He'll do whatever he can to irritate me—including drive the woman in my life crazy by banging his acorn against the window when we're enjoying the afterglow of the most phenomenal sex in the history of the universe. Go away, Herman," he snarled at the creature, who pinched his mouth as if he wanted to snarl back.

Melissa struggled to assimilate Derek's words. *The most phenomenal sex in the history of the universe*—yes, that sounded reasonably accurate. The squirrel being his nemesis seemed somewhat exaggerated.

But that other thing he'd said, about the woman in his life. Was that how he saw her? As the woman in his life?

She wanted to hug him, to pepper him with kisses, to exclaim that she was so glad she wasn't the only one caught up in a romance that seemed awfully whirlwind but utterly right. She wanted to be the woman in his life. She wanted it more than she could remember ever wanting anything else.

Even if being the woman in his life meant she had to take his side against the most adorable squirrel she'd ever seen.

"How can you say he's from hell?" she asked. "Look at those cute little eyes."

"The eyes of Satan," Derek muttered, then waved his hand at the window as if to flick the squirrel off his perch. "Get out of here!"

The squirrel smacked the acorn against the glass one last time, then poked his nose in the air and spun away, whipping his thick tail against the pane as he went. Derek leaned forward and squinted through the glass, then scowled and shook his head. Before he could close the drapes, Melissa glimpsed the droppings the squirrel had left behind.

"All right," she conceded. "So he's messy. He's still very cute."

"He wants me dead," Derek insisted, though his tone was mild. "I should have done him in yesterday when I had the chance. I could have skated over him, but I didn't. I avoided him—and wound up hurting myself. See?" He gestured toward the purple bruise that darkened his left knee. "If I'd skated over him, I could have spared myself that."

"But you wouldn't have been able to live with yourself," Melissa pointed out, not at all persuaded by his bluster. She didn't think Derek could ever kill a squirrel, even one he loathed.

"I could kill him without a moment's qualm," he boasted, his smile assuring her he was joking. "But if I did, you'd never forgive me."

"You're right about that." She took his hand and led him back to the bed. "Now you just lie right down and tell me if there's something I can do to make that bruise hurt a little less."

His smile deepened as his gaze merged with hers. "Hmm," he murmured, gliding his hand tantalizingly up her thigh and under the loose tails of the flannel shirt. "I can think of a few things you can do."

They kissed, and she was willing to bet that his bruised knee was the furthest thing from his mind.

CHAPTER SIX

"THERE'S A GALLERY opening tonight, if you want to come," JoAnn told Melissa. They were sitting side by side on the couch in their tiny living room, sharing take-out tubs of Thai chicken and rice that Melissa had picked up on her way home from work. Melissa still had on the dress she'd worn to the office, but her shoes were off and her stockinged feet rested upon the storage chest/coffee table. JoAnn's feet rested there, too, but she was wearing garish green-vinyl mules—no doubt some shoe designer's ghastly mistake.

Melissa chewed thoughtfully on a spicy chunk of chicken. "Maybe. But I can't stay too late. It's a work night."

JoAnn laughed. "I bet you always went to bed early on school nights, too. When your parents said, 'Bedtime, Melissa,' you never kicked up a fight. So, do you think Loverboy might want to join us?"

Melissa sighed. No, there was no chance Derek would want to join them on a Thursday evening.

Life was so close to perfect with him. They

had spent every weekend together, Friday and Saturday nights and all day on Sundays. Some days they went on outings—to a museum, a movie, downtown to Battery Park for a ride on the Staten Island ferry. Other days they stayed closer to home, strolling through his Upper West Side neighborhood, browsing in the shops along Broadway, dining at intimate tables in romantic cafés. One Saturday when the air had warmed with a premature hint of spring, they brought a picnic lunch to Central Park. One Friday night, they'd accompanied JoAnn and a costume designer she occasionally dated to a rowdy party on an unused theater stage. Melissa and Derek had danced half the night away and awakened with sore legs the next morning.

One Sunday, they'd traveled out to Sunnyside for a dinner at her parents' house. Derek had brought a huge bouquet of spring blossoms for her mother and a bottle of brandy for her father. He'd charmed them silly. Her mother had humiliated her by dragging out the photo album and showing Derek pictures of a very young Melissa mugging for the camera. In one photo, she stood shakily in the driveway, scarcely balanced on the colorful clip-on roller skates her grandmother had given her for her fifth birthday.

Her parents adored Derek. JoAnn approved of him. Melissa was falling madly in love with him.

So close to perfect—except for one thing: Derek didn't want her to spend any nights other than Friday or Saturday with him.

JoAnn thought Melissa was stuffy when it came to partying on weeknights, but Derek was much worse. Sunday evenings, he would accompany her to her apartment. His farewell kiss would always be deeply passionate, wistful, almost despairing. When he got home he'd phone her to wish her a good-night and sweet dreams.

But he wouldn't let her spend Sunday night with him.

If anyone understood the difficulties of functioning at work after a night with too little sleep, Melissa did. But surely she and Derek could exercise some discipline if they spent the night together on a work night. They could limit themselves to only one bout of lovemaking—probably.

But Derek refused even to consider it.

At first she worried that he might be dating another girlfriend during the week. However, she honestly didn't see how he could manage that, not when he phoned her most evenings. Not when he occasionally showed up at her office, surprising her with a single yellow tulip or an array of chocolate bars from the cheapest no-name brand to the most elegant Swiss or Belgian import. The first time he'd shown up, he'd greeted Tom Trumbull as if he were a long-lost brother, which had surprised her; she hadn't realized they'd ever met before. But subsequent visits found Derek being the one greeted warmly. The foundation had decided to invest some money through his firm, and in the two months he'd worked with their funds, their investment had returned an excellent profit. Ronald Towers himself had shaken Derek's hand and mentioned that he'd like to discuss some personal investments with him.

Melissa was proud that her colleagues and her boss respected Derek's expertise. She knew he was brilliant, and it pleased her that the people she worked with recognized his prowess, as well. But being in love with the Wizard had its drawbacks.

"I don't know how to explain it," he'd said when she pressed him about his refusal to let her sleep over on a weeknight. "It's just the way I work. I've got to be on track. My mind has to be focused. I have these morning routines, and if I don't get through them I can't function. I make such high-pressure decisions, Melissa—I just need to have my head in the right place if I'm going to do the job right. Having you here would distract me."

She supposed wizards had their rituals. But Derek *knew* her. Did he really think she'd interfere with him if he wanted to spend his breakfast guzzling coffee and memorizing the stock charts? Or sipping herbal tea and meditating? She had no idea how wizards started their days, but she loved

Derek. She would never do anything to distract him from his wizardry.

When she pictured her future, he was in it. Prominently. Centrally. In her ideal picture, they were married, sharing a home every day of the week. Nothing in Derek's behavior indicated that she was insane to imagine such a thing. When they were together, he treated her with love and affection. When they were apart, he stayed in touch, telephoning to ask her about her day, laughing at her funny anecdotes and consoling her about her frustrations.

She had no reason to believe he didn't love her as much as she loved him. Correction: she had *one* reason.

He wouldn't let her spend a weeknight in his bed.

For the first two months of their relationship, she'd accepted it. But now April was warming the horizon, and it was really beginning to bug her.

As her closest friend, JoAnn knew how much it bothered her. She lowered her chopsticks and eyed her couch-mate, her face shadowed with concern. "Melissa, Derek is the best thing that ever happened to you—maybe the best thing that ever happened to either one of us. Don't blow it just because he won't go to a gallery opening with you on a Thursday night."

"Oh, he'd probably go with me," Melissa muttered. "But then he'd see me home, kiss me goodbye and go back to West Sixty-ninth Street." She sighed. "I bet he spends his week-nights torturing that poor squirrel. He just doesn't want me to witness his cruelty."

JoAnn laughed. "Well, if he's going to have all that fun with his squirrel, you ought to come to the gallery opening with me and have some fun yourself. We can stay till about ten-thirty and then you can come home and get your beauty rest. How about it?"

Melissa wasn't in the mood to sip cheap wine shoulder to shoulder with a bunch of artsy types in a small, crowded gallery. But if she stayed home, she'd spend the evening alone, wondering why Derek didn't want her with him on a Thursday night.

"Sure," she said, forcing a smile. "I'll go with you." She'd have JoAnn for company to-night, and Derek would have Herman. Definitely his loss.

"HI," JOANN'S VOICE chirped on the answering machine. "Melissa and JoAnn can't take your call right now. We're either working, sleeping, shopping, washing our hair or painting the town red. Leave a message if you're not too envious."

Derek heard the beep, signaling that the ma-chine was ready to record his message, but he didn't speak. He lowered the phone onto its cra-dle and scowled because Melissa wasn't avail-able to talk to him.

He missed her.

His apartment seemed too big when he was alone. He used to think it was on the small side. Now, since Melissa, he couldn't use the kitchen without wishing she was in it—on a Saturday morning, perhaps, clad in one of his old flannel shirts and nothing else, her hair tousled and her hands wrapped around a steaming mug of coffee. He couldn't wash his face without hearing her rhapsodize about his antiquated bathroom fixtures. He couldn't take a shower without imagining her standing under the hot spray with him, the water streaming through her hair and down her body as she soaped his back, then his front.

And now she was off somewhere, unable to answer her phone. It was his own fault, too.

She wanted to spend more time with him. She'd told him as much. One of the best things about their relationship was that she was forthright about her wants. If she wanted to make love, she didn't act coy and bashful; she simply wrapped her arms around his neck, kissed his lips, and whispered, "Let's go to bed." Or the couch, or the floor, or wherever the spirit moved them to go. If she was hungry, she said so. If he asked which video they should rent, she never said, "Whatever you want, darling." She told him which video she preferred, and if they disagreed, she fought for her video.

He was the one being less than honest. If he were as forthright as she was, he'd tell her why he couldn't have her sleep over on weeknights: he couldn't let her learn the truth about his investment strategy.

She thought he was some kind of genius. Hell, everybody did: his partners, the firm's clients, even Melissa's co-workers and her boss, Ronald Towers himself. When Melissa introduced him to Derek, he'd mentioned how impressed he was by the performance of the fund in which Towers Foundation money was currently invested. ''I might have some pocket change for you to play with,'' he'd remarked. The man was worth billions of dollars. Pocket change for him would be millions, at least.

Would Ronald Towers entrust Derek with his pocket change if he knew Derek divined his investments from the horoscope page in *America Today*? Would Melissa still think he was a genius?

If she were someone else, he'd take her into his confidence, and she'd laugh and enjoy being his co-conspirator. But she was so damned earnest. She took things seriously—for instance, Derek's reputation as a miracle man when it came to investing. He simply couldn't bear to think of what she'd do if she woke up one weekday morning, came into the kitchen and found him sitting with the newspaper open to the astrology column, his Palm Pilot at his elbow, while he counted the number of words in the first sentence and noted all the nouns. He usually wasn't afraid to take risks—but he wasn't prepared to risk Melissa's respect for him.

So here he was, all alone on a Thursday evening, while Melissa was downtown somewhere. He prayed that she wasn't painting the town red without him.

If she was, he had only himself and his bizarre stock strategy to blame.

THE ART GALLERY was as awful as she'd anticipated. The paintings were pretentious, canvas after canvas of vivid streaks with a Roman numeral inscribed in black in the lower right corner of each. What did it mean? Why was the red canvas numbered "IV" while the green one was "MDC"?

If Derek had accompanied her, she would have had a blast. He would have come up with an elaborate theory for the Roman numerals "Actually, the 'IV' on that canvas doesn't represent the number four. It stands for 'intravenous,' and the red paint is supposed to make you think of blood. 'MDC' isn't sixteen hundred in this context. It's someone's initials. Or no—it stands for the artist's summation of his life's work. 'My Dopey Canvas.'"

Without him to joke with, she'd spent the time sipping from a plastic glass of wine that tasted even worse than she'd feared. And she'd listened to the art fans around her pontificate about the spiritual significance of Roman numerals. Well before ten o'clock, she'd signaled JoAnn that she was ready to leave.

She should have stayed home. But if she had, she would have spent the evening wondering why she wasn't with Derek.

She wanted to trust him as much as she loved him—not just trust him, but believe that he trusted her equally. If this relationship was going to succeed, Melissa needed reassurance that Derek wanted her around as much on a weekday morning as he did between Friday night and Sunday evening.

And if he didn't want her that much, then she'd be better off ending the relationship now, before she fell even more deeply in love with him.

She didn't sleep well that night and the cheap wine left a headache in its wake. Her mind kept churning all night long, refusing to set aside her apprehension about Derek and the future of their relationship.

By 6:00 a.m. she was tired of tossing and turning. She arose in the milky-dawn light, downed a cup of coffee, and dressed in a trouser suit of spring-weight wool. She pinned her hair back from her face, added some makeup and her simple pearl earrings and checked the contents of her briefcase. By six-thirty she was out the door.

The subway platform wasn't as crowded as it usually was when she caught the train to her office, and she actually got a seat on the uptown local. In fifteen minutes, she emerged from the station into the pale spring sunlight and strolled the few blocks to West Sixty-ninth Street.

A plump, cheerful-looking squirrel guarded the stairs that led to the front door of Derek's building. Melissa wasn't convinced that a specific squirrel named Herman existed—all squirrels looked alike to her, and she suspected that Herman was in fact a horde of nearly identical critters. But if this fellow was Herman, he was certainly a lot friendlier than the fiendish beast Derek muttered about. The squirrel dropped the bread crust he'd been snacking on and bounded from the steps to the wrought-iron railing. He scampered up it to the door, where he sat calmly, his head cocked as if to say, "Come on in!"

She had never been welcomed anywhere by a squirrel before. The experience made her smile. Surely Derek's paranoia about squirrels was unrealistic. If this was Herman, he was quite the pleasant host.

She stepped into the vestibule of his building and reached for the intercom button for his apartment. Before she could press it, the inner door opened and the lawyer who lived in the apartment across the hall from Derek's filled the doorway, decked out in jogging clothes. She had met John and his partner a few times since she'd started spending her weekends with Derek. He greeted her with a big grin. "You're up early, aren't you?"

She returned his smile. "So are you."

"Gotta get my daily run." He held the inner door open for her, then darted out of the building and headed down the street in a loping gait. The squirrel, she noticed, was gone.

She climbed the stairs to Derek's floor and pressed the button at the center of his door. After a brief wait she heard the dead bolt click, and the door swung inward. "Melissa," Derek murmured.

He was more or less dressed for work, in crisp slacks, dark socks and an Oxford shirt, a tie dangling loose around the collar. His hair glistened with moisture from a recent shower, and his freshly shaven cheeks smelled of his familiar aftershave. His eyes were bright but his lips were not smiling.

Had she interrupted something? God help her if it was something with another woman. Was barging in on him going to wind up embarrassing them both?

"I missed you," she said.

He wrapped his hand gently around her upper arm, pulled her inside and shut the door. Then he enveloped her in his arms and kissed her—a greedy, penetrating kiss that reassured her he didn't have another woman lurking in his bed. "I missed you, too," he whispered. "I called you last night and no one was home. I figured you and JoAnn were painting the town red."

"We were painting it drab gray," she told him

between kisses. It felt so good having his arms around her, so good having his lips brushing her cheeks, her forehead, the tip of her nose. Why couldn't they start every day like this? He obviously wanted to as much as she did.

Feeling inordinately better, she leaned back and gazed into his face. Love bathed her in its shimmering warmth. "Offer me a cup of coffee and I'll say yes."

"Coffee," he muttered, his smile vanishing.

Her inner warmth vanished just as quickly. Why was asking for a cup of coffee at 7:30 in the morning a problem? Maybe the other woman was lurking not in his bed, but in his kitchen.

"You're having coffee right now," she pointed out. She'd tasted it in his kiss. "Did you not make enough to share?"

"No, I—" He glanced away.

The longer he hesitated, the greater her anxiety grew. "All right, skip the coffee. I'll settle for tea," she said, hearing a tremor of panic in her voice even as she tried to joke.

"I have plenty of coffee," he said, turning back to her. He stepped away from the door, a look of resignation sliding down over his face. "If you want coffee, you'll have coffee." He pivoted and stalked into the kitchen.

She realized he'd been telling the truth about his morning rituals, his need to stick to an unvarying routine before work. Now that he'd gotten past his initial joy at her unexpected appearance on his doorstep, he was angry with her for having messed up his schedule. Fair enough. She was so relieved that he wasn't with another woman, she could handle his wrath.

She followed him into the kitchen. The aroma of fresh-brewed coffee hung thick in the air, and sunlight streamed through the window by the table, across which a copy of *America Today* was spread open. Next to the newspaper sat a mug of coffee, a plate with a toasted English muffin on it, and Derek's Palm Pilot.

She wasn't sure what she'd expected. An exercise mat on the floor, maybe. Some free weights. A Beethoven symphony. Incense. An encyclopedic volume on stock trades. Something a bit more esoteric than the sorts of things that might be found on the kitchen table of any normal, non-wizardly person.

Derek folded the newspaper and tossed it aside, clearing space on the table. "Would you like an English muffin, or some toast? Or a bowl of cereal—"

"No, thanks," she said, startled by his nervous energy as he darted around the kitchen to fill a mug with coffee for her.

"Sit." He pointed toward the chair across from his. He set the mug down in front of her, then carried a carton of milk from the refrigerator to the table.

"I drink it black," she reminded him, bewildered. Every Saturday and Sunday morning for the past few months, he'd seen her drink her coffee black.

"Right." He rolled his eyes and hustled back to the refrigerator to put the milk away. "What else can I get you? A multivitamin?"

"Derek." She laughed at his edginess. "Relax. Sit and finish your breakfast. It's just me."

"Right." He stopped opening and shutting cabinet doors and returned to the table. He slumped into his chair, took a deep breath and smiled at her.

"I saw a squirrel outside. Do you think it was Herman?"

Derek looked wary. "How did he act?"

"Very friendly. He practically escorted me to the front door and waved me inside, like he really wanted me to barge in on you."

"That was Herman," Derek grunted, turning to the window as if he didn't want her to suffer the full force of his frown.

"Are you all right?"

"I'm fine. Just a little off balance. I wasn't expecting you."

"I know." She took a sip of coffee and sighed. "For us to see each other on a weekday morning is unheard of."

He obviously understood what she was getting at. "I'm sorry, Melissa. I know you want us to spend more time together."

"If I'm being pushy—"

"No. I want us to spend more time together, too. It's just that I need my mornings."

"Am I that big a distraction?"

He let his gaze wander slowly over her face. A helpless laugh escaped him. "Yeah," he admitted. "You're an incredible distraction."

Her cheeks grew warm from his flattery. "But I'm not a distraction when you call me from your office."

"It's different. I use my mornings to set myself up, to plan out what I'm going to do that day. You love to plan things out, so you should understand. Once I've got my plan settled in my mind, the day falls into place. At that point, a little distraction isn't going to throw me off."

"My being here now—it throws you off?"

"I'm afraid so." He looked sad oddly enough.

She drank some coffee and tried to sort her thoughts. Derek was the least rigid person she knew. Spur-of-the-moment activities delighted him. She was the organized, orderly one in their relationship.

How could he be so unyielding at 7:30 a.m. when he was so flexible the rest of the time?

And what would happen if her dreams came true and they decided to get married? Would he move out of their home on weekdays and return only on the weekends, so she wouldn't throw him off?

"I love you, Derek," she said, her voice steady and sure. "But I don't understand this."

"I love you, too." He reached across the table and covered her hand with his. "And I just can't explain this."

"Why not?"

He sighed, lifted her hand to his mouth and kissed her fingertips. "Because," he admitted, "I don't understand it myself."

CHAPTER SEVEN

HE WAS IN BIG trouble.

He sat at his desk in the office, staring alternately at his computer monitor and his blank Palm Pilot. He didn't know what to do.

No nouns. No word counts. He hadn't had a chance to read his horoscope, let alone to make note of the relevant information, before Melissa had rung his bell that morning. Without his horoscope, he was at a complete loss.

A crutch, that was what the daily Capricorn write-up was. He wasn't proud of himself for needing it, but damn it, it worked. For three years—since before he, Stan and Abby had established their firm—he had used astrology to determine his day's transactions. It had worked then, and it worked now, and he wasn't about to toss the crutch aside.

And he'd still have his crutch today—if Melissa hadn't asked if she could steal his copy of *America Today*. "I left home so early, I didn't have a chance to read the paper. Can I filch yours to read when I get to my office?"

Like an idiot, he'd said, "Sure."

He was a coward. He should have come clean, told her about the horoscopes and let her learn that the man she loved was no wizard. Any stock investor could do what he did: pluck the nouns from the astrology column and find stocks on the market that sounded like the nouns.

But he loved the fact that Melissa loved him—and he knew her love was based in part on his alleged wizardry when it came to investments. He couldn't let her find out the truth about him.

He clicked through the files of his computer until he got to his data on the overall holdings of his major stock fund. He supposed he could leave it unchanged for one day, just let everything ride. Doing nothing might be better than doing the wrong thing.

But what if the market took a downturn? What if action was necessary?

He shoved himself to his feet, stuffed his Palm Pilot into his pocket and stalked out of his office. Passing Gloria's desk, he shouted over his shoulder, "I've got to go out for a minute."

"How long will you—?"

"A minute," he repeated, then bolted from the office suite before she could interrogate him further.

He waited impatiently for the elevator to arrive, fidgeted during the trip down to the first floor, and charged out into the echoing lobby. A variety of stores lined the perimeter. He passed the sandwich shop, the barber shop, the one-day dry cleaner, and headed directly to the newsstand. Assorted newspapers were for sale, but *America Today* was sold out.

Maybe it was a syndicated column, and one of the other newspapers carried it. He lifted a copy of the *Post* from the stack and thumbed through it in search of the horoscope page.

"You gonna read that? You better buy it," the newsstand operator barked at him.

Derek dug into his pocket for a few coins, handed them to the man, and continued thumbing through the paper. He found the horoscope column, but it wasn't written by the same astrologer who wrote the column in *America Today*. This other horoscope might work, but Derek wasn't optimistic. The write-up for Capricorn was very brief and lacking in nouns.

"Hey, Derek!" Abby's familiar voice wafted over to him. "What's up?"

He quickly shut the newspaper and spun around.

Abby's smile faded as she perused his face. "Is something wrong?"

"No," he lied, hiding the newspaper behind his back—although the motions of her eyes indicated that she could see the newspaper without any difficulty.

"I'm just back from breakfast with the Mulroneys. They insisted on taking me out to celebrate their returns on the investment of theirs we're managing. They've seen a twenty percent increase in value in less than six months, and they're ecstatic."

"I'm so happy for them," Derek muttered grimly. If he didn't find a copy of the right horoscope soon, the Mulroneys might wind up a little less ecstatic by the end of the day.

"Are you sure nothing's wrong?" Abby appeared concerned. "Everything's okay with Melissa, isn't it?"

"Sure. Everything's fine. We had breakfast together this morning, too." And he'd gazed at Melissa and thought about how crazy he was about her, instead of spending his breakfast doing what he had to do to keep clients like the Mulroneys ecstatic. "Look—I've got to run an errand. I'll be back in the office in a few minutes, and then you can tell me all about the Mulroneys." He stretched his mouth into a smile so phony it hurt his cheeks.

Perplexed, Abby backed toward the elevator bank. Derek waved at her, then turned away. He stuffed the *Post* into the nearest trash can and hurried through the revolving door and out onto the sidewalk.

He stopped at three newsstands. None of them had *America Today*. He wondered if it had an Internet edition. If it did, he might be able to salvage the day.

He ran back to the building, felt his pulse slow while waiting for the elevator to arrive, and paced the tiny car as it carried him up to the eighth floor. Barreling through the firm's reception area, he waved and nodded in Gloria's direction while she hollered after him that she had three messages for him. Still nodding, he hurled himself into his office, slammed the door, and flung himself into his chair.

He tried every search engine he could think of. *America Today* had a Web site, but he couldn't find the horoscope column. Thousands of other horoscope sites were available, and he opened a few. Several offered only yearly and monthly forecasts. Most of them listed daily horoscopes, but none of them sounded right to him.

The wrong horoscope might be worse than no horoscope at all.

Cripes. He could guess what his horoscope that day might be: "Your life is about to come crashing down around you. The woman you love will lose all faith in you once she finds out the truth about you, which she'll learn thanks to the intervention of a monstrous squirrel."

Life, he thought, collecting the nouns of his imaginary horoscope. *Woman, faith, truth, squirrel.* The first four nouns could be the four points orienting his world: life, woman, faith, truth. The four most important sources of strength and joy, the four anchors that kept his soul steady. He could never invest in a stock based on one of those profound, powerful nouns.

Maybe there was a stock that related to the word squirrel.

If there was, he vowed to sell every last share of it in his fund.

MELISSA COULDN'T HELP noticing Derek's sullen mood as they ate dinner that evening. Usually he was buoyant on Friday nights. Much as he and she both enjoyed their jobs, the arrival of Friday night meant the end of the work week and the start of their time together.

Obviously, he wasn't excited about their time together tonight. Seated across from her in a Japanese restaurant in his neighborhood, he poked at his tempura and nursed his bottle of Kirin beer.

"Bad day?" Melissa asked sympathetically.

"Horrible," he confirmed.

"I'm sorry."

"You should be. The Tower Foundation lost a nice piece of change."

She sat straighter. He looked so miserable—but for heaven's sake, he shouldn't. "All funds have their ups and downs," she pointed out. "Your fund will recover. In any case, even after today, I'm sure your clients are way ahead of where they would have been if they'd invested elsewhere."

"Yeah, right." He sighed, took another pull of beer from the bottle, and lowered it to the straw place mat in front of him. "Maybe I've lost my touch."

"After one bad day?"

"Who am I kidding?" he muttered. "I don't have a touch. I've just been lucky all this time."

"Now, don't you put yourself down," she scolded, reaching across the table and giving his hand a squeeze. "You're the Wizard. Just because you've had an off day doesn't mean you aren't brilliant. You are."

He managed a feeble smile. "I'm glad you have faith in me."

"I do," she swore.

Determined to not let him ruin the whole weekend moping about his funds having lost money, Melissa decided to keep his mind off work. She insisted on a walk after dinner. They ambled around the courtyards at Lincoln Center, strolled down to Columbus Circle, then took Central Park West back uptown to Derek's block. The park carried the fragrance of early spring, new grass and budding leaves. By the time they'd reached Derek's apartment, he was in a marginally better mood. And Melissa knew how to make his mood even better, once they were inside. She unbuttoned Derek's shirt, unstrapped his belt, unzipped his fly—and got him into a very good mood, indeed.

ON SUNDAY EVENING the boom fell.

They'd just finished cleaning up from dinner, and the clock showed a few minutes past seven. By seven-thirty, Derek would be escorting her from the subway station to her apartment and kissing her goodbye. By eight he'd be back here, alone, wishing he were a true wizard so he wouldn't have to hide his astrology habit from Melissa.

"I want to stay tonight," she announced.

He swallowed and cautioned himself to stay calm. He should have realized, when she'd shown up uninvited at his apartment Friday morning, that something was going on with her—that something was going on between them.

He couldn't flat-out refuse to let her stay. If he did, he'd lose her, and he couldn't bear that.

He had to handle this carefully—because there was no way she could spend the night without learning the truth about him. For the sake of his clients, he couldn't afford to ignore Monday's horoscope the way he'd ignored last Friday's.

He draped the dish towel over the door handle on his wall oven and turned to her. "I'd love for you to stay, Melissa," he said, meaning it. "But—"

"I have clothes for tomorrow," she told him, gesturing toward the overnight bag she'd brought with her. Every weekend, she brought that bag. But this was the first time she'd ever packed clothing for work in it.

"Melissa."

She pulled herself up to her full height. Her eyes were fiery, her marvelous chin poked out at him. "I want to be with you, Derek," she said in a low, even voice. "Not just on the weekends but during the week, too. I thought you were hiding something from me by not letting me spend a weeknight here. But I came Friday morning, and I didn't see anything you need to hide from me.''

That was because he'd hidden it—to the detriment of his clients and his career.

"I don't know what the hang-up is, Derek. If there's a legitimate reason you don't want me with you during the week, I need to know it now, before—"

"Before what?"

At last she lowered her eyes. "Before I fall even more deeply in love with you."

He felt something shatter inside him. It might have been his heart. He loved Melissa, too. He wanted to be with her all week long, every night.

But she was right. He was hiding something. And it was standing in the way of their love.

"Okay," he conceded, taking her hand and leading her out of the kitchen and into his small living room. He sat on the couch and pulled her down next to him. "I've told you about my morning preparation," he reminded her. "The way I prime myself for work—"

"I know about that, Derek. I don't see what the big deal is. You're brilliant. Whatever you do to hone that brilliance—it's not going to affect me."

"I'm not brilliant," he argued.

"Of course you are. You're the Wizard." She smiled, and he felt his heart shatter all over again.

"I read my horoscope," he blurted.

She stared at him for a minute, then burst into laughter. "Your horoscope?"

"Listen, Melissa, I—"

"*That's* the big deal? Derek, millions of people read their daily horoscope. Personally, I learn more about life from Ann Landers, but if you want to read your horoscope, so what? It's just a little meaningless fun."

"It isn't meaningless."

"You believe in it? Well, that's all right, too." She laughed again. "Lots of people believe in it."

"I don't believe in it." He sighed, released her hand and turned to face the wall across the room. "I don't know whether I believe in it or not. All I know is that I need it to manage the funds I oversee."

"You mean—you look to astrology to predict how the stocks will perform?"

"Sort of. No, not even that." He shook his head, disgusted by his inability to come right out and tell her.

Sucking in another deep breath, he forced himself to explain. "I pick words out of the daily Capricorn horoscope in *America Today*. They have to be nouns. I compare the nouns to the names of stocks coming onto the market. If there's an even number of words in the first sentence of the horoscope, I sell. If there's an odd number, I buy. I use that number to determine the percentage of the fund to work with. Then I go with the nouns."

He dared to glance at her. She was gaping at him, her mouth hanging open. "You're kidding."

"No, I'm not. It started as a game. I did it as a joke. But I kept getting good results, and people wanted those results, so I just kept doing it. I work out this stupid formula every morning and use it to manage the funds. I'm no wizard. I'm not brilliant. I've just been incredibly lucky."

She continued to stare at him, literally speechless.

"Come on, Melissa. Say something."

"My success at the Towers Foundation is based on your making money by counting the number of words in a horoscope?"

"Just the first sentence," he said, attempting a smile.

She didn't return it. "I talked the foundation into investing money with a lunatic?"

"I'm not a lunatic! It's worked, hasn't it?"

"Because you've been lucky! You don't study the markets? You don't track the trends? You don't do the research?"

"I haven't had to. My funds make plenty of money this way."

"I can't believe this!" She pushed herself off the couch and marched in a circle around the room, apparently too distraught to sit still. "Derek, I pushed to get the foundation to invest with you. I fought hard for it. If that investment turns sour, so does my reputation. Maybe my job."

"I don't think—"

"And if that happens, how am I going to help my parents out? I need this job, and I need to be good at it so I can get a raise and help my father to retire. I trusted that the foundation's money was in good hands with you."

"You were right. I've done well for them so far, haven't I?"

"Through a horoscope! As a joke! For crying out loud, Derek—you said it was a game!"

"And I've won that game. So I keep playing. As long as I make money for your foundation, I don't see why it should matter to you how I do it."

"You know it matters. That's why you hid it from me. That's why you didn't want me to see you in the morning, playing this…this *game* with your horoscope."

"I hid it from you because I didn't want you to react the way you're reacting."

"You hid it from me because you wanted me to believe you were a genius," she retorted.

He met her gaze for just a moment. It was too painful to face that accusation. Yes, he'd wanted her to believe he was a genius. What man wouldn't want that?

"You're a fraud," she said. "That's what you are."

"I've never cheated anyone."

"You cheated me. You let me believe things about you that weren't true." All the fire seemed to leave her, and her voice cracked when she said, "You're not the man I fell in love with."

He couldn't think of anything to say to that. He wasn't the sort to beg. He'd presented his defense, and he hadn't persuaded her. She thought he was a fraud—and maybe she was right.

He watched as she strode to the kitchen, lifted her overnight bag, and carried it to the front door. She paused to put on her jacket, then let herself out of the apartment. She didn't ask him to accompany her home. She didn't even look at him.

She wanted a wizard. She wasn't going to settle for him.

CHAPTER EIGHT

"So, WHY ARE YOU HERE?" her mother asked.

Melissa sighed and glanced up from the ledger book she had spread open in front of her on a small desk at the rear of the store. "You know why I'm here, Mom. It's almost tax time, and you still haven't filed your taxes. It has to be done."

"I hate it that you're here on a beautiful Saturday," her mother lamented. "You should be out with Derek."

Melissa lowered her gaze to the rows of numbers on the page in front of her. Her mother had decided long ago that Derek was the man for Melissa. Unfortunately, Melissa had decided the same thing—and she'd been wrong.

A week had passed since she'd learned the truth about him: that he wasn't the Wall Street whiz, the investment prodigy, the mutual-fund maestro she'd imagined him to be. He was a stargazer, a superstitious eccentric. He didn't even use astrology the way it was intended, as a predictor of the future. No—he counted words and picked out the nouns. It was all a stunt to him.

She'd wanted to believe he was a wizard. A fool was more like it.

Her mother was still hovering behind her. "Mom, do you want me to do these taxes, or don't you?"

"I want you to be happy. You don't look happy to me."

"Doing taxes is the exact opposite of being happy."

Her mother shook her head. "For once in my life I'm not worrying about your father. I'm worrying about you. Something's wrong. I knew it the minute you walked into the store this morning. Mothers know these things. Did you and Derek have a fight?"

"No," Melissa said. "We just had a parting of the ways."

"Why? He was such a nice man. And handsome. And crazy about you. That much was obvious."

Melissa really didn't want to have this discussion. She shoved up the sleeves of her cotton sweater and jiggled one sneakered foot. "I've got another hour's worth of work here—"

"So why did you have a parting of the ways?"

She knew her mother was going to badger her until she got an answer. "It turned out that he wasn't what I thought he was."

"What did you think he was?"

Was her mother ever going to leave her alone? She stared pointedly at the paperwork in front of her. Refusing to budge, her mother hovered behind her, throwing a shadow across the ledger pages and across Melissa's mind.

Melissa sighed, set down her pen and swiveled to face her mother. "He misled me into thinking he was a genius. He wasn't. He deliberately deceived me so I wouldn't find out."

Her mother shrugged, unimpressed. "Who needs a genius? What a woman needs is a man who loves her and respects her and does what he can to make her happy. Derek made you happy, Melissa, just like your father makes me happy. And now you and he have had this parting of the ways, and excuse me, but you aren't happy. And don't tell me the taxes have anything to do with that."

"Fine. I'm not happy. There's a customer." Melissa gestured toward the front of the store. Uncle Eddie was manning the cash register, so her mother wasn't needed. But at last she took a hint. After giving Melissa's shoulder a loving pat, her mother walked away.

She attacked the tax forms, poked at the buttons of her calculator, added, multiplied, took percentages. Her accounting degree and the fact that she'd been keeping the store's books all year made filling out the tax forms relatively simple— tedious and time-consuming, but not mentally challenging. Which was unfortunate, because that left her mind free to wander.

It wandered to thoughts of Derek.

He wasn't what she'd thought he was—but what had she thought he was? She'd been in awe of his reputation, but the first time she met him, he'd failed in a grand way to live up to that reputation. Late and limping, he'd seemed more a gimpy goofball than an investment dynamo. The second time she'd met him, he'd been sweet and contrite, wooing her with wit and chocolate. The third time, he'd courted her with in-line skates. He'd urged her to take a chance, and he'd made her laugh.

She'd believed him to be a wizard, but that wasn't what had made her fall in love with him. What she'd fallen in love with was his humor, his grace, his attentiveness. His enchanting eyes. His hypnotic smile. His passion.

Not his wizardry. Never that.

So he was superstitious. So he didn't apply logic to his investment decisions. The thought that they were based on such flimsy reasoning— or lack of reasoning—frightened her a little. Lately, when she'd tried to picture her future, she'd seen herself being fired from the foundation staff after their investment gurgled down the drain, frittered away by a broker who was fixated on astrological nouns.

But investment companies that relied on econometric projections and intensive research lost money for their clients, too. Was relying on a horoscope all that much riskier?

She scribbled the last few numbers onto the

tax form, carried the total profit from the store onto the first page, and ran the final calculations. Her parents had paid estimated taxes all along, and they wouldn't owe much, thank goodness.

She stuffed the forms into an envelope and tucked in the flap. Then she stood, wiggled her head from side to side to loosen her neck muscles, and started toward the front of the store. The windows were filled with golden sunshine that made everything inside, the cans and jars and bottles, the foil bags of potato chips and the pyramids of fresh fruit, look fresh and appealing. Melissa realized she hadn't been eating much lately. She'd been too depressed.

Her mother was helping her father unload ice cream into the freezer case at the back of the store. Melissa smiled at her uncle. "Did you sell out all your newspapers?" she asked, peering over the counter to the rack where they were on display.

"There's probably a couple still out there. Help yourself."

She circled the counter and studied the selection of newspapers. Some of the editions were sold out, but she picked up a copy of *America Today*. Pulling the paper from the rack, she flipped through the pages, ignoring the articles about world crises, city corruption, and a heartwarming tale about a cat that had gotten lost during a family vacation and wound up traveling twelve hundred miles to get home. On the page after the cat story, she found the horoscope.

She had to read the dates alongside each sign to recall that she was a Taurus. "Bullheadedness has its value, but it also has its costs. Your stubborn mind can get in the way of your yearning heart. If you take the easy way out, you may not forgive yourself. With an open mind, you can turn an enemy into a friend."

Mumbo jumbo, she thought. Platitudes. Stating the obvious. Of course stubbornness could be a bad thing as well as a good thing. Of course an open mind could make dealing with an opponent easier.

She smiled sadly. Even her reading of her horoscope was marred by her bullheadedness. She definitely needed an open mind.

"Here." She rummaged through her purse for her wallet and pulled out two quarters.

"No," Uncle Eddie objected, refusing to accept the money. "Don't pay for it. We owe you so much for doing the taxes, honey—don't insult me by paying for the newspaper."

Grinning, she kissed her uncle's cheek. "I've got to go. Tell my folks the tax stuff is in the envelope on the desk."

"Here, take this, too," he said, handing her a hot pretzel from the case behind the counter. "You look skinny, Melissa. I hope you aren't on a diet or something."

She didn't want to quarrel with her uncle over

a pretzel. "I guess I can use a snack," she
agreed. "Thanks, Uncle Eddie." Tucking the
newspaper under her arm, she headed out the
door.

Spring warmed the air. The sky held a few
high, puffy clouds. She gave herself a minute to
study them, searching for recognizable shapes. A
cotton ball. Another cotton ball. She was definitely the least creative thinker she knew.

That was another reason she'd fallen in love
with Derek: he thought about things in creative
ways. If he were here, he would never have
looked at those clouds and seen cotton balls.
He'd have seen a lobster and a motorcycle and a
lopsided Christmas tree—and maybe a pair of
skates.

It was definitely time to silence her stubborn
mind and heed her yearning heart.

HE WAS SKATING FOR SPEED, for exercise, for the
chance to burn off some fury. He wore his helmet, wrist guards and knee pads, because in-line
skating on the perimeter road of Central Park was
a tricky enterprise. He had to share the track with
bikers, joggers, and pedestrians moving much
slower than he. A collision with one of them
could inflict a lot more damage than a collision
with a squirrel, even if the squirrel was Herman.

The afternoon was warm. Derek wore shorts
and a T-shirt, but despite the light clothing, he
was sweating. He pushed himself, pushed harder,

wishing he could push Melissa Giordano out of his mind.

His heart thumped at a brisk, steady pace. He zoomed past a couple of slower bladers, veered around a parade of joggers, and charged up a hill, feeling the strain in his thigh muscles. His legs ached from the exertion, and his fingers felt stiff, even though he flexed and unflexed them as he moved. One more circuit, and maybe he'd call it quits.

Or maybe not. Maybe he'd keep going until he collapsed on the doorstep of Tavern on the Green and passed out from exhaustion. That would be one way to put Melissa out of his mind for a while.

He circled around the top of the hill and tucked into the descent, letting gravity do some of the work for him. Near the bottom of the hill he spotted an obvious beginner. Her back was to him. She was standing with her arms extended from her sides, struggling for balance on her in-line skates and looking like a slightly tipsy wedding guest doing the hokey-pokey.

Her long, curly black hair reminded him of Melissa's. Her slender figure did, too. So did her awkwardness on the in-line skates.

But he knew Melissa would never strap on another pair of in-line skates. The woman reminded him of Melissa only because he was still obsessed with her.

The grade of the hill increased his speed too

much. He zigzagged to slow himself down, then scraped a brake along the pavement to slow down further. He was supposed to be skating for speed, but he couldn't resist checking out the woman with hair like Melissa's.

He zoomed past her, then spun around, curious to see her face. When he saw it he was so startled he lost his balance and landed on his butt in the grass.

"Derek! Are you all right?" Melissa shrieked, moving cautiously over to him, her hands jerking at her sides as she struggled to remain upright.

"What the hell are you doing here?" he asked.

She tried to bend over without losing her balance, but the in-line skates carried her feet out from under her and she tumbled into his lap. His body immediately shot to attention, and he cursed at the understanding that he was a long, long way from getting her out of his system.

"I thought I ought to learn how to in-line skate," she said in a breathless voice. She tried to push herself out of his lap, pressing one of her hands against his thigh and the other against his shoulder. He suddenly decided he didn't care if she'd sat in judgment of him and found him lacking, if she'd walked out on him, if she'd taken a piece of his heart with her when she'd left. It felt too good having her sprawled out across his lap.

He fought against his physical response to her. "Why do you want to learn how to in-line skate?" he asked, wishing his voice didn't sound so husky, wishing the delicate brush of her hair against his chin didn't crank up his arousal even more.

"There were these clouds, Derek—and they looked like nothing to me, but I thought if you were looking at them, they'd look like skates to you."

"Skates?"

"I don't know how to read clouds. Or stars. Or constellations." She sighed. "Or stocks, for that matter. I'm the most unimaginative person in the world. And I thought I wanted you to be just like me."

"You're not unimaginative," he argued, allowing himself to run his fingers through her hair. It felt like rippling silk.

"The only things I can imagine are boring, sensible things. Where I'll be in three years. What job I hope to have. How much I need to be earning. How many school loans I'll have left to pay off. That's not imaginative."

"It's sane," he said.

"I need to accept that other people do things in other ways—sometimes ways that don't make any sense to me." She shifted off his lap, and he almost reached out and hauled her back onto him. But she turned to face him, resting on her knees and easing his helmet off his head. The air felt cool against his sweat-damp hair, and he decided that looking at her was almost as satisfying as holding her. "I read my horoscope for today," she said. "It told me that with an open mind, I could turn an enemy into a friend."

He gazed into her dark eyes, remembering all the times he'd looked into them before—when he and she talked, when they bickered over Edam versus Gouda or Tom Hanks versus Brad Pitt. When they made love. "I've never been your enemy, Melissa," he swore.

She smiled and shook her head. "I think the enemy I turned into a friend was Herman."

"Herman? The death-star squirrel?"

"I went out and bought these in-line skates, and then I went to your house. You weren't home—obviously. But Herman was there. Or some squirrel was. He was sitting on the railing, chattering and playing with an acorn."

"Sounds like Herman," Derek confirmed. "He was probably scoping out a target to throw the acorn at."

"I rang your bell in the foyer, and when it was clear you weren't home, I went back outside. I had this pretzel in my pocket that my uncle gave me, and I broke off a piece and gave it to Herman."

"You gave him food? What are you, crazy?"

"Probably," she said, grinning. "Anyway, he ate the piece of pretzel, and then he scampered down to the sidewalk. And he looked over his shoulder at me, as if to say, 'Follow me. I know where Derek is.'" So I gave him another piece of pretzel, and he ran down the street, and I followed him. I followed him all the way to this spot, but then I ran out of pretzel and he disappeared.''

"Typical. He's your buddy until you stop feeding him. Then he abandons you.''

"But he abandoned me here, right where he knew I'd find you. I strapped on my skates and practiced in-line skating around this little area until I felt confident enough to look for you.''

He stroked her hair back from her face, then trailed his fingertips along her chin. "And what were you going to do when you found me?''

"Tell you I love you,'' she whispered.

"Even though I'm not the Wizard?''

"I don't want a wizard, Derek. I want you.''

That was good enough for him. He leaned forward and touched his lips to hers. "You aren't going to tell my colleagues how I pick stocks, are you?''

"It'll be our secret.''

"I like your horoscope,'' he said, then kissed her again, a little longer, a little deeper. "I even like Herman, if he brought you to me.''

She smiled against his lips. "I need to practice skating, Derek. Help me to my feet.''

"I'd rather sweep you off your feet,'' he murmured, but he pushed himself to stand, gripped underneath her arms and eased her up. He could have let go once she seemed stable, but he didn't want to. He never, ever, wanted to let go.

So he slid one arm around her, holding her close, and they skated down the path together.

Dear Reader,

Novellas are always so much fun to write. Besides being a change from the longer Harlequin Temptation novels that I usually write, creating a story for an anthology gives me a chance to work with other authors, fashioning plots and characters around a common theme—this time, astrology.

Although I don't read my horoscope daily, I can't deny the fact that a lot of astrology rings true. I'm a typical Leo, possessing all of the best—and the worst—qualities of this fire sign. I'm determined, but can often be stubborn. I love to be in charge, but I'm sometimes impatient when things don't go my way. I strive for perfection, yet I find myself getting obsessed with silly details. And as a Leo, I surround myself with those of my kind—my three cats, Tani, Tibby and Tally, who seem to share many of those classic Leo qualities.

I hope you enjoy my contribution to *Written in the Stars*. And I invite you to visit my Web site at www.katehoffmann.com to learn more about my upcoming releases for Harlequin.

Happy reading,

Kate Hoffmann

Kate Hoffmann

SHOOTING STARS

Kate Hoffmann

CHAPTER ONE

THE INSIDE OF THE BARREL cellar was cool and dark. The thick stone walls, built into the hillside, and the tile roof, kept the temperature consistently cool all year round. Early morning light filtered through the tiny windows set just beneath the timber rafters, catching dust motes kicked up by Spencer Reid's footsteps. This was his favorite part of the workday, the easy stroll past the high stacks of oak barrels to his office in the far corner of the building. He could have chosen a route that would take him around the outside of the building, but this walk always gave him a satisfied feeling, a feeling of accomplishment.

On one end of the barn, the barrels filled with wine from last year's harvest lined the racks. The Merlot from the previous year was already bottled and warehoused for aging in another cave beneath the winery at the bottom of the hill, proof that Shooting Star's Merlot was about to become not just a good wine, but a great wine.

On the other end, Alberto Castillo, Spence's right-hand man, waited near a scarred oak table. Spence slowed his pace when he saw a bottle of

the '98 Merlot sitting in the center of the table.
Alberto had been urging him for the past three
months to send the wine to market, but Spence
had been reluctant to let it go too soon. This was
the wine that would change the reputation of
Shooting Star. Like a father unwilling to allow
his child to cross the street, Spence had held on
to it as long as he could.

"It's ready," Alberto said. He didn't bother to
say more.

Spence could guess what he thought. Two
thousand cases of wine at seven dollars a bottle
wholesale wasn't making them any money gathering dust in the cellars. But bottle aging was a
tricky business and Spence wanted to be sure the
time was right. "I'll try it," he replied before
Alberto turned and walked out.

The winery had been in his family since 1970,
when his parents had formed a partnership with
Joe and Sophia Santini in the rundown Sonoma
Valley vineyard. Back then, the Sonoma Valley
was a magnet for San Francisco hippies, and California wine was still trying to gain a reputation.
With David Reid's marketing talent and Joe Santini's knowledge of wine-making, the two had
quickly produced a passable Cabernet. Though
the winery had always turned a profit, Shooting
Star had never really lived up to its potential.

Spence's parents were now retired, living in
Arizona to be closer to his older sister and the

grandkids. Joe had died the year before Spence's parents' retirement, leaving his wife, Sophia, to carry on the Santini side of the partnership. Sophia Santini still worked at the winery as Spence's assistant manager. But she was so much more—a friend, a surrogate mother, a valued partner. And she was a touchstone to the past, reminding him of the days when Shooting Star had just been a dream.

He took another step toward the table. The single green bottle stood next to an empty goblet, the wine uncorked an hour earlier by Alberto. Spence grabbed the bottle and the goblet, then turned toward his office, too nervous to take the first taste. Would it live up to its potential? Would the investment he'd made in French oak barrels pay off? Or would it simply be an ordinary wine from an ordinary vineyard?

He reached for the bottle, but the tension of the moment was interrupted by an odd sound. Spence stopped and cocked his head. Sound was always distorted in the cavernous interior of the barrel room, but the racket sounded suspiciously like a dog barking. It came nearer, the skittering paws very close by. An instant later, he looked down to see a fuzzy white dog scampering around his feet, yipping and snapping at his leg.

"What the—"

At the sound of his voice, the dog backed up, growling now. Then suddenly it lunged for his leg and sunk its sharp little teeth into Spence's jeans. Tugging and twisting, ears flopping, the dog wouldn't let go, even when Spence picked his foot up off the ground and the dog hung in midair. "Hey, get off my—"

"Gaby! Gaby, stop! *Arrête! Maintenant! Mauvais chien!*"

Spence looked up at the dog's owner. He opened his mouth to lodge an icy rebuke but the words stopped in his throat about the same time the dog let go of the leg of his jeans. There'd been precious few women who could take his breath away, but this woman had done it in record time. Even in the dim light, he noticed the stunning profile, the straight nose and the lush lips, the dark hair and smoky-green eyes.

She was dressed all in black, from the jaunty black beret on her head to the trendy leather boots on her feet. Along the way, Spence appreciated her slender figure and long, shapely legs. The woman bent and picked up the little dog, then scolded it in softly murmured French. "I'm so sorry," she said, her words completely free of an accent. "She doesn't understand much English."

"I— What— Can I—" Spence cleared his throat and began again. Good grief, he sounded like a babbling fool. "Can I help you?"

She smiled, her face lighting up with surprise. "No. I'm fine."

It wasn't the answer he was expecting, at least not from a stranger. So he offered another question. "Are you looking for someone?"

"Actually, I was. But I'm not anymore." She hugged the dog, nuzzling her face in its soft fur as she watched Spence with a coy gaze. Then she nodded toward the wine bottle he held. "What's that?"

"Merlot," Spence answered.

"Vintage?"

"It's a '98."

"May I?"

Still a bit unnerved, Spence nodded, then splashed a bit of the wine into the goblet and held it out to her. She sniffed the wine, then swirled it in the glass. Spence had done the same thousands of times in the past, but watching her do it, every movement seemed exotic and seductive. He nearly moaned out loud when she raised the goblet to her lips and took a sip. As she let the wine slide over her palate, a tiny smile curled the corners of her mouth. It was only then that Spence realized he was holding his breath again.

"Very nice," she said. "In fact, quite extraordinary." She took another sip, then lazily drew her tongue over her bottom lip. Spence found himself transfixed.

"More?" she asked, holding out the glass.

"Mmm," he said. Just once more, along her upper lip this time, just until it glistened with moisture and— He blinked, startled by the direction of his thoughts. Her smile widened and he realized she found his behavior amusing.

Spence cursed inwardly. He was damn tired of her silly little games. Not that they weren't a pleasant diversion. But if this went on any longer he'd make a complete ass of himself. "What is it you want?" he asked.

"I'd like more wine," she said, holding out her glass.

"That's not what I—"

She put on a playful pout. "Please?"

Grudgingly he sloshed a bit more into her glass, but she shook her head and urged him on. "More," she murmured. He added an extra sip or two. "More," she said. Frowning, he continued to pour.

When the wine neared the rim of the goblet, he stopped. "Enough?"

She giggled softly, then nodded. *"Oui. Merci beaucoup."* With that, she turned neatly on her heel and started off in the direction of the door. He called out to her but all he heard was a distant *"À bientôt!"* and a lighthearted laugh before the room went silent.

Frowning, he sniffed at the bottle, then took a sip. The wine, like liquid velvet, slid over his tongue and the flavors of black cherry and currant burst in his mouth. It was ready, finally. But rather than call out for Alberto, Spence continued to stare into the shadows, his mind still focused on the woman.

"Good morning, good morning!"

Spence turned as Sophia Santini appeared beside him. She smiled broadly, deep crinkles bracketing her eyes. Even though her hair was steel-gray and she was nearing sixty, she still looked girlish. As always, she had the morning newspaper tucked under her arm and a mug of coffee clutched in her hand. She clinked her mug against the bottle he held. "Is this the '98 Merlot? Alberto told me you were finally ready to taste it."

Spence nodded, distracted. "Did you see her?"

She glanced around. "See who?"

"The woman. With the little white dog and the…" He pointed to his head. "The French hat. What's it called? A…"

"Beret?" Sophia asked.

He nodded again. "She was just here. She had a little white dog. And she was…beautiful."

Sophia's expression turned skeptical. "I didn't see anyone." She sat at the table. "But I do have good news. Though, I'm not sure I should tell you."

Spence shook his head, trying to rid his brain of her image. Who the hell was she? And where had she come from? He couldn't have imagined her, could he? He glanced down at the leg of his jeans. The impressions from the dog's bite were still there. "Tell me what?" he asked, distracted.

With a sly smile, she held out an envelope. He glanced at the return address and noticed the logo of *Wine Connoisseur.* "What is this?"

Sophia could contain her excitement no longer. "It's Jonathan Cartwright. He reviewed the '97 Merlot." She picked up the magazine and read out loud. "'If '97 is any indication of the future of Shooting Star then their Merlots are sure to become one of the great Sonoma wines.' He gave it eighty-nine points out of a hundred. We need to strike now, get the '98 to market while people are still buying our '97. And we're going to have to rethink our pricing. Oh, and one of their editors called and wants to do a profile of the winery."

Spence gasped, then slowly sat at the table, the letter still clutched in his hand. "He gave it eighty-nine points?" The cachet of a good review in *Wine Connoisseur* was exactly what the vineyard needed! But a good review and a profile of the winery were more than Spence could have ever wished for. It meant he'd arrived, he'd made a name for himself beyond those of Joe Santini and David Reid.

"It's time to ship the '98," she said. "We can't wait any longer. I'll call our distributor as soon as we set a firm price." Sophia unfolded her paper. "Now, let's just see what your horoscope says today. I bet it will be full of good news.''

Sophia started the day the same way every day. She sat at the old table with Spence, read his horoscope and hers from *America Today,* then moved on to the business at hand. But he didn't want to move on. He wanted to savor this moment. Yet try as he might, he couldn't think about the business success waiting just around the corner. His mind was still flooded with thoughts of the woman who had wandered into his life for a few moments then disappeared.

"Here it is," Sophia said. "'Capricorn. You run the risk of making a fool of yourself today. Be careful around animals and members of the opposite sex. An unexpected opportunity will pass you by if you don't act on it. Someone in a hat may bring luck—but remember, luck sometimes comes in many guises and isn't always easy to recognize.'"

Spence laughed skeptically. "Let me see that." He grabbed the paper and reread his horoscope. But there it was. The day had barely begun and he had already made a bumbling fool of himself with a beautiful woman. She had a little dog and she was definitely a member of the opposite sex. And the opportunity to find out who she was had slipped right through his fingers. She wore a hat and the review in *Wine Connoisseur* was astounding luck.

He raked his fingers through his hair. "This is...spooky. It's exactly what happened."

Sophia took the paper and sent him a smug smile. "Now do you believe in the power of the stars?"

Though Spence wasn't sure about the stars and destiny, Sophia was a true believer. The story had been repeated over and over again, how his parents and the Santinis had discussed buying an old vineyard for nearly a year. They'd been eating a late dinner in the Santinis' backyard, spinning their entrepreneurial dreams, when Sophia had noticed a shooting star streaking across the sky. She'd taken it as an omen and just two months later, they'd taken possession of crumbling buildings and outdated equipment on a gentle hillside in the Sonoma Valley. The vineyard was at the perfect elevation for the Cabernet and Merlot grapes that Joe wanted to grow, the grapes that were left for Spence to tend.

He stood, the chair scraping against the stone floor and echoing through the barrel room. "I believe we have a lot of work to do if we're going to be profiled by *Wine Connoisseur*. Tell Alberto I want to see him. I'm ready to ship the '98. We'll wholesale it at nine dollars a bottle."

As he walked toward his office, the words of the horoscope drifted through his mind. He wasn't one to believe in such silliness. But the coincidence was pretty amazing. One thing was missing from the horoscope though.

There'd been no mention of whether he'd see this beautiful stranger again.

"HE DIDN'T EVEN RECOGNIZE me, Aunt Sophia. Have I changed that much?" Francesca Payton saw the answer to her question in her aunt's smile. "Funny, but the moment I drove up the road to the winery, I started to feel like the shy, gangly teenager who used to spend summers with my uncle Joe and auntie Sophia. In Paris, they call me Cesca. Here I'm just plain old Frannie."

The house was so silent that she could hear Sophia sigh. "You've grown into a beautiful woman, Francesca. So sophisticated and confident. Your mama was right to send you away to France all those years ago."

In truth, Francesca had hated her mother for choosing a European education for her daughter. Her entire first year at the Sorbonne had been terrifying. She'd been homesick and lonely and her high school French didn't seem nearly as fluent as she'd thought it was. She'd been tempted to come home after just a few weeks. But her parents had scrimped and saved to give her the opportunity and she'd had no choice but to be grateful.

Over time, she'd learned to love Paris. She'd been anxious to come home that first summer, to show off her newfound sophistication to her family. But when school chums had invited her to travel through Italy, she'd decided to see where her mother's family—the Santinis—had come from. After that, she came home for a few weeks each year to visit her parents, having made a life for herself in Paris. Her summers at the winery had become part of a childhood she'd left behind.

But she had always remembered the sunny days she'd spent wandering the vineyards at Shooting Star. The long, solitary walks through the rows of twisted vines, the quiet afternoons reading and sketching on the stone terrace of Joe and Sophia's cottage, and the time to dream. And then there'd been Spencer Reid—the handsome son of the vineyard's co-owners.

She'd first seen him the summer of her eleventh year, fourteen years ago. Her mother had sent Francesca to Joe and Sophia, hoping that having a child around might help ease the void in their lives. Joe and Sophia had no children of their own. She'd also hoped that by cutting the apron strings, Francesca might become a bit more independent.

And here she was again. Only this time, she wasn't sitting at her aunt's kitchen table in the stone cottage at the end of the drive. She was now at Spencer Reid's kitchen table in the spacious main house. Since Uncle Joe's death and the Reids' move to Arizona, Sophia had lived at the house on the hill, renting her little cottage to Alberto and his wife.

"He thought he was seeing things," Sophia said. "You were a vision to him, *cara*. I think you made quite an impression."

Francesca smiled, her mind wandering back to that morning. She'd been fresh off the plane and had decided to see how kind the years had been to Spencer Reid. Francesca had remembered him as a handsome young man with sun-streaked hair and a profile worthy of a Greek god. Her first summer at the vineyards he'd been fifteen, four years older than she, and what her friends had called "hot." She hadn't really known what they'd meant, only that whenever she caught sight of him, her heart started to pound and her palms began to sweat.

He'd been charming back then, already aware of his power over the opposite sex. And whenever he'd seen her, he had turned on that charm, teasing her and making her fall even more madly in love with him. He used to call her the "little girl with the big name." His teasing had always brought a blush to her cheeks and a stammer to her voice. But as the summers passed, she saw less and less of him. Once he got his driver's license, he spent time with his own friends and later, as a college man, he had more important things to occupy his time—like parties and pretty girlfriends.

"He hasn't changed much," Francesca murmured. "He's still as handsome as ever."

"And he knows it," Sophia countered. "He's quite popular with the ladies, a regular heartbreaker. Although, over the past few years he hasn't dated nearly as much. Not since that awful Linda."

"'That awful Linda'?" Francesca asked, her curiosity piqued.

"She was more interested in the money than the man. Once she found out that the vineyard wasn't going to provide her with adequate spending money and that Spence had no intention of marrying her, she found herself another bank account and moved on. Since then, Spence has been consumed with the winery. He's determined to make Shooting Star into a first-class vineyard. And he's almost done it."

Francesca smiled. "I tasted the '98 Merlot. It's wonderful." She glanced up at the clock then moved to check the bread that she'd put in the oven. The kitchen was already filled with the tantalizing scent of yeast and warm bread, and she still had another pair of baguettes waiting to be baked. Already, she felt comfortable here, doing what she did best.

"So, now that you're back, what are you going to do with yourself?"

Francesca shrugged. "Well, I've scrimped and saved, and with the inheritance I got from Grandmother Payton, I thought I might open a French bakery. Maybe in Santa Rosa. I was an apprentice *boulangère* at a shop in Paris, the bread capital of the world. I can make a mouth-watering croissant and the perfect baguette. And I'm pretty good with pastries and tortes. I thought I'd drive over in the morning and check out the town."

She pulled a baking sheet out of the oven and tapped on the crusts of the baguettes with her fingernail. It was nearly midnight but she was still on Paris time. Gaby, on the other hand, had settled into California time. The little bichon frise was sound asleep on the kitchen floor in front of the refrigerator. "Why don't you go to bed," she said to her aunt. "You look exhausted. I'm going to be up for a while yet. It will take me a few days to adjust."

Sophia stood, then crossed the kitchen. She pressed a kiss on Francesca's cheek, then wandered off into the dark house. "I'll see you tomorrow, *cara*. Sleep well."

Francesca listened to her aunt's footsteps fade in the quiet house. Then she plucked the baguettes off the baking sheet and dropped them on the cooling rack. The bread hadn't turned out badly considering she'd been using unfamiliar ingredients and tools, and had been stuck with a noncommercial oven.

She put the last pair of baguettes in the oven, then sat on a kitchen stool and sipped at her tea.

After so many years in Europe, it felt odd to be back in the U.S. Just listening to her native language was strange. And everything moved so much faster than she remembered. But the vineyard hadn't changed at all, and now that she was here, it seemed as though only weeks had passed since she'd left.

Francesca heard footsteps returning to the kitchen and she smiled, wondering what little detail her aunt had forgotten to tell her. Sophia had been worrying about her comfort ever since she'd arrived that morning. But when she turned to assure her aunt that she had plenty of towels and blankets, she came face-to-face with Spence Reid.

He froze the moment he saw her, his hand clutching a bottle of wine. Francesca couldn't help but smile. She knew what was going through his mind. He was wondering who she was and what she was doing in his kitchen, her face streaked with flour, her feet bare. He was probably also wondering about the delicious smells coming from the area near the oven. "Hello," she said.

"It's—it's you," he murmured.

"It's me," she repeated. She really ought to come out and tell him who she was, before he started to doubt his own sanity. But it was fun to have the upper hand for once, especially with a certified ladies' man like Spence Reid. After all, she had become quite an accomplished flirt in Paris, putting her on equal footing with Spence.

But the playful flirtation took a serious turn when he reached out and touched her cheek. His fingertips lingered for a long moment before he pulled his hand back, frowning. "You're real. After this morning, I wasn't sure."

His touch sent her pulse racing and Francesca wondered how that could be after all these years. How could he still make her feel like a silly schoolgirl? But as she stared into his eyes and watched the confusion in their depths, she also wondered whether she'd made a serious mistake in coming back to Shooting Star.

CHAPTER TWO

"I—I SHOULD CHECK my oven," she murmured, stepping just out of his reach. For the first time since they'd met, she seemed rattled. Spence watched her open the oven and spray the interior with water. When she turned back to him, her composure had returned.

"Actually, that's *my* oven," he said, ignoring the flood of heat that raced from his fingertips through his body. She was real and so was the desire that flamed inside of him. "And this is *my* house. And you're baking bread in my house. Don't you find that a little strange?"

A coy smile quirked her lips again and Spence had the impression that she still found him amusing. "It's what I do." She handed him one of the long skinny loaves, then turned and retrieved a small plate of cheese from the counter. "Go ahead, try it."

While he was tearing off a piece of the baguette, she grabbed the bottle from the counter and searched the cupboards for a pair of wineglasses. When she found them, she quickly pulled the cork and filled the glasses, then handed him one. He took a bite of the bread and the crust exploded, sending crumbs over the countertop. But that didn't stop him from moaning softly. The bread was warm and yeasty, like nothing he'd ever tasted before. He took another bite and the crumbs scattered again.

She giggled. "Don't worry, it's supposed to do that. It's the mark of a good baguette." She held out the plate of cheese. "Try some of this. It's French."

Spence grabbed a slice, then slid onto one of the kitchen stools and watched her as she tidied the kitchen. "You expect me to believe you just wander the neighborhood breaking into houses and baking bread?"

"And drinking wine," she teased as she took a sip of the Merlot. "And this isn't a strange house. I've been here before."

Spence felt his impatience rising. He was a master at witty banter with the opposite sex, but he wanted to know who she was and where she came from—now, before she disappeared again. Spence set down his bread and wiped his hands on his jeans. "Ah, now we get to it. You've been here before and you're insulted because I don't remember you."

She shrugged. "I've changed a lot."

"Are you going to tell me your name?" he asked as he chewed. "Or am I just supposed to guess?"

"You're supposed to tell me how you like the bread," she countered. "I complimented your wine, now you should return the favor."

"It's very good," he replied. "Better than good. Great. Now, what's your name?"

His words seemed to please her. "I'm the little girl with the big name."

"What is that supposed to mean?" he asked. But as his gaze skimmed her features, her words hung at the edges of his memory, hauntingly familiar. *The little girl with the big name.* He'd said those words before, in the distant past. But the image that flashed in his mind didn't match the woman standing in front of him. He saw braces and gangly limbs, hair pulled back in a severe ponytail and ill-fitting clothes. And a blush that never seemed to go away. Then it came to him in an instant and he gasped. "Frannie?"

A smile lit up her face and suddenly all the pieces fell into place. Of course it was her, all grown up and in this house where her aunt now lived. She'd spent summers at Shooting Star when she was young, but Spence would never have made the connection between this beautiful woman and the clumsy young girl.

She laughed, a sweet and musical sound that echoed through the silent house. "I should have told you this morning in the barrel cellar. But it was fun to tease."

"You've grown up," Spence said, his comment an understatement. She hadn't actually grown up, since she was the same height as she was as a teenager. But she'd definitely grown in other ways—she was confident and witty and gorgeous and accomplished. And she had a body that— He swallowed hard. That would make any man weak in the knees. "So, what have you been doing for the past…seven or eight years?"

"Do you want all the details or just the highlights?"

"The highlights for now," Spence said with a grin. "We'll make time for the details later."

Frannie shook her head. "You haven't changed a bit, Spence Reid. You're still the biggest flirt in the county." She broke off a tiny piece of the baguette and nibbled on it as she collected her thoughts. "I went to study art in Paris at the Sorbonne and after I graduated, I went to cooking school. I've been apprenticing at a bakery on Rue Jacob in Paris for the past two years."

"So how long is your visit?" Spence asked.

She shook her head. "I'm not here to visit. I'm here to stay."

"Here?" he asked.

"Not here here. Well, yes, here, for a while until I find a place of my own. I want to open up a French bakery, maybe in Santa Rosa. I'm driving there tomorrow to look at some properties. I want it to be a real artisan bakery, where the breads are so good you can't help but come back every day. And maybe I'll add a coffee shop so it will become a gathering place for the locals in the morning.''

Spence lost himself in the sound of her voice and in the excitement in her words as she told him about her dreams. He could barely believe that the ugly duckling had turned into a graceful swan. His gaze dropped to her hands as she fiddled with the stem of her wineglass. He fought the urge to reach out and take her fingers in his, just to touch her again, to make sure she was real.

But now she wasn't his mysterious, alluring stranger anymore. She was Frannie, the little girl he'd teased, the one who had watched him with such curious eyes. She was Frannie, Sophia's favorite niece. She was the closest thing he had to a little sister, yet no matter how hard he tried, he couldn't think of her as anything but an alluring and stunningly beautiful woman.

"I'd come every day," he said as he watched her take the last loaves of bread from the oven. "Listen, why don't you let me take you tomorrow? We can drive over to Napa and visit Sonoma, too. We'll make a day of it.''

She thought about his invitation for a long moment, then nodded. "All right," she said, dropping the loaves onto a rack. "But we'll need to go a little later. I'm still getting used to the time change." Frannie rubbed her eyes, then sighed. "I have to get to bed or I'll never adjust."

"Then I'll see you tomorrow," Spence said. "I'll just wait until you're up. You can come down to the office when you're ready."

She nodded, then turned away. But he caught her arm at the last moment, then bent near and brushed a kiss on her cheek. The kiss surprised her and he instantly regretted being so forward. "It's nice to have you back, Frannie."

"It's nice to be back," she said with a winsome smile. With a soft sigh, she walked toward the east wing of the house, where Sophia had her rooms. A few moments after she left, Spence wished that she'd return. He hadn't had enough of her musical voice or her luminous beauty, he wanted to look into those gray-green eyes for just a minute longer.

He grabbed his wineglass and wandered in the direction of the library. Sophia had lit a fire earlier to take the chill out of the damp January night. The blaze was just embers now, but he stretched out on the leather sofa and enjoyed the warmth from both the wine and the fire.

Yes, it was definitely good to have Frannie back, he mused. It had been a while since he'd had a woman in his life. And though she really was like a member of the family, her return promised to make life a whole lot more interesting at Shooting Star.

"You look very pretty," Sophia said as Francesca walked into the kitchen.

Francesca twirled in front of her aunt, showing off her pale pink sweater and skin-skimming black pants. "I slept so well last night. Usually it takes me days to recover from jet lag. But I feel wonderful, energized."

Sophia studied her shrewdly. "Is that French perfume I smell?"

A tiny smile quirked Francesca's lips. Maybe she had taken particular care with her appearance this morning. But it wasn't to attract the attention of a certain handsome vineyard owner. It was simply to prove to him that she wasn't the same goofy kid whom he'd ignored for years. "Spencer came in after you went to bed last night," she said, pouring a mug of coffee from the pot on the counter. "He finally remembered who I was."

"Funny," Sophia said. "I saw him this morning and he didn't mention it. He just told me that he'd be gone for most of the day."

Francesca nodded, then searched the kitchen for Gaby's food. "He's taking me to Sonoma and Napa to look for a spot for my bakery." At Sophia's worried look, Francesca reached out and patted her aunt's shoulder. "Don't worry. I'm not Frannie anymore. I'm not going to suddenly turn into a lovesick teenager. It's just that it makes me feel good when he looks at me like a woman.'' Francesca glanced up at the clock. "I should go. He's probably waiting for me." She bent and picked up the dog, then gave her a kiss. "Feed Gaby for me, will you?"

"Take a jacket. The sun hasn't burned the chill out of the air yet."

Francesca handed Sophia the dog, then hurried out the front door of the house, ignoring her aunt's advice. The day was glorious, bright with a crisp bite to the air. She strolled down the road toward the stone barn. A tiny shiver of anticipation prickled her skin. She shouldn't feel this way, but she couldn't help herself. She had expected to be lonely for all her friends in Paris, but with Spence here, she had at least one person she could look forward to seeing every day.

Still, Sophia was right. Francesca knew all too well of Spence's reputation with the ladies and she certainly didn't want to be one of his conquests. She had to find a way to keep her distance. Maybe she could just think of him as an older brother—a very handsome, sexy older brother.

Francesca sighed. It had been a while since she'd had a man in her life. Her last year in Paris had been filled with plans for returning to the States. She had almost avoided men to keep from falling in love and changing her decision. But now that she was here, maybe it was time to find a social life. Perhaps Spence could introduce her to some of his friends.

A roar sounded from behind her, then the beep of a horn. She jumped, startled, then turned to find Spence pulling up beside her in his Jeep. He wore sunglasses and a canvas jacket. His sun-streaked hair was windblown and he sent her a rakish smile. "Hey, little girl. Can I give you a ride?"

Francesca giggled, then ran around the front of the Jeep and hopped into the passenger seat. Before he started off, Spence slipped out of his jacket and draped it around her shoulders. And then with a boyish yell, he hit the accelerator and they took off through the vineyards, kicking up dust behind them.

They bumped along between the rows of vines, the wind turning her cheeks cold and making her breathless. When he finally pulled to a stop, Francesca's heart was pounding in her chest. He hopped out of the Jeep, then circled to help her out. "What are we doing here?" she asked.

"I wanted to check on something before we left. Come on." They hiked up the hill, her hand tucked in his, through the vines to a remote corner of the vineyard. When they reached a wide section of scrawny vines, he bent and examined them carefully. "This is the future of Shooting Star," he murmured. "A new variety of Merlot grape I can blend with our other grapes. We'll make a reserve out of this, maybe three hundred cases. People will beg for a bottle of Shooting Star Merlot Reserve.''

"How long will it take?"

Spence straightened. ''Maybe another two or three years for the grapes. Then three more to get it right.''

"That's a long time to wait," Francesca commented. "With my bread, it takes three or four hours. Instant gratification.''

He sat back on his heels. ''But starting your own bakery, that's a dream that you've waited for, isn't it?''

Francesca looked down into his blue eyes. She suddenly felt as if he could see inside her soul. She had dreamed about her own place for such a long time, but buying her own bakery in Paris had been beyond her financial means—bakeries were handed down from generation to generation. She had other dreams, too. Dreams she'd put far into her future—a husband, a family, and a happy home. But those dreams were vague and unfocused, unlike the bakery, which was close enough to touch.

"It is," she murmured. Her gaze drifted down to his mouth and the urge to kiss him was strong. It wasn't so much desire that drove her, but curiosity. She wondered what it was that he did that had made all the girls crazy over him. But a tiny voice reminded her of her aunt's warnings. Instead of taking such a risk, she smiled. "Maybe we should go."

He rose, then reached out and took her hand as they walked back to the Jeep. Francesca knew that this would be a perfect day. It already was and they'd barely started. Perhaps she'd find a spot for her bakery today. Perhaps she'd take another step toward her dreams.

Whatever happened, Francesca knew that she'd made the right decision in coming back— coming back to the States, coming back to Shooting Star. And coming back to old friends like Spence Reid.

THEY GOT HOME just as the sun was sinking toward the horizon. Spence had dropped Frannie off at the house, then promised to return for a glass of wine once he'd checked in at the office. He drove the Jeep down the hill to the barrel room and winery offices, and parked it near the side door.

They'd driven through all the small towns in the Napa Valley, from Napa to Calistoga. Then they'd taken a route west and come down through the wine country of Sonoma County, stopping for dinner at one of his favorite spots in the village of Sonoma. Over seafood, they'd discussed the pros and cons of three different spots they'd looked at for Frannie's bakery. Throughout the discussion, he'd hoped she'd choose the little brick building near the restaurant, the closest spot to his vineyard.

He imagined driving over every morning for coffee and a croissant, or perhaps meeting her for lunch, or picking her up after closing time for an intimate dinner. Already he was making plans for them to spend time together and after only a day with her. Since seeing her in the barrel room, that first morning, he'd been attracted to her. But once he'd learned who she really was, he'd tried to bury that attraction, as if it were somehow improper. It wasn't impropriety that was worrying him, it was Sophia's reaction to a potential romantic entanglement.

He opened the office door and stepped inside, intending to flip through the mail and his messages before heading back to the house. But when he found Sophia waiting for him, a wary look in her eyes, Spence knew that he was about to find out exactly how she felt.

"Don't look at me like that," he murmured, taking a wide berth around her desk to get to his.

"She's just come back," Sophia said, her voice even. "She's a little lonely and you're too charming."

"We're just friends," he insisted.

"Make sure it stays that way," Sophia warned. "If you hurt her, I'll guarantee you that the Reid family line will end with you."

He grabbed the stack of envelopes on his desk.

"Nothing happened today. We just took a drive and found a few spots for her bakery. And I promise I won't hurt her. Hey, she's Frannie. She's like my little sister." But as he said the words, Spence knew that his feelings for Frannie had started as brotherly and taken a sharp turn in the opposite direction sometime during dinner.

Sophia didn't seem satisfied with his answer, but let it go. "I didn't read you your horoscope this morning," she said. "I think you ought to hear it now." She laid the paper out in front of her. "'Capricorn. Business success is on the horizon, but your social life must take a back seat. Though old friends may distract you, don't lose your focus. Attention to selfish needs will only cause you and those you love pain. An older woman offers sound advice.'"

Spence tossed the mail down on his desk and headed for the door. "I don't believe for a second that's what my horoscope says," he called. Still, he took her veiled threats seriously. Sophia was his business partner and her opinion mattered to him. Before he made any move toward Frannie, he'd better be damn sure he knew what he was doing.

He left the Jeep at the office and walked back to the house, taking the time to rewind the day in his head. He couldn't remember having so much fun with a woman. They'd fallen into an easy companionship, talking about their pasts and their futures without hesitation, laughing and teasing as if they were the oldest and dearest of friends.

She'd captivated him with her sense of humor and her cool sophistication. Frannie was a study in contrasts, contrasts that intrigued, that made him want to spend more time with her. As he approached the house, he saw her standing on the stone terrace, staring out at the western horizon at what promised to be a beautiful sunset.

As he walked through the house, he pulled a bottle of Shooting Star Cabernet from the wine rack, grabbed two glasses and stepped up to the French doors. Gaby was sprawled at her feet and the little dog looked up at him but didn't bark. He stood there for a long moment taking in the details of her profile, the way she brushed her hair from her eyes, the subtle tilt of her chin as she stared out at the sky, the lush shape of her lips.

Spence walked up to her and smiled. "Come on. I've got a much better place to watch the sunset. If we hurry, we'll make it there just in time."

They set off up the hill behind the house, climbing the knoll to a rocky outcropping, Gaby scrambling up behind them. Spence set the bottle and glasses down and helped Frannie climb up onto the flat surface of a rock. When she'd settled in beside him, he opened the wine with a corkscrew he kept on his keychain and filled her glass.

"I forgot how beautiful the sunsets were from here," she said.

"You've been here before?" he asked.

A pretty blush stained her cheeks. "A few times. But not nearly as many times as you. And all those girls," she added.

"What girls?"

"Lisa Ventano," she said. "You kissed her right over there, under that tree. She had that little high-pitched giggle that could break glass. And I believe you kissed Mary Graff right here on this rock. And when you tried to get to second base, she slapped you."

"How do you know that?"

"I had my own special rock," she said. "Right over there. I'd come up here to draw—and to spy on you. I used to watch you all the time. You taught me everything I knew about kissing boys. That is, until I moved to Paris."

"And did you kiss a lot of men in Paris?" The thought of Frannie kissing any man brought an unbidden surge of envy. What did her mouth feel like? How did she taste? Would her kisses be as tantalizing as her laugh and the sound of her voice?

"I kissed a few," Frannie teased. "But I think you're probably still way ahead on that score. I mean, with girls, not with French men."

Spence chuckled, then leaned back against the rock and stared out at the sunset. They watched in silence, sipping their wine as the sun dipped below the horizon, setting the sky on fire. They didn't need to speak, they'd talked themselves out during the day. It was perfect to just sit beside her and enjoy the silence of the evening, with Gaby nestled between them.

When the sky turned an inky blue, he heard her take a sharp breath. She pointed to the north. "Look," she cried. "A shooting star. Make a wish, quick!"

She turned to look at Spence as he closed his eyes and did as he was told.

"So, what did you wish for?" Frannie asked.

"I'm not supposed to tell," he murmured, his gaze dropping to her lips, stained red by the Cabernet.

"That's birthday wishes. You can tell a shooting star wish. It'll still come true."

"All right," Spence replied. "I wished I could kiss you. Right here and right now."

She swallowed, then smiled. "Then I guess I'll have to make your wish come true." Frannie set down her glass and slowly wrapped her arms around his neck. And when her mouth met his, it wasn't just a kiss to fulfill a silly wish. It was a kiss tinged with desire.

With a soft moan, he pulled her closer and opened his mouth, their tongues touching and tasting, the kiss whirling out of control. As she skimmed her fingers through his hair, Spence's mind spun. So much for thinking of Frannie Payton as a little sister. After a kiss like this, he'd be lucky if he'd be able to stop thinking about her at all.

CHAPTER THREE

IT WAS NEARLY TEN when Francesca decided to get up. Though she'd been awake since eight, she'd been caught in a delicious contemplation of last night's activities. She and Spence had stayed out until almost eleven, strolling the vineyards by moonlight and talking—and kissing.

As a young girl, she'd often fantasized what it might feel like to capture the attention of Spence Reid, to have him turn the full power of his charm upon her. She'd watched other girls lose all their common sense when it came to Spencer. Last night she'd found out why.

Kissing Spence was wonderfully exhilarating, like being caught in a whirlpool of excitement and need that became more thrilling with every minute that passed. His experience with women was evident, for he was quite possibly the best kisser she'd ever kissed—including a fair number of Frenchmen, who were supposed to be known for their approach to the art.

Spence made a kiss so much more than just a touching of lips and tongues. He had a way of looking into a girl's eyes, until she could see exactly what he wanted. But he didn't kiss her then. Oh, no. He waited, his gaze flitting back and forth between her eyes and her mouth, his fingers toying with her hair, or smoothing along her neck, his words soft and seductive. And then, when she just couldn't stand it another minute longer, he bent closer, his breath teasing at her lips before capturing her mouth.

Francesca moaned softly, then scrambled out of bed. She hadn't felt this way for years, so silly and breathless, like an inexperienced schoolgirl. In truth, she'd become rather jaded by romance, wondering if she'd ever find the right man. Not that she thought Spence was the right man. She was as surprised as he was at the intensity of the attraction between them.

But she knew better than to turn Spence Reid into the man of her dreams. Sooner or later, as with all the girls in his life, she'd be cast aside for someone more intriguing. For now, an occasional kiss couldn't hurt, could it? The anticipation certainly added a little excitement to her time here at Shooting Star.

She tugged on a sweater and pair of blue jeans, then raked her fingers through her tangled hair before heading downstairs. The smell of French coffee drifted through the house, a gentle reminder of the life she'd left behind. In Paris, she'd almost be finished with her workday. Once everything was laid out for the next morning at the bakery, she'd grab her things and head to her usual sidewalk café for the morning paper and a café crème—a wonderful mixture of rich espresso and hot milk.

Funny, Francesca mused. The coffee was the only thing she really missed about her old life. Since she'd returned, she'd barely thought of her friends or her little apartment on the Rue Bonaparte or the bustle of Parisian life. She paused, then frowned when she realized that her thoughts had pretty much been consumed with Spence Reid. Francesca made a silent vow to try to occupy her mind with more mundane matters. It wouldn't do to let herself get all wrapped up in a romantic fantasy that would never happen.

She found her aunt Sophia in the conservatory, a tiny little alcove off the great room that was once used for plants. Gaby sat at her feet, waiting for a treat from the breakfast table. *"Bonjour, chère Sophia,"* she said as she slid into a spot across the table from her aunt. *"Bonjour, Gaby."* She reached down and patted the little dog's head, then grabbed the coffee and poured herself a cup.

Sophia glanced up from the work she had spread in front of her. "Morning, *cara*. Did you sleep well?"

Francesca sipped at her coffee. "Mmm." She reached out for a muffin, examined it, then tossed it back into the basket, making a note to herself to bake something decent for tomorrow's breakfast, perhaps *pain au chocolat* or some little *tartelettes aux pommes*.

"How's the coffee?" Sophia murmured, her eyes cast down on her work. "I know you don't like American coffee, so I used the coffee you brought from Paris, but I wasn't quite sure how you made it."

"It's fine," Francesca replied. She studied her aunt for a long moment. Usually Sophia was so cheerful in the morning. "Is everything all right?"

"Everything is fine," her aunt said.

"Are you sure? You look upset."

"I'm not," Sophia insisted.

But Francesca knew her aunt well enough to know she was lying. Sophia stared at her fingers, as if she were suddenly afraid to look Francesca in the eye. "You want to talk to me about Spence?" Francesca asked.

A long sigh slipped from her aunt's lips. "You know how much I love you, darling. You're like a daughter to me. I just don't want you to get hurt. And with the way you feel and the way he…behaves, I know that might happen."

"How could I get hurt?"

Sophia looked her straight in the eye, her gaze unwavering. "You've been in love with Spence Reid since you were eleven. And now he's paying you all this attention. But he does that with all his women. And sooner or later, he moves on. I love Spence like a son, but when it comes to romance, he isn't a man I'd wish on my worst enemy's daughter.''

Francesca reached over the table and grabbed her aunt's hand. ''I'm a big girl now and you don't need to protect me.''

''And Spence Reid is too charming for his own good—and yours.''

''But I'm not the same girl who left here eight years ago. And if Spence Reid wants to spend his time chasing after me, I'm not going to tell him not to. In truth, I kind of like it. The roles have reversed and it's fun. That's all—just fun. I'm not about to let him catch me.''

''Then you aren't falling in love with him?''

''No!'' Francesca cried. But though she answered the question emphatically, she couldn't deny that as a teenager she'd been completely infatuated with him. And when she thought about her first love, Spence always came to mind. But she was an adult now, and she'd left that foolish infatuation behind when she'd left Shooting Star the last time. ''We're just friends.''

''So there's been no...''

''We kissed,'' Francesca admitted. ''But that's all.'' She didn't bother to explain that they'd kissed more than once. And that it wasn't just a platonic peck on the cheek, but a passionate experience that had left her reeling. ''It was all because of that shooting star,'' she added, trying to minimize the effect of her admission.

''Shooting star?'' Sophia asked.

Grateful that her attention had been deflected, Francesca nodded. ''Before he kissed me, I looked up in the sky and saw a shooting star and I told him to make a wish. And he said he wished he could kiss me. So it was all because of the star.''

Sophia's eyes widened. ''Right before Joe kissed me for the first time, I saw a shooting star,'' she murmured. ''And then there was the night we decided to buy the vineyard with the Reids. A shooting star is an—''

''Here you are. I should have known I'd find you in Sophia's favorite spot. We've got to be going or we'll be late for that appointment with the real estate agent in Sonoma.''

Francesca's gaze shifted away from her aunt, over to the door where Spence stood. As always, he was dressed in casual work clothes, but he looked as though he'd just stepped out of a men's fashion ad—rugged and sexy. With Spence, it came naturally. An unbidden smile touched her lips. ''Hi,'' she said. ''I'm almost finished with my coffee. Can you give me fifteen minutes? I'll meet you outside.''

He nodded, then gave Sophia an odd look before he turned and strode through the great room. Francesca realized she'd been holding her breath, then let it out slowly. "So, you have nothing to worry about," she said, focusing her attention on Sophia again. "I have everything...under control."

But as she hurried back to her bedroom to get ready, Francesca couldn't ignore the pounding of her heart or the slightly giddy feeling she got whenever Spence came near. She couldn't ignore the memories of the kisses they'd shared and the desire that fluttered in her stomach—or the warmth that seeped through her bloodstream.

She had everything under control, she reassured herself. At least, she would, once she could catch her breath and keep her heart from beating out of her chest every time she looked at Spence Reid.

THE TINY BRICK BUILDING just off the plaza in Sonoma was cluttered with remnants of the previous tenant—a florist who had gone out of business nearly two months ago. Francesca slowly walked through the storefront imagining her bakery filled with early morning patrons.

The old mosaic tile floor would gleam with a fresh coat of wax and the tables would be covered with colorful and casual linens. The wide plate-glass windows would gleam and the quaint center entrance would lure customers in from the street. She'd have to buy some cases for the baked goods and maybe a refrigerated display for the desserts, but the basic structure of the building was perfect.

She slowly wandered into the back room. It was littered with scraps of dried flowers and foliage, crumpled tissue and crushed boxes, but once the room was cleared out, there would be plenty of room for her commercial ovens and prep tables. The electricity would have to be upgraded, but beyond that, it was perfect. Francesca wanted to jump up and down and giggle with glee. Instead, she maintained her blasé expression. Unfortunately, Spence didn't do the same.

"It's perfect," he said, grabbing her hands and giving them a squeeze. "It's close enough to the plaza to draw a lot of the tourists, yet far enough away to appeal to the locals. And the building is sound. This plumbing is almost new and the electricity has been updated."

"It is perfect," Francesca agreed.

"So you'll take it?" the agent asked, her voice suitably hopeful.

"Yes," Spence said.

"No," Francesca countered.

Spence blinked in surprise. "No? But, Frannie, this is everything you've been looking for."

She tugged her hands from his and smiled at the agent. "I really need to look around a little more," she said. "Do a bit more research. And the rent is a little beyond my budget. I—I'm not even sure people here would like a French bakery."

The agent shrugged, then handed her a sheet describing the property. "My number is on the top. This place won't be available for long. I've got two other interested parties." She spun on her heel and walked to the door, her high heels clicking on the tile floor. Francesca saw her pull out her cell phone and quickly dial and she imagined that she was calling the two other "interested parties" to inform them that there was a third interested party now.

Francesca folded the paper and put it in her purse. "We can go now," she said, starting for the door.

But Spence caught her arm and turned her around to face him. "Tell me why you don't like this place."

She shrugged, trying to appear indifferent to both his touch and his question. "It's not that I don't like it. I just want to look around—I need to go to San Francisco and Sophia told me I should try Monterey. There are all sorts of possibilities. I don't want to settle on something before I've had a chance to check them all out."

"Monterey is at least two hours away," Spence said. "And if this place is out of your price range, San Francisco will be even worse."

Francesca didn't have to listen hard to hear the true meaning behind his words. He wanted her near. Two hours was too far. How could they possibly carry on a relationship when she worked and lived miles away? Sonoma was close enough for him to drop by and see her whenever he wanted. His reaction wasn't surprising, for it was classic Spence Reid. When he found a woman he wanted he simply tossed aside all caution and pursued her with single-minded zeal.

But she'd already made a promise to herself to not fall for his charms again. It would be so easy and so incredibly stupid. "This is a big decision," she murmured, "and I don't want to be hasty."

"Frannie, what is this really about?"

She sighed softly. "Things are moving just a little fast, that's all. I just got home a few days ago."

"Sophia talked to you," he said bluntly. "She's not happy that we're spending time together."

Francesca nodded. "It's not that she doesn't love you, she's just concerned for me."

"Hell, I'm not carrying the plague," he said after a muttered curse. "So my track record with women isn't so good. I just haven't found the right woman yet. And it's not like we tumbled into bed the moment we saw each other. We kissed. A few times. Well, maybe more than a few."

"I know. And maybe that's where it should

stop. Sophia is your business partner, Spence, and she's my aunt. If things didn't work out, it would put her in an awkward position. She'd be forced to choose between us.''

''So where does this leave us?''

''As friends?'' Francesca ventured, reaching up to touch his face. ''Old friends?''

''Hell, Frannie, we barely know each other. How can we be old friends?''

She sighed. ''We've known each other for years. Maybe we should concentrate on that and try to avoid any…romantic entanglements.''

She sent Spence an encouraging smile and he reluctantly nodded. ''Maybe you're right,'' he murmured. But even though he said the words, there wasn't a trace of conviction in his tone. She suspected that the very next time he felt like kissing her, he'd do just that.

Francesca grabbed his hand and gave it a squeeze. ''Come on, I'll treat you to lunch. Or maybe we'll go Dutch. After all, that's what friends do, isn't it?''

''NOW, REMEMBER the differences? These are all made from the Chardonnay grape, but from three different countries—France, California, Australia.'' Spence held out a goblet to Frannie. ''Concentrate on what's beneath the flavor, the undertones, the subtleties of the wine.''

He watched as she took the goblet in her slender fingers. A pair of candles flickered on the table, the only illumination in the dim interior of the tasting room. The flames cast her beautiful face in an intriguing play of warm light and deep shadow and Spence couldn't keep from staring, from memorizing every perfect detail of her features.

She took a sip and closed her eyes, her brow knitted in concentration. "I taste the oak right away, so it's either California or French."

"And what else do you taste?" he asked, his gaze focused on a tiny droplet of wine on her lower lip, the moisture gleaming in the soft light from the candles. He fought the urge to lean forward and kiss it away, to taste the wine and then her mouth.

"Rich, sweet fruits. Pear and mango." She smiled, her eyes still closed. "It's French." Frannie opened her eyes and sighed. "I've always loved white wine, but have never known much about it. Let me try another."

Spence chuckled. They'd already opened seven different bottles from his private cellar and Francesca was getting a bit giddier with each sip. But the uneasy distance they'd put between them earlier that afternoon had dissolved, and they were once again laughing and teasing, the desire palpable between them. "All right." He splashed white wine into another glass, then handed her a piece of bread to clear her palate. "This is one of my favorites."

She took a sip, but this time she didn't close her eyes. Instead, she stared into his, her expression filled with confusion. Then a slow smile curled the corners of her mouth. "This isn't a Chardonnay," she said.

"What do you taste?"

Frannie closed her eyes again and took another sip. "Fruit, but not citrus. Mmm...peach. No, nectarine?"

"Good," he murmured, leaning closer.

"And something else. It's like fresh herbs."

"Very good," he said, his eyes drifting over her face and stopping at her lips.

"And just a touch of...licorice?"

"Anise," he whispered.

She opened her eyes and gasped softly, surprised to find him so close. But before she could pull back, Spence captured her mouth with his in a soft, urgent kiss. He could still taste the wine on her lips and he took her bottom lip between his and sucked gently.

A tiny moan slipped from her throat, but she didn't resist. Spence wove his fingers through the hair at her nape and pulled her back into the kiss. He didn't want to stop, but he knew he should. Just hours ago, they'd agreed to be friends. But it was a stupid plan, made for stupid reasons. If Francesca Payton was going to tempt him with her sultry eyes and her coy smile, then he had no choice but to respond.

Spence deepened the kiss, his hands snaking around her waist. At the first sign of resistance, he vowed to end the kiss. But there was none there. Her tongue tangled with his and her hands skimmed over his chest. His lips traced a path from her mouth along her jawline and, anxious to discover the taste of her shoulder, he fumbled with the top buttons of her sweater.

When they were opened, he pushed aside the cashmere and pressed his mouth to her bare skin, nibbling around the tiny strap of her camisole. She tipped her head and a soft sigh slipped from her throat. And then, her hand grasped his and she slid it beneath her sweater. Her skin was like silk and he ached to touch her further. His hand moved up to her breast and he cupped her flesh in his palm, the satin fabric of her bra a poor barrier to his touch.

Her breathing suddenly stopped and Spence froze, realizing he'd gone too far. Slowly, he pulled back to find her staring at him, her eyes wide, her color high. She swallowed hard, then forced a smile. "Wha...what was that?"

He frowned. "I'm sorry. I shouldn't have—"

"I meant the wine," she murmured with a tremulous smile. "What was it?"

Relief washed over him. She wasn't angry.

"Oh." He chuckled, then reached for the bottle. "It's a Napa Valley Sauvignon Blanc."

"I should go," she murmured. "It's late and I—I should go." She pushed her stool back and stood, wavering slightly. Her fingers fumbled with the buttons of her sweater.

Spence reached out to steady her. "I'll walk you back."

She shook her head. "I'm fine. I—I'll see you tomorrow." With that, she hurried to the door.

It swung shut behind her, the sound echoing through the tasting room. Spence closed his eyes and raked his hands through his hair. How the hell was he supposed to act like her friend when all he could think about was pulling her warm, supple body against his? How could he put aside thoughts of slowly undressing her, of exploring every inch of her skin with his lips and his tongue? From the moment she walked back into his life, he'd been infatuated. His mind was filled with thoughts of her. And no matter how hard he tried, he couldn't stop wanting her.

"Working late?"

Spence spun around to find Sophia standing in the shadows. "Have you been spying on me?"

"Of course not. What would be the point? You and Francesca will do what you want to do, wherever you choose to do it."

Spence groaned and shook his head. "I don't need scolding from you."

"I wasn't going to scold you," Sophia said. She pulled up a stool and sat. "In fact, I think I've changed my opinion about you and my niece."

"You have?" he asked, blinking in surprise.

She nodded as she straightened the bottles of wine and studied the labels. "I may have been a bit hasty in my objections. She obviously enjoys your company and you enjoy hers. There's no reason why you shouldn't…see what develops. Explore your cosmic connection."

"What is all this about?" Spence asked, suspicious of Sophia's sudden change of heart. "We decided to be friends because of you. And now you're telling me it's all right if we're more than friends? Why?"

"Let's just say I've had reason to reconsider."

Spence nodded, realization suddenly dawning. "I know what this is," he said, shaking his finger at her. "It's reverse psychology. You think if you give your approval, then I'll suddenly lose interest."

"And will you?" Sophia asked.

He raked his hands through his hair. "I don't know. For the first time in my life, I don't know what the hell I'm doing. Frannie is beautiful and smart and sexy, and I know that I should stay away. But something draws me to her. And I swear, if it were the same thing that drew me to all the other women in my life, I'd turn around and walk away. But she's different. Don't ask me to tell you why, but she is.''

"And what about you?"

He shrugged. "I'm still working on that." He grabbed Sophia's hands and gave them a squeeze. "Trust me on this. If either one of us starts to fall in love, we'll come right to you and you can slap us silly."

Sophia tugged her hands from his, then placed her palm on his cheek. "If either one of you falls in love, it will be too late for my help." She pushed back from the table and slowly walked to the door.

Spence stared after Sophia and shook his head. He should have known this would be complicated. He couldn't make a move without Sophia scrutinizing his motives. He wanted Frannie to stay in Sonoma, but he wasn't sure why. He wanted to make her happy, but he wasn't sure how. And he felt as if he was working against the clock. He needed time; time to let this overwhelming desire cool a bit, time to regain some perspective, time for Frannie to see that friendship wasn't always better than desire.

Spence turned and grabbed the phone on the wall. Then he pulled a business card out of his shirt pocket and dialed. There was a way to buy a little time and it wouldn't cost that much.

The real estate agent answered after three rings. He identified himself, then mentioned their meeting that morning in Sonoma. "I want to rent the brick building just off the plaza," he said. "I'd like to come in and discuss a lease."

When he hung up, Spence realized that he'd made the only decision he could make. Forget the doubts and confusion and Sophia's reverse psychology. Forget his track record with women. Something was going on between him and Frannie Payton and until he knew what it was, he wasn't taking any chances. He'd give her all the time she needed, wait for her to come to him, and when she did, he'd prove his case for romance.

Spence sighed. "We'll see just how long this friendship lasts."

CHAPTER FOUR

FRANCESCA STOOD in the kitchen and stared down at the croissant dough on the granite countertop. With a soft curse, she attacked the dough with her rolling pin. Making croissants took careful concentration, turning and folding and chilling the dough at precise intervals. But though she tried to keep her mind on the task at hand, her thoughts kept wandering.

After the wonderful exhilaration of her first few days at the vineyard, the past week had seemed dull in comparison. Spence had been friendly, but they'd barely spent any time together. A relationship that seemed to be heading in one direction had suddenly made an about-face. Where there was once attraction, there was now indifference.

She'd begun to wonder whether she'd imagined a romance between them, whether the kisses they'd shared had been part of some delusion. But there was one hint that they hadn't. Though Spence tried to maintain his distance, whenever she caught him looking at her, she saw the desire there in his eyes.

Francesca tossed aside the rolling pin and tried to remember what turn she was on. Maybe he was actually serious about becoming her friend. Though her suggestion had sounded like a sensible plan, after just a few platonic days together, Francesca didn't want to be sensible! She wanted to fall into his embrace and kiss him until her head spun and her knees wobbled. She wanted to feel his hard, lean body against hers.

Now, she was left to deal with hurt feelings, even though she had no right to show them. She'd sworn to Sophia that everything was under control. It was blatantly clear that she'd been lying—both to her aunt and to herself. She glanced down to find Gaby sitting at her feet, staring up at her with wide, unblinking eyes. "At least he hasn't broken my heart," she murmured. "Maybe bruised it a little."

Sophia could finally put her concerns to rest. And Francesca could turn her attention back to her career. She stared down at the croissant dough and frowned. Her skills as a *boulangère* had suddenly deserted her. She gathered up the dough and wrapped it in plastic, then sat on a kitchen stool.

"Buon giorno, Francesca!"

Francesca looked up to see Sophia hurrying through the kitchen. She carried a small package and stack of mail, along with an empty coffee mug.

"Morning," Francesca replied.

Sophia stopped short and stared at her. "Why so gloomy on such a beautiful day?" She set the package down on the counter and began to sort through the mail. "Did you and Spence have a fight? He's been moping around the office for the past week."

"Me and Spence? A fight? Why would we fight?"

"Because that's what people in love sometimes do," Sophia murmured distractedly.

Francesca gasped, then shook her head. "I'm not in love with Spence, Aunt Sophia. We're just...friends. Nothing more." She couldn't keep regret from coloring her words. "We see each other a couple of times a day, we chat, but we haven't—well, since you told him to stay away from me, he hasn't even tried to—you know."

Her aunt glanced up from the pile of mail. "I didn't tell him to stay away from you. I told him I thought it would be a good idea for you to see how you feel about each other," Sophia explained.

Francesca's jaw dropped and her eyes went wide. "You what? Why would you do that?"

"Well, there was that shooting star you two saw," Sophia explained, as if it made all the sense in the world. "And his horoscope on the day you arrived. You can't just ignore the heavens, *cara*. I was stupid to have done so. When the stars speak, you have to listen."

"Listen to what?"

"The forces of the universe. You and Spence are destined to be together. I'm sure of it now."

"And you told him this?"

"No. I'm hoping he'll come to that conclusion on his own. When it comes to the stars, it's not good to interfere. There are cosmic forces at work here."

Francesca groaned. "Well, throw away your star charts and your horoscopes, Aunt Sophia. I don't think it's going to happen. The stars are wrong on this one."

Sophia laughed out loud. "Oh, it will happen. You just have to be patient, dear. And open yourself up to the possibilities. You were a sweet girl, Francesca, and you've grown into a beautiful woman. Spence Reid would be lucky to have you. And the next time I talk to him, I think I'll tell him that."

Francesca wagged her finger at her aunt. "I don't want you interfering anymore, do you understand? If Spence Reid wants to be friends, then that's exactly what we'll be. And the stars will just have to accept that." She grabbed her croissant dough and threw it in the refrigerator, then wiped her hands on a kitchen towel.

"If you can take a little more interfering, I have a suggestion," Sophia murmured.

"If it has to do with Spence, I don't want to hear it."

"Actually, I think it might be nice if you got out and met some people." Sophia slid an envelope across the counter. "It's the invitation to the Vintner's Ball. It's an annual event for the Sonoma winemakers and every year it's held at a different winery. I tried to talk Spence into going with me, but he refused. Maybe you'd like to go with your aunt? It will give you a chance to meet some people your own age. If you're going to settle here in the valley, it would be good for you to make some friends."

Francesca picked up the invitation and examined it closely. A formal event—black tie, fine wine, sparkling conversation, and maybe a few handsome men to dance with. Suddenly the prospect of a night out, away from Spence and the winery, seemed irresistible. After all, she didn't want to appear as if she were just waiting around for him. "Of course, I'll go. You're sure Spence won't be there?"

"No," Sophia said. "He hasn't gone for the past few years, not since he took that awful Linda person and she told everyone they were engaged."

Smiling, Francesca tapped the vellum invitation against her fingertips. She was already contemplating what to wear. She needed something perfect, something subtle yet sexy, something very French. And she needed to get her hair and nails done, and a facial might be nice. A tiny smile curved her lips. Yes, this was exactly what she needed to get her mind off of Spence Reid.

And after an exciting night out, she'd have a whole new outlook on life in the Sonoma Valley.

SPENCE STARED at his reflection in the rearview mirror of his Jeep, then adjusted his bowtie. The party was already in full swing. The parking lot at the Simon Creek Winery was packed with cars, and music drifted through the night air. The fact that Simon Creek was hosting the ball was proof that the winery had managed to turn a tidy profit last year. They'd produced one of the area's top-ranked Cabernets, much to Spence's chagrin.

It wasn't that he begrudged a fellow wine-maker his success. But this was Tom Simonson. He and Spence had gone to high school together, and though they'd been friends, they'd also been rivals—on the playing field, in the classroom, but most especially with the girls. Tom had stolen any number of Spence's girlfriends and Spence had returned the favor in kind. And after all these years, they were still competing with each other, producing the same varieties of wines for the same markets.

As Spence walked inside, he surveyed the room. One look told him he knew most of the people attending. The wine-making community in Sonoma was a tightly knit group and this was their big night. The old timber warehouse at Simon Creek had been transformed by tiny white lights and linen-draped tables, yet cases of wine were still stacked high against the walls, a reminder of what brought them all together.

As he grabbed a glass of champagne from a passing waiter, his gaze fell on a group near the center of the room. Tom Simonson stood in the middle with his usual circle of friends, most of them young and single, the females making up the extent of the dating pool in the valley. But there was one person Spence didn't recognize, a woman standing next to Simonson, her back to Spence.

Her dark hair was swept into a mass of curls, revealing the tantalizing length of her neck. His gaze trailed down, the cut of her dress revealing the curve of her back, from nape to the intriguing hollow at the base of her spine. Though the dress was perfectly appropriate for a formal event, Spence didn't know any women in the wine crowd with the guts to wear a dress quite so... revealing.

Spence smiled. This was exactly what he needed to forget his troubles with Francesca Payton—an attractive woman, the challenge of luring her away from Tom Simonson, and a dance floor that offered the opportunity to touch her without worrying about propriety. He gulped down the rest of his champagne then started across the room, ready to turn on the charm. But halfway there, the woman turned slightly and he stopped, his progress halted by a flash of familiarity. Her head tilted slightly to the right as she listened. And then she laughed and he knew he was lost.

"Francesca," he murmured.

Spence fought the urge to turn around and leave. This was all Sophia's doing! He'd come here hoping to forget Frannie for an evening and lose himself in the attentions of a willing female. And now he was sure to be tortured, watching Frannie flirt with Tom Simonson, watching as Simonson plied her with champagne and pawed her on the dance floor. Well, there was one way to make sure that didn't happen.

Spence crossed the room in measured strides and when he reached Frannie, he let his hand drop possessively on her bare shoulder. She turned, her smile fading when she realized it was him.

"Francesca." He didn't bother with pleasantries; no questions about what she was doing here and who she was doing it with; no compliments on the way an errant strand of hair brushed the sweet angle of her shoulder or the way her dress dipped just low enough to see the swell of her breasts.

"Spence," she replied, pasting the smile back on her face. "I didn't think we'd be seeing you tonight."

"We?"

She nodded, then stepped aside. It was only then that he caught sight of Sophia on the other side of Tom Simonson. Amusement glimmered in Sophia's eyes and she lifted her champagne glass to Spence in a silent toast. He cursed inwardly. How had Sophia known he'd show up? He hadn't known himself until just an hour ago.

"Well, it's nice to see both of you here," he said, trying to remain indifferent. The effort was nearly impossible considering the damned dress Frannie was wearing. He nodded a greeting at the rest of the group just to drag his eyes away from the perfectly kissable spot of skin on her shoulder.

"Reid," Tom muttered. "We haven't seen you at one of these events in ages. Some of us thought you'd taken up with the monks."

Spence chuckled dryly. "I couldn't very well miss a chance to dance with the two most beautiful women in the Sonoma Valley." He directed a pointed gaze in Sophia's direction, then turned to Frannie. "But I've got a problem. I'm not sure which beautiful woman to dance with first."

"Well, I've had too much champagne to dance," Sophia said with a wave of her hand. "Why don't you ask Francesca? She hasn't danced at all yet."

Spence held out his hand, his gaze meeting Francesca's with an unwavering challenge. He wagered she wouldn't refuse his invitation in front of her new friends, but he knew the odds were about even either way. "I guess it's just you and me, then."

To his relief, she placed her fingers in his and

he led her to the dance floor, secretly pleased with the look of irritation on Tom Simonson's face. They moved through the crowd of couples swaying to the music of a big band orchestra. Spence wasn't sure what song they were playing when he pulled her into his arms, only that it was as perfect as the way her body felt against his.

"You're the last person I expected to see here," he murmured, breathing in the sweet scent of her hair.

She stiffened slightly in his arms. "I got tired of hanging around the house."

He'd done his best to keep her at arm's length during the past week, testing both his resolve and the depth of his desire for her. But now the whole effort seemed ridiculous at best. What had he hoped to accomplish? Did he really think he could forget his feelings for her? Hell, he'd already decided he wanted Frannie in his life, so why was he trying so hard to prove himself wrong?

He'd done it so many times before, talked himself out of relationships, certain that sooner or later he'd become restless and his eye would begin to wander. But he wasn't going to do it this time! Frannie was different.

"I thought it might be nice to make some new friends," Frannie added.

"New friends?" He turned his face slightly, until his chin grazed her temple. The contact was surprisingly intimate and Spence was tempted to press his lips to the spot. "Then you've decided to stay in the Sonoma Valley?"

"I—I haven't decided anything."

"It certainly looks like Simonson would be pleased if you stayed," Spence commented.

"He's a very charming man," Francesca said, pulling back to study his face. She frowned. "Are you jealous?"

"Me? Not a chance," he lied. In truth, he wanted to keep Frannie on the dance floor all night long, just to keep her out of Simonson's arms. "We're old friends."

"You should be happy for me. I've stopped hanging around the house, mooning over you." He glanced down at her only to see a sarcastic arch to her eyebrow.

"And aren't we friends?" he said, staring over her shoulder, hoping that she couldn't see the lie in his eyes. Hell, they were a lot more than friends. A man didn't go to bed every night with the image of a mere friend branded on his brain. And a man didn't wake up in the morning with an ache so bad that the only way to soothe it was to lose himself in the soft body of "a friend."

"Yes, we are," she replied. "Very old friends. Friendly friends. I just thought it was time for a few *new* friends. Besides, you're ready to move on."

"Move on?" Spence asked.

"Oh, please, don't play dumb! It's standard operating procedure for Spence Reid. With you, it's all about the chase. Without the chase, it's no longer fun. I guess I just should have kept running. I would have kept you interested a little longer.''

Stunned by the anger in her voice, Spence opened his mouth to reply, but a firm tap on his shoulder stopped the words in his throat.

"Step aside, buddy. I'm cutting in."

He turned from Frannie, only to find Simonson standing behind him. "We're not through dancing."

Tom stole Francesca's hand and pulled her into his arms. "That's why they call it cutting in."

Spence reluctantly stepped away and watched as Francesca moved across the dance floor with another man, his irritation growing with every smile Frannie turned Tom Simonson's way. The two of them danced as if they'd danced together for years. Had he been an objective observer, he'd be forced to admit that they looked good together.

His jaw tightened and he bit back a curse. Maybe he should just let her go. She was probably right; once the thrill of the chase wore off, he'd find himself looking for something new. But Spence couldn't imagine ever becoming bored with Frannie Payton. Since Frannie had come back into his life, there'd been only one woman on his mind. And he couldn't fathom finding a more exciting or alluring woman to love.

Spence sucked in a sharp breath. Love. He hadn't really thought of their relationship in that way before. But the word seemed completely right considering his feelings for her. He'd fallen in love with Frannie Payton. The concept ought to feel strange, but it was as if he'd known all along. Perhaps Sophia was right. Their destiny had been written in the stars.

He stared across the dance floor. Their destiny wasn't going to be helped along by another man. Spence tugged on the lapels of his tuxedo jacket, then started toward Francesca. They didn't see him coming and when he clamped his hand on Tom's shoulder, he made sure it hurt a little. "I'm cutting in," Spence said.

"Come on, Reid, we just started dancing," Simonson protested.

"That's why they call it cutting in," Spence muttered, easily spiriting Frannie back into his arms. The look he sent Tom as he retreated was enough to send a clear message. There'd be no more cutting in. "Now," he said. "About this chase business, I—"

"Listen," Frannie interrupted. "I don't care what silly ideas Sophia has been shouting in your ear, I'm perfectly happy with our friendship. I'll admit, I might have had a little crush on you when I was younger, but I got over that a long time ago."

"Good," Spence said. "Because we were kids back then. And we aren't kids anymore."

"She thinks because of some shooting star we're meant to be together and I think—"

"That stars have nothing to do with how we feel," Spence finished.

"Right."

His gaze dropped to her mouth and he fought a sudden urge to kiss her. Hell, *this* was crazy, this silly attempt to ignore the desire between them. He wondered what it would take to shake her resolve. He reached up and smoothed his fingers along her jawline. She turned just slightly into his hand, her eyes closed and Spence bent nearer, determined to capture her mouth with his.

But then at the last moment, she opened her eyes and he froze. "You really shouldn't do that," she warned. Gently, she pulled out of his arms. "And I should get back to my new friends."

Spence didn't want to let her go. So he grabbed her hand, pulling her toward the tall oak doors on one end of the barn. He yanked open the door and led her outside. When he finally looked down at her, he saw her shiver. But he didn't touch her. He was afraid that if he put his hands on her there'd be nothing to stop him from pulling her into his arms and kissing her.

Instead, he tried to put his feelings into words, to explain the desire that seemed so overwhelming. But in the end, all he could do was warn her. "You don't know Tom Simonson," he murmured.

She gazed up at him with wide eyes. "And that's why I'd like to at least complete one dance with him. He seems like a very nice guy."

"He's not," Spence muttered. "He's got a real reputation with the ladies and I—"

Frannie laughed, then shook her head. "I suppose you would know. It takes one to know one."

"I just don't want you to get hurt," he said.

"No, Spence. You just don't want me to be hurt by another man. You'd prefer to do that on your own."

He reached out and grasped her arms, giving her a gentle shake. "I'd never hurt you, Frannie. I swear. I only want you to be happy." *And the only way you can be happy is with me,* Spence thought.

"Then just leave me alone, Spence. Let me go back inside and dance."

She was gone before he had a chance to protest, slipping back through the doors and disappearing into the crowd. Spence let out a long breath and leaned back against the low stone wall. Maybe she was right to be suspicious of his motives. He'd never actually had a committed relationship with a woman before. How the hell was he supposed to know if his feelings for Frannie would last?

Spence raked his fingers through his hair. "I know," he murmured. "I don't know *how* I know, but I know that I love her. And once she realizes I'm not interested in the chase, then maybe she'll decide that it's time to stop running.''

CHAPTER FIVE

FRANCESCA SLIPPED INTO the dark house. She kicked off her shoes as she closed the front door, then tiptoed to the kitchen, her feet aching. Three-inch heels had seemed like a good idea earlier that evening.

Sophia had left the party hours ago and Francesca would have returned home with her, but Tom had insisted that she stay, offering to drive her home himself. She would have rather left with her aunt, but had stayed to prove a point— to Spence and to herself.

She stopped at the kitchen sink and rubbed her eyes. Spence. Why did her thoughts automatically go back to him? She'd spent the evening with a very charming man, yet she'd passed most of her time cataloging Tom Simonson's deficiencies against Spence Reid's considerable assets.

Tom was handsome, but Spence was the kind of gorgeous that made a girl dizzy. Tom was clever, but Spence dazzled with his wit. And Tom had given her a chaste peck on the cheek when he'd dropped her off at the front door. Spence would have taken advantage of the moment and swept her into his arms—kissing her until her mind spun and her heart raced and they tumbled into the nearest bed.

"I was wondering if you were going to come home at all."

Francesca jumped at the sound of Spence's voice coming at her from the shadows of the kitchen. She pressed her hand to her chest then saw him perched on one of the kitchen stools. He still wore his tux, but his bowtie was unknotted, hanging loose around his neck. "You waited up for me?" she asked.

He ignored her question and slowly stood. "Did you have a good time?"

"I had a very nice time," she replied.

"And are you going to see him again?"

"Tom?" Francesca took a long breath. "I thought we decided to be friends, Spence. If we're friends, then that's really none of your business."

He took a step toward her. "If we're friends we're supposed to share, aren't we?" he countered in a soft voice.

Francesca raised her chin defensively. "Then I don't want to be friends anymore."

He smiled. "Good. I think we should scrap that plan. I never liked that plan anyway."

"Funny. I thought you were quite happy with it," she murmured. "Until someone else started paying attention to me. You haven't changed a bit, Spencer Reid. I used to watch you and Tom

Simonson compete for the affections of every beautiful girl in the valley. As soon as Tom showed any interest at all, you'd do your best to steal her away. Well, we're adults now and those kinds of games won't get you anywhere with me.''

"You think Simonson is really interested in you?" Spence asked. "He knows you're living here. He probably suspects we're involved. And he's making his move."

"But there's one flaw to your reasoning," Francesca said.

"And what's that?"

She gave him a dismissive shrug. "You and I are not involved. And because we aren't, I'm perfectly free to see whomever I choose."

"How French," Spence muttered.

They stared at each other for a long moment and Francesca fought the maddening impulse to throw herself into his arms and kiss him. It always came down to an undeniable need for physical contact, the urge to touch him and to taste him until she finally had enough. Would she always be left wanting? Years from now, would the thought of Spence's hands on her body still make her tremble?

Francesca moaned inwardly. There was only one way to make sure that didn't happen, one chance to rid herself of a future filled with doubts about Spence Reid. After all, she'd imagined this solution hundreds of times in the past. Why not take a chance? "Maybe we should just get this over with," she said in a defeated tone.

"Is that what you want?" Spence asked, his voice cracking slightly.

"It's the only way," she murmured.

He cursed softly. "So you're just going to walk away and pretend that there's nothing between us?"

"That's not what I meant," she replied. "I meant we should just get *it* over with."

"It?"

"Sex. We should have sex."

His gasp shattered the silence of the kitchen. By his expression, she could tell that suggestion had taken him completely by surprise. Though he tried to cover, she hadn't missed the flicker of desire in his eyes at the mere mention of the two of them together...in bed.

"Sex?" he repeated.

"That's really what's standing between us," Francesca explained. She kept her expression bland, almost clinical, realizing how ridiculous—and desperate—her suggestion sounded. But she was tired of the tension between them, tired of wondering what it would be like. And once they satisfied their curiosity, then they could both get on with their lives, Spence with his winery and she with her bakery.

"Do you really think that's the solution?"

She shrugged. By the look on his face, he obviously didn't. "Probably not. It would only complicate things more."

"Maybe," he murmured.

"I just thought if we satisfied our curiosity there wouldn't be all this...well, we could get it over with and still be friends."

"Friends."

Francesca cursed inwardly. If all he could manage was one-word replies, she'd hate to think of his level of enthusiasm in bed. Why had she made such an impetuous suggestion? A flood of warmth rushed to her cheeks and she was thankful for the dim light in the kitchen, glad that he couldn't see her embarrassment.

"Is this something particularly French?" Spence asked. "I mean, do Frenchmen find this seductive?"

Francesca shrugged, bristling at the sarcastic edge in his voice. "I don't know. I never tried it on a Frenchman."

"Because it sounds like you're approaching the most intimate moment we could ever share with as much excitement as you'd give a root canal. I gotta tell you, Frannie, that doesn't do it for me."

"I was just saying that it might make things easier between us. I was obviously wrong."

He stepped in front of her and stared down into her eyes. "Or maybe you were right."

Francesca's breath caught in her throat. The look in Spence's eyes caused a shiver to course through her. He wanted her as much as she wanted him, it was there in his eyes. But was it for the right reasons? Or would they simply share a physical release together and nothing more. "I—I'm really tired," she murmured. "I should get to bed."

Spence reached up and skimmed her cheek with the back of his hand. "Maybe that would be best."

She fought the urge to turn into his touch, to press a kiss to his warm palm to see where it might lead. She ached for the sensation of his hands on her body, for the taste of his mouth and the smell of his skin. With every ounce of determination she possessed, she stepped away from him and began to walk out of the kitchen.

"Frannie?"

Francesca turned. His striking profile was illuminated by the dim light from above the stove. Her breath caught at the sight of him and she felt weak and foolish. No, it would be reckless to give in to these feelings. "Yes?"

"It wouldn't be just sex," he said. "And I can assure you, once would never be enough."

And then Spence turned and walked out the back door, leaving her with just shadows and shattering realization. "He's right," Francesca murmured. "Once would never be enough."

FRANCESCA'S HANDS were still trembling as she slipped out of her dress and tugged on her cotton batiste nightgown. The cool fabric felt good on her flushed skin. She sat on the edge of the bed and took a shaky breath.

They'd come so close, just a nod away from giving in to their desires. But once again, they'd both walked in opposite directions, away from what they craved the most. Francesca wasn't sure whether to feel relief or rejection. She smoothed her hands over the bedspread, a sudden image of them together flashing in her mind.

He'd be beautiful, all hard muscle and smooth skin. And the passion would sweep them both into another world, a world of soft moans and fevered caresses. She could almost feel his weight above her, could anticipate the sensations that would course through her body when he—

The sound of the floor creaking outside her bedroom door brought Francesca out of her brief fantasy and back into the real world. She stood and approached the door, then pressed her ear against the wood. Was he there, waiting outside her bedroom, filled with as much indecision and desire as she was? She reached out to open the door, then pulled her hand back. Every shred of common sense told her to jump into bed and pull the covers over her head, to keep herself safe from Spence Reid's touch.

She stepped back, then slowly sat on the edge of the bed again. Gaby jumped up beside her and Francesca idly scratched her behind her ears.

"Why don't I just admit it?" she murmured. "I'm in love with him."

All her resolve, all her determination, hadn't made a difference. Somewhere between the time she'd arrived and this moment, he'd swept her into another crazy infatuation. But this time, it wasn't just a simple crush on an unattainable teenage boy. This time, the feelings were so deep and stirring that she couldn't make them stop.

Francesca groaned softly. When it came to Spence, she had never been able to think straight. He wasn't outside the door, waiting for her to open it. She'd been so edgy since their encounter in the kitchen, she was probably just hearing things. To prove the point to herself, she jumped up from the bed, reached out and yanked the door open, fully expecting an empty hallway.

Her heart froze and her breath died in her throat. He stood against the opposite wall, still dressed in his white pleated shirt, though it was pulled from his tux pants and open to the waist. For a long time they stared at each other, both unable to move or to speak, gauging the importance of the next word or action. Finally, he broke the silence and the stalemate.

"I want to put an end to this," he said, taking a step toward her.

She released a tightly held breath. "Me, too," Francesca replied.

They met with such raw need that the heat of his mouth on hers stole the breath from her lungs.

Spence's fingers slipped through her hair as he molded her lips to his, his tongue tasting and teasing, then turning insistent and demanding. She sank into the kiss, her head spinning and her knees weak.

There was no reason to speak; they didn't need words. Frantic sighs punctuated every breath, and every kiss brought whispered moans. The heat from his hands branded her skin through the thin fabric of her nightgown. In truth, she was afraid to speak, for fear that a single word might bring them both back to reality. Kissing Spence, raking her fingers over his naked chest, wasn't the sensible thing to do. But it felt so right and he felt so perfect.

When he pulled away, Francesca looked up into his eyes. Though Spence hadn't said the words, she knew, at least in this place in time, that he loved her. And she loved him. She'd never stopped, not since that day so long ago, when she'd first seen him. Back then, she'd dreamed about kissing him, chaste kisses that ended after a few seconds. But the dreams of a schoolgirl had given way to the desires of a woman. And kissing wasn't enough.

Francesca bent her head and pressed her lips against the hard plane of his chest. Slowly, she traced a path up to the notch in his neck and then down again, brushing his shirt off his broad shoulders. When it fell to the floor, she opened her eyes and stepped back. The sight of his naked torso, skin gleaming in the soft light from the bedside lamp, brought a ragged breath to her lips. She remembered the boy, the gangly limbs and skinny body. But he'd left boyhood far behind.

A smile touched the corners of his mouth as she ran her fingertips down his chest to his belly. Her touch had power over him and when she reached the button of his pants and began to work it open, he groaned softly and closed his eyes.

She was unprepared for the surge of desire that heated her own blood, dissolving the last hint of inhibition. She wanted to wrap her fingers around him, to tease him until he ached for release.

But Spence reached down and took her hand, stilling her descent into more intimate territory. His gaze held the question. *Are you sure?* Francesca didn't bother to answer for she didn't have the power to say no. They'd already gone too far and the need raging inside her was too much to deny. She pulled her hand from his and flipped open the button.

A low growl rumbled in Spence's throat. He scooped her into his arms and carried her over to her bed. Gently, he set her down, then stood over her. For a moment, he hesitated, and Francesca thought he was about to turn and walk out of the room. But then she held her hand out to him in a silent invitation.

Spence pulled her up to kneel on the bed in front of him. He bent his naked chest brushing against her breasts through the fabric of her nightgown, sending jolts of desire through her limbs. His fingers bunched the thin cotton at the hem, then slowly, deliberately, he dragged the nightgown up along her hips.

With each inch of skin revealed, Spence explored, with his fingers and his lips and his tongue. When he bared her breasts, he paused, taking each nipple into his mouth before moving on. And when he finally pulled the fabric over her head and tossed it aside, Francesca felt the last vestige of her control shatter.

This was more than just a dream, more than the fantasy she'd built in her mind over the years. Every caress was so real, every sensation so intense. She wanted to savor each moment, but Francesca couldn't stop them from rushing headlong toward their release. One moment he was still half-dressed and the next, he was lying naked beside her. One moment his body was pressed along the length of hers and the next, he was moving inside her.

All at once Francesca wanted to stop time, yet hurdle into the future. And when she felt her climax near, time did seem to slow. For a long delicious moment, they hung on the edge, each second, each heartbeat, becoming slower and slower until everything stopped. Through passion-glazed eyes, Francesca watched him, the mix of pleasure and pain suffusing his face, his need holding him captive. And then, with a soft moan, Spence arched above her and drove into her and together they found release—aching, shattering, breathless release.

And later, after Spence had fallen asleep beside her, his leg thrown over her hips and his face tucked into the curve of her neck, Francesca realized that no matter what happened between them, she'd never regret opening that bedroom door. For as Sophia had insisted, it was their destiny to be together.

But not even the stars could predict how long their time might last. For now, one night would have to be enough.

THOUGH THEIR NIGHT together was supposed to put an end to all their desire, Spence knew it was only the beginning. He stretched lazily, brushing the tangled sheet from around his waist. He'd never wanted or needed a woman as much as Frannie. And last night only proved what he'd known since the moment she'd walked back into his life. They belonged together.

He reached up and rubbed his eyes, then turned onto his side, expecting to see Frannie asleep next to him, ready to wake her with his kisses. Instead, he found Gaby staring at him from Frannie's pillow. He reached out and patted the dog on the head. Gaby cocked her ears, then scrambled off the bed and sat in front of the bathroom door.

A moment later Francesca emerged, completely dressed except for her shoes. She didn't realize he was awake and was trying her best to not make noise. But as Frannie passed the bed, she stubbed her toe. A string of whispered curses split the silence of the room, many of the words in French.

Spence pushed up on his elbow as Francesca hopped across the room to the door. It was then that he noticed her suitcase with her shoes sitting neatly next to it. "Good morning," he said. "You're up early."

Startled by the sound of his voice, she spun around to face him, nearly losing her balance. "I—it's not that early," she murmured, frozen to the spot in front of the door.

Spence nodded toward her suitcase. "Are you planning a trip?"

A blush crept up her cheeks, as if she'd been caught red-handed. "Actually, I am. I'm going to San Francisco today. I need to look at some locations for my bakery and I—"

"This morning?" Grabbing the sheet, Spence pulled it around his waist then stood. "You have to leave this morning?"

"No. But...but after last night, I think it would be best if—"

"If we spent the rest of the day in bed," Spence finished. He crossed the room in a few short steps and slipped his arm around her waist. "The bakery can wait. The vineyard can wait." Spence nuzzled her neck. "I'm not sure we've really put an end to this and I think we should keep trying, don't you?''

Francesca slipped out of his embrace and stepped around him. She hurried to the dresser, then busied herself by pulling jewelry out of a small leather case. "I really need to—"

"Frannie, what's wrong?" She was doing her best to avoid his eyes and his touch. Spence frowned. "I thought we settled everything last night. I know how I feel and I know how you feel." He raked his hand through his hair. "You don't have to go to San Francisco today. You can stay right here with me."

"I have to look for a spot for my—"

"Bakery. I know." He leaned back against the door, his mind spinning an image of Francesca, naked, in his arms. He imagined himself unbuttoning the dress she wore and toying with the French silk underwear he'd probably discover beneath. His head was already filled with the scent of her hair and the taste of her lips. "And I have the perfect spot. That building off the plaza in Sonoma. Now that we have that settled, come back to bed."

"That shop's not available anymore," Francesca countered. "I called the agent a few days ago and her assistant told me it was leased."

"It is. To me," Spence said. He moved to the dresser and grabbed Francesca's hand, then tried to pull her to the bed. But she resisted.

"You rented the shop?" she asked. "Why?"

"Because I knew you weren't ready to make a decision. And I didn't want you to lose it. It's the perfect place, Francesca."

"I see," she said. "So you made the decision for me?" She scooped up the pile of jewelry from the dresser then stuffed it back into the small bag. "That's just fine. I'm glad you know what I want more than I do. But that's typical, isn't it? You decide what you want and you go after it. I'm just supposed to fall down at your feet and thank my lucky stars that Spence Reid has turned his attention on me."

He gasped, taken aback by her sudden show of anger. "What the hell is that supposed to mean? I rented the bakery because I thought it would be a great place for your business. I'm not trying to run your life."

"Good. Then you can break the lease."

He reached out and grabbed her elbow as she crossed to the closet, spinning her around to face him. "What is this really about? Because, if it were about us, we wouldn't be shouting at each other. We'd be kissing...and touching...and talking about what we're going to do today and next week and for the rest of our lives."

"We had an understanding," Frannie said, her words measured. "Last night was just one night. That's all. It's over. We satisfied our curiosity."

"And that's just an excuse, because both you and I know that last night was never meant to be the end of it."

"You were the one so determined to be friends. Is it that easy to turn your passion on and off? Forget about last night. What about last week? You did your best to keep me at arm's length and now you change your mind?"

Spence shook his head. "That was different. That was a...a test. I tried to stay away, Frannie, but I couldn't."

She tipped her chin up and stared at him stubbornly. "You know that sooner or later this will end. You'll get that look in your eye and you'll start wondering if there's someone more exciting, more beautiful, out there, just waiting to meet you."

The notion of someone more exciting and beautiful than Frannie was so ridiculous that it made him laugh out loud. "I don't think that will happen, considering that I'm head over heels in love with you."

His admission brought her up short and her eyes went wide with disbelief. She slowly shook her head. "No. You just think you love me. But you'll get over it. You always do."

"I'll never stop loving you, Frannie." The words had come so naturally to him that he knew in his heart they were true.

"Don't say that," she demanded. "Don't lie to me."

He stared at her for a long moment, then reached out and took her hand. Now was not the time to convince her of his love. No matter what he said, she wouldn't listen. Frannie needed time. It had taken them fourteen years to get to this moment and now that she was here, she didn't want to believe it was real.

He took her fingers and wove them through his. "I'm not lying, Frannie. And I think, in your heart, you know that. But I came to you last night certain that I loved you. And when you realize how you feel, you're going to have to come to me." Spence dropped her hand. "Go to San Francisco and try to find a life for yourself there. And when you don't, you can come back here, because I'll be waiting for you."

Spence crossed to the door, then picked up her shoes and suitcase and held them out to her. Frannie stepped toward him and reached out to take them, then hesitated. His breath froze as he waited for her decision, praying that she'd stay. But in the end, she grabbed her things and hurried out of the room.

With a soft curse, Spence closed the door, then leaned back against it, angry that he couldn't convince her of his feelings. Still, he didn't care how long he had to wait. He knew that Frannie was the only woman he wanted in his life. But she'd have to come back on her own.

He sighed, then rubbed the sleep from his eyes. "I sure hope you don't keep me waiting long, Frannie. Because we do have a future together and I want it to start as soon as possible."

CHAPTER SIX

FRANCESCA HAD BEEN summoned to the tasting room by a note from Sophia, which she'd found taped to the coffeemaker.

She'd spent the morning explaining to her aunt why she had to leave, then spent the afternoon convincing herself she shouldn't. And now, when she'd finally decided that she was doing the right thing, she'd be forced to explain herself to Sophia once more.

Though she hadn't decided on a permanent residence yet, San Francisco seemed like a good choice for the moment. If starting a bakery proved to be too expensive, there would be plenty of jobs for someone with her skills. In truth, she could have chosen any city anywhere—just as long as she left. She and Spence needed time apart, time for the memories of their night together to fade.

What had ever possessed her to make love with him? She'd thought it would clarify everything, her feelings, his feelings, all the confusion between them. But instead their encounter had brought a startling realization—no matter what she did, she couldn't keep from loving Spence Reid. And even though he'd confessed his feelings to her, she still couldn't trust him. Sooner or later, if she didn't get away from Sonoma Valley, she'd get her heart broken into a million pieces.

Francesca pushed open the heavy oak door of the tasting room and stepped into the dimly lit interior. Her mind immediately returned to the night she'd kissed Spence, right here, in this very room. She should have stopped him then, put an end to their unchecked rush toward intimacy. None of this would have happened and she wouldn't be left to question her own common sense.

The room was quiet and her footsteps echoed on the stone floor. A light from the office filtered into the room and she saw a figure sitting at the scarred table. Francesca stopped short when she realized it was Spence and not Sophia.

He turned at the sound of her footsteps and his smile faded. "What are you doing here? I thought you'd left."

Francesca shrugged and met his unwavering gaze. "I was about to. Where's Sophia?" Memories flashed in her mind: the feel of his hands on her body, the way he caressed her naked skin with his fingers and his lips. The easy weight of his body as he sank inside her and the sensations that rocked her as they reached their peak. She swallowed hard and glanced around. "I—I've got to go. Tell Sophia I'll call her when—"

"Sit," Sophia ordered as she appeared out of the shadows. She pointed to the chair next to Spence. "I need to talk to both of you, together. I have some news that I'd like to share." She set an uncorked bottle down on the table, along with three wineglasses. Carefully, she poured a small amount of wine into each goblet, then pushed a pair across the table at Francesca and Spence.

"A toast," Sophia said brightly, holding up her wine.

"To what?" Spence asked.

"To me," she replied. "I have a rather important announcement."

"It's probably just another message from the stars," Spence muttered.

"Well, now that you mention it, my horoscope said I'd make an important decision today and I have," Sophia explained. "I've decided to retire."

"What?" The word burst out of Francesca's mouth at the exact instant Spence uttered it.

"Retire? But why?" Francesca asked. "This vineyard is your life. You love it here."

"Sophia, you can't retire. I need you."

"I can and I will retire," Sophia said. "I want to travel, maybe go back to Italy and visit relatives. Besides, I have a perfectly good plan for the vineyard. I'm going to leave my half to Francesca."

This time the "What?" increased in volume and was tinged with an edge of hysteria on Francesca's part and disbelief from Spence. When the sounds stopped echoing through the cavernous tasting room, an uneasy silence fell around them. "But...but I don't want your half of the vineyard," Francesca protested.

"I don't care," Sophia said. "I've decided to give it to you. And it's not polite to refuse a gift, especially not one so dear."

"You can't do this," Spence said. "She doesn't know anything about running a vineyard."

"I taught you," Sophia replied. "And you can teach her. After a year, if Francesca doesn't care to keep her half, then she has my authority to sell her shares to anyone she chooses. She can use the money to buy a bakery in Paris if she wants."

"The hell she will," Spence said, pushing to his feet and slamming his hands down on the table. "I've invested my future in Shooting Star. I don't want her selling your half to some stranger who'll come in here and mess up what I've built."

"Then you better learn to work with your new partner," Sophia replied.

Francesca sighed and twisted her fingers together in front of her. "You can't make us love each other," she murmured. "Just because you want it, doesn't mean you can make it happen."

Spence turned to Francesca, his gaze piercing

hers. "You'll sell to me and no one else," he ordered.

She bristled at his demand. "Don't tell me what I will and won't do," she replied, setting her jaw in a show of determination that, in truth, was sorely lacking. "I'm tired of both of you trying to run my life. You with that lease for the shop in Sonoma. Sophia with her half of the vineyard. I have my own life and I'd be grateful if you'd both butt out of it." She shoved her chair back and braced her hands on the table. "I won't take the vineyard."

"You don't have a choice," Sophia repeated.

"Why are you doing this?" she said in a wavering voice. "You know how I feel." The last was said in barely a whisper. Yes, her aunt knew precisely how Francesca felt, how she'd fallen in love with Spence Reid when she was eleven and had never really stopped loving him. That was the problem. But nothing Sophia did, not even making them partners in the vineyard, would keep Spence from leaving her in the end.

"If this is the only way I can keep you two together long enough for you to figure out you belong together, then so be it," Sophia said. "Now, if you'd like to discuss your new partnership, I'll leave you to it."

SPENCE WATCHED Sophia leave, stunned by her news, angered by his reaction, and frustrated by Francesca's indifferent attitude. He cursed softly, then kicked his chair away. "She shouldn't have done that," he muttered as he paced the floor. "I don't want to force you to stay here if you don't want to."

Francesca let out a long sigh. "And I don't want half of your vineyard. She's got some misguided notion that we're destined to be together. Something about your horoscope and that shooting star we saw."

Spence shook his head. "It's all that astronomy stuff she's—"

"Astrology," Francesca said with a soft laugh. She turned to face Spence. "If she gives me her half—which I'm not sure she'll actually do—but, if she does, I'll give it back to you. Free and clear. I have enough for my bakery. I don't need your help."

He released a tightly held breath, and along with it, his anger. Hell, he really didn't care if Francesca owned half his vineyard. If it kept her close, then he'd give her every damn acre. "I'm sorry I went off like that. It's not about the vineyard."

"It's all right," Frannie murmured. "Sophia can be stubborn when it comes to something she really wants. And I guess she wants us to be together. No matter what the circumstances."

Spence reached out to touch her face and saw her stiffen. How could they have shared such intimacies last night, yet be as uneasy as strangers today? Instead, he grabbed her hand. Immediately a wave of desire washed over him. He needed time with her, time for them to put aside their doubts. "I don't want you to go," Spence said. "We have a lot to talk about."

"What?" Frannie asked. "This? Or last night?"

"First, this. I'll buy your half of the vineyard, Frannie. Whatever you want. It may take me a while to pay you everything it's worth, but it will give you more for your bakery. You could even buy a place in San Francisco...or you could afford the shop in Sonoma."

"I—I don't know what I want," Frannie murmured. "But I know, I don't want your money." She glanced around the room and he was suddenly aware of how close they were standing. Close enough to smell her perfume. Close enough to feel the heat from her body. Close enough to lower his head and kiss her. "Frannie, I—"

She took a step back. "I—I should go. I've got a long drive ahead of me."

"About last night," he insisted.

"We meant to put an end to it," she said with a weak smile. "I guess we did."

"You can't go."

"Why not?"

Spence cursed softly. This was not coming out the way he wanted it to. He wanted her in his arms, not standing at a safe distance with a wary look in her eyes. "Because...because you can't.

You're meant to stay here. With me. Last night proved that.''

"Now you're beginning to sound like Sophia," Frannie said.

"Well, maybe I am. And maybe she's right."

She bit her bottom lip, her eyes downcast. "This isn't real," she finally said. "For a little while, we lived a fantasy. But it can't last. It isn't meant to." She turned on her heel and hurried toward the door, but he couldn't let her go.

"Frannie," he called as she reached for the doorknob.

She froze, but didn't turn around. "Yes?"

"I love you. Whatever you believe about us, you have to believe that."

Her shoulders slumped and for a moment he thought she'd turn around and come running back into his arms. But then she stiffened, yanked open the door and walked out.

Spence leaned back against the edge of the table. He fought the urge to go after her, to force her to see the truth in his words, to kiss away her doubts and fears. Women had come and women had gone over the years, but Francesca was different. She was the one who was supposed to stay.

He rubbed his forehead. It had all been handed to him—her return to Shooting Star, their instant attraction to each other, the passion they shared. He should have been able to make it work. Yet, once again, he'd come up short and the regret was acute.

But he couldn't blame Frannie for her hesitation. He just prayed he'd have another chance to prove he wasn't the same Spence Reid she thought she knew. And to prove he was through with the chase now that he'd discovered the true prize.

THE HOUSE WAS QUIET by the time Francesca was ready to leave. She'd expected Sophia to hover over her in a last-minute attempt to convince her to stay. Obviously, her aunt had given up the cause, just as Spence had.

She reached down and picked up Gaby, tucking the little dog under her arm. Though the rental car had been dropped off earlier that morning, she couldn't bring herself to toss her bags inside and head for San Francisco. Instead, she felt the same mixture of longing and loss that she had felt every August, when it had been time to leave Shooting Star to go home to her life with her parents and her school friends.

But this time, she really didn't have any reason to leave. Everything she wanted was here, in this beautiful place, everything she'd ever wished for in her schoolgirl dreams. Yet she hadn't been brave enough to reach out and grab it—or to believe in it.

She pressed her face into Gaby's soft white fur. "You have to stay here with Aunt Sophia," she murmured. "She'll take good care of you. But I'll be back to get you very soon. I promise." The little dog sniffed and wriggled until Francesca put her down. She scampered to the back door and scratched at it. Francesca sighed. The afternoon light was waning and if she didn't get on the road soon, she'd be forced to navigate the complex maze of San Francisco streets in the dark.

"Come on," she said, opening the door. "One more run around the vineyard and then I have to leave."

Gaby gave her a playful bark then raced into the bushes dotting the hill behind the house. Following the little dog, Francesca hiked up the hill, drawn to the spot where she and Spence had gone to watch the sunset. He'd kissed her there, in the same place where he'd kissed so many others. She tried to remember that—all those girls who had come before her and all the women who would come after her.

Francesca raked her hands through her hair, then tugged her jacket more tightly around her to ward off the evening chill. Somehow, her rationalizations no longer made sense. They were simply the feelings of a rejected teenager, a girl who harbored secret jealousies and insecurities. But Francesca wasn't that girl anymore. She was a woman with a heart capable of true love. And though she fought it with every breath, she loved Spence Reid.

She stopped short, Gaby continuing her joyful race to the top of the hill. If she was no longer that lovesick girl, why did she continue to believe that Spence was that fickle boy? Was she so mired in the past that she couldn't see what the future held? "He's not a boy, he's a man," she murmured. "A man who knows what he wants. And he says he wants me."

Suddenly she needed to see him, to reassure herself that his feelings were true. "Gaby!" she called. "Come. Gaby, come here." She whistled for the dog as she walked, searching through the scrub. Her heart pounded in her chest and she had to force herself to remain calm. Spence Reid loved her; he'd said the words that she'd waited years to hear. And she'd walked away!

"I'm so stupid," Francesca muttered. "What was I thinking?"

Up ahead, Gaby barked, then growled. Francesca broke into a run, wondering whether the dog had cornered a rabbit or had encountered something more vicious. But when she emerged from behind a high shrub, she found her dog hanging on to Spence Reid's leg with her little teeth.

They stared at each other for a long moment, neither one of them moving, both of them aware that this was where they'd started. If only they could begin again, Francesca mused. She'd never walk away, not this time.

Gaby continued to tug at Spence's jeans, but

his attention was so focused on Francesca, so unshakable, that he barely noticed the dog. "You're back," he said.

Francesca swallowed hard. "I—I couldn't bring myself to leave. Not until I took one more walk."

"I remember when you were a kid, you used to spend your last day wandering the vineyards. One year, it was pouring rain and you still managed to cover every inch of the property."

"I was so happy here," she murmured.

"You still can be," he said. He stepped up to her, dragging Gaby along with him, a wry smile curling the corners of his mouth as the dog fought his progress. "I can make you happy here again."

Francesca held her breath, afraid to speak, afraid she might somehow ruin this chance she had. And when he pulled her into his arms, she didn't have the power to resist. This is where she belonged, Francesca mused. She'd always belonged in Spence's arms—it had just taken them fourteen long years to figure that out.

"I'm afraid," she said, her eyes moist and her voice wavering.

He pulled back and brushed the hair from her temple, then wiped an errant tear from her cheek. "Of what? You don't have to be afraid of me," Spence said. "Because I swear on my life, I will never, ever hurt you, Frannie."

"I—it's not that. I'm afraid that when you realize I'm not really the woman you see, you'll move on. Like you did with Danielle Eaton and Cathy Walters.''

"Then, who are you?"

"In some ways, I'm still that gawky teenage girl who carried a torch for you all those years. I may dress differently and act like I know what I'm doing, but sometimes I still feel like you could break my heart so badly it could never be mended. I don't think I've ever stopped loving you, Spence. In truth, I've loved you for more than half of my life. But I don't know what I'll do if you don't love me back."

"Sweetheart, from the moment I met you all those years ago, I knew we'd end up together. I knew when it finally came time for me to fall in love, for real, it would be you, Frannie. Those other girls, they were just for marking time. Until you grew up and came back." He pulled her hand up to his lips and kissed her wrist. "Marry me."

Her eyes went wide. "Marry you?"

Spence nodded. "You don't have to answer now. But I'm going to keep asking until you say yes." He paused, then dropped a kiss on her lips. "You could say yes right now," he suggested.

Francesca giggled and shook her head, unable to believe what she'd just heard. She'd dreamed about this moment, but her dreams had been so cliché, silly fantasies of the perfect proposal. As she stared up into Spence's eyes, she realized that it was the love there that made his proposal perfect, not a candlelit dinner or a huge diamond ring.

"You made me wait fourteen years," she said. "I think maybe I should return the favor."

Spence frowned. "You're going to make me wait fourteen years?" His expression fell. "Well, if you—"

She tipped her head back and laughed. "Fourteen years is a long time."

"A hundred years wouldn't change the way I feel about you."

"I was thinking maybe fourteen days? Ask me again in two weeks, Spence."

He gazed down into her eyes then kissed her, his mouth capturing hers. Francesca sank into him, losing herself in the kiss, a kiss that she never wanted to end. When he finally pulled away, she could barely draw a breath. A devilish twinkle glittered in his eyes. He grazed her bottom lip with his teeth. "Fourteen days?"

A tremor raced through her and she moaned softly. She had to at least make some show of resistance, didn't she? "All right," Francesca muttered. "Ask me again in fourteen hours."

"Agreed," he said. "I can wait for fourteen hours. But not a minute more." With that, he pulled her into another kiss, a kiss that sealed her destiny. And when they finally paused to take a breath, the sun had disappeared below the horizon and the sky was a deep midnight-blue.

Francesca stared up at him, unable to drag her gaze from the man she loved. "You're not marrying me because you want my half of the vineyard, are you?"

Spence took her hand and tugged her along with him. "No, I think you should keep your half. We need to be equal partners. Besides, I'm really bad with the books so you're going to have to do them."

"Sophia has to stay," Francesca insisted. "I can't run my bakery in Sonoma and help run the vineyard. I think we'll have to give her an ultimatum. An offer she can't refuse."

Spence laughed as they hiked the rest of the way up the hill, Gaby scampering around their feet and nipping at Spence's boots. They found the spot where they'd first kissed, then climbed up on the rock. When she'd settled herself in his arms, Francesca stared up at the first stars to light the evening sky. She stopped, then pointed toward the eastern horizon. "Look," she said, glancing over at Spence.

But he wasn't looking at the sky. His gaze was fixed on her. "I am looking," he said. "And I like what I see."

"No," she insisted. "I saw a shooting star. Right over there."

He groaned and pulled her back into his embrace, kissing her neck. "I don't know how Sophia did that, but she probably has contacts at

NASA. Maybe she had them shoot down a satellite.''

''I think it's an omen,'' Francesca teased.

With a low growl, Spence grabbed her around the waist and pulled her on top of him. ''All right,'' he shouted. ''I give up. If it's written in the stars, then it has to be so.''

He kissed her, long and hard, until she was giddy with joy. Whether stars had a hand in their destiny or whether their love had come of its own accord, Francesca knew that their feelings were true and sure. And as long as the stars shone in the night sky, she would love Spence Reid. Now and forever.

Dear Reader,

Readers frequently ask me if I ever include events from my own life in my books. My answer is always the same—I write fiction. I don't deliberately use real people or circumstances because it is much more fun to make them up. But, of course, I am often inspired by things that really happen to me. Arkansas and the surrounding states were hammered by ice storms in the winter of 2000-2001, leaving my family stranded—on more than one occasion—in our home without power or access to so many of the luxuries we've become accustomed to. So it was natural for me to remember those experiences, and to draw upon them, when I wrote a winter storm into "Star Crossed."

Who, at some time or another, hasn't read her horoscope and wondered if there was some chance the predictions could come true? I certainly have. It's fun to at least pretend to believe in magic. As Keely and Michael find out in this story, the most powerful magic isn't conjured by the stars; it comes straight from the heart. When I write, my twenty-five-year marriage also serves as another real-life inspiration. So the answer to that frequently-asked question is that my stories are made-up, but that I draw at least some elements from my own experiences when I create them. I hope you enjoy the results as you read "Star Crossed."

Gina Wilkins

Gina Wilkins

STAR CROSSED

Gina Wilkins

CHAPTER ONE

"*Ooh,* is it cold out there!" Keely Parker shivered as she tossed her morning newspaper onto the table and made an eager grab for the coffee carafe. Her icy skin tingled when the steam from her coffee wafted across it. Her red-tipped fingers were stiff as she wrapped them around her favorite Garfield mug.

"That's what happens when you go running at sunrise in January," her older brother, Jonah, drawled from the other side of the table. "If you'd stay in bed with the covers over your head until the last minute like normal people do, you wouldn't be in danger of freezing any important body parts. Southerners just don't do winter."

She spread cream cheese on a bagel, savoring the warmth of the toasted bread. "I like running in the mornings—even in the winter. I enjoy watching the world wake up."

"You're welcome to it. I'll stick to my routine of hitting the gym during my lunch break a couple of times a week."

In response to a sound from the kitchen doorway, Keely turned her head. A familiar flutter somewhere in the vicinity of her heart made her smile ruefully. She supposed it was one of the inevitable consequences of living with an absolutely gorgeous male. Sometimes her hormones just went berserk at the sight of him, even though she thought of Michael Gordon as an almost second brother. Or at least, that was the way she tried to think of him, since he had always treated her as if she were his little sister.

Michael was dressed for work, though his red tie hung loosely around the neck of his white dress shirt and he hadn't yet donned the jacket that matched his crisply tailored navy slacks. His dark hair was tousled around his face, and his midnight-blue eyes were heavy-lidded from sleep. "Coffee," he said, as articulately as always first thing in the morning.

Keely nudged the carafe toward him. "It's still hot."

He nodded, poured a cup, and downed a third of it. Only then did he look at his housemates and say, "Good morning."

Jonah looked up from the legal briefs he'd been studying while he'd wolfed down an enormous bowl of sugar-frosted cereal. "Both of you remember that I'm leaving for Birmingham this afternoon, don't you? I'll be back Tuesday."

"It's a shame you have to leave on a Friday," Keely remarked. "You're going to have to spend the whole weekend in Birmingham."

Jonah shrugged. "It couldn't be helped. We

have a big meeting late this afternoon, and another early Monday morning. But I'll be busy doing research during the weekend.''

''Better hope this storm they're predicting doesn't hit sooner than expected.'' Michael nodded toward the kitchen window, through which they could see the dark gray clouds covering the morning sky. The Memphis, Tennessee, weather forecasters had been predicting a winter storm for days, something rare enough in their area to cause a sensation. ''The airport's going to be in chaos if we get the sleet and freezing rain they've been talking about all week.''

''I'll try to get an earlier flight just in case. Keely, remember, if we do get an ice storm, don't try to get out on the roads. If you need anything, go get it this morning so you won't have to leave the house in bad weather.''

Keely rolled her eyes. ''Yes, Dad,'' she muttered, opening the nationally published tabloid she always picked up on her way back from her daily run. She turned to the horoscope section first. It had become a habit for her to read her horoscope, her brother's, and Michael's out loud every morning during breakfast.

Jonah usually found the ritual entertaining, and Michael tolerated it, though he had little patience for such foolishness. Practical, levelheaded, ambitious attorney Michael didn't believe in any fate he didn't create for himself. Keely had gravely assured him that his attitude was typical of Capricorns, which had only made him shake his head in exasperation.

"So, what's in the stars for us today?" Jonah asked, closing his folder and looking expectantly at his sister.

She read her own first. "'Taurus. You are blessed with wisdom today, but what counts is convincing others.' Oh, I like that."

"You would," Jonah muttered. "You always think you know what's best for everyone else anyway."

Michael didn't comment, but the look on his face told her that he agreed with her brother.

She wrinkled her nose at both of them and continued to read, "'An argument could lead to an emotional breakthrough. Your heart's desire is within your grasp, but your hidden insecurities could prevent you from achieving your goals. Don't let your fears guide your actions.'"

"You? Insecurities?" Jonah snorted inelegantly. "Yeah, right."

Keely lowered the paper to glare at her brother. "Excuse me? Are you accusing me of being conceited?"

"Not conceited. Just...self-confident," he revised quickly.

She had already turned her attention back to her horoscope. "Maybe I'll get a call from the art gallery today offering me a show of my own. That's always been my goal, but it would be rather intimidating. I suppose fear could cause me to make a mistake about that.''

"Now you *are* reaching.'' Michael shook his head as he poured milk over his cereal. "If there's one thing you're ready for, it's a show of your own. When it comes to your art, you have no fear. You're just trying to make that stupid horoscope sound believable.''

"I'm not trying to prove anything,'' she retorted. "I'm simply reading what it says.''

In an obvious effort to avert a very familiar quarrel, Jonah asked, "What does mine say? I hope it doesn't make any dire predictions about air travel.''

With a flourish intended for Michael, Keely lifted the paper again. "'Cancer. Duties and responsibilities rest heavily on your shoulders today. Do your best, but accept your limitations. Take time for yourself this evening. Read a good book, enjoy a fine meal, and recharge your energies.' Did you pack that new mystery novel I bought you yesterday?''

"I packed it. And I'll try to make time to read it after a fine room-service meal,'' he assured her, looking rather pleased with the advice the stars had given him. "It sounds like a great way to spend the evening.''

"The astrologist was apparently in a good mood the day she wrote those,'' Michael commented with typical cynicism. "According to her, everyone's going to have a glorious day today."

Keely looked at him over the paper. "You haven't heard yours yet."

Jonah grinned. "Uh-oh. Sounds like you're in trouble, Mike."

Michael shrugged and swallowed a mouthful of cereal. "I'd be in more trouble if I actually believed in that stuff."

"What does his say, Keely?"

In response to her brother's prompting, Keely read out loud, "'Capricorn. You run the risk of making a fool of yourself today.'"

Laughing, Jonah teased, "And how would that be different from any other day?"

Michael responded with a cereal-muffled mumble that might have been a rude suggestion.

Ignoring them both, Keely continued. "'Be careful around animals and members of the opposite sex. An unexpected opportunity will pass you by if you don't act on it. Someone in a hat may bring luck—but remember, luck comes in many guises and isn't always easy to recognize.'"

Michael made a face. "Someone in a hat? Give me a break."

Keely folded the newspaper and looked at him. "You have to admit she's been right pretty often lately. Remember last week when she said you would find something you thought was lost? That very afternoon you found the cuff link you thought was gone forever.''

''It had fallen behind my dresser. When I moved the dresser to vacuum, I found the cuff link. It was just a coincidence that I happened to vacuum that day.''

''And what about this past Tuesday? Your horoscope said you'd get good news by mail, and that very afternoon you got a letter telling you your sister's going to have a baby. And the one Wednesday that said Jonah might hurt himself and he cut himself on that broken glass? And yesterday mine said I would come into unexpected money and, sure enough, I got that refund from my accidental insurance overpayment.''

''Coincidence,'' he repeated. ''Nothing more, nothing less.''

''Well, I'd be careful around animals today if I were you,'' she advised him sternly. ''As for making a fool of yourself—are you still planning to have dinner with Laurel tonight?''

Jonah groaned and sank more deeply into his seat, as if he knew what was coming.

Michael set his spoon down. ''Don't start with that, Keely.''

''I'm not starting anything.'' Trying to look nonchalant, she picked up her coffee mug. ''I told you I wouldn't say anything more about her being absolutely, totally, *completely* wrong for you, and I won't. Unless you want my opinion, of course.''

"I'm well aware of your opinion."

"It isn't just *my* opinion, either. Your horoscopes have been warning you about her ever since you started dating her a month ago. Several of them specifically said you're involved with the wrong person. Even today it warns you to be careful around her."

"Since you're so into the astrology/psychic thing, maybe you should try reading my mind right now." The gleam in his eyes told her she'd probably rather *not* know what he was thinking.

"As entertaining as this is," Jonah said, standing, "I've got to get moving. Keely, I was serious about you staying in the house if that ice storm hits. Driving on ice is just asking for disaster."

"No problem. I'll just sit here and wait for all my dreams to come true."

"Let me know when you come into all that money. I've got some dot-com stock I want to sell you," Michael drawled. "It has to do with ocean-front development in Kansas." He gathered his empty dishes as he spoke.

Keely wrinkled her nose at him again. "You're implying that I'm gullible?"

"If the shoe fits…" He smiled at her good-naturedly as he passed her on the way to the dishwasher, bringing their squabbling to an end for the morning.

Left alone in the kitchen a few minutes later, Keely sighed and sipped her coffee as she turned her attention back to her newspaper. She scanned headlines and read the stories that interested her, ending up on the same page that held the daily horoscopes. She couldn't resist reading Michael's again. Something about it made her nervous. It didn't exactly predict catastrophe—but close, she decided. For Michael, making a fool of himself would be tantamount to disaster.

It was important to Michael, who had turned twenty-nine only the week before, to be in control at all times. Everything he had done for almost his entire life had been carefully planned, all angles and outcomes taken into consideration. He was now completely focused on making partner at the prestigious law firm where he and Jonah both practiced. She hoped the unexpected opportunity that might pass him by didn't jeopardize the career advancement that meant so much to him.

It wasn't that she was a strong believer in astrology, she assured herself, folding the paper again. She didn't let her horoscopes guide her actions. It was just fun to read them every day.

And yet—the coincidences had been rather dramatic lately. What if Michael passed up something wonderful just because he was too stubborn to listen to her?

Maybe she should try again to get him to pay attention to his horoscope. Just this once, it wouldn't hurt him to keep an open mind. And if he decided that the signs pointed to Laurel being a bad match for him—well, all the better.

It was only because Keely cared for him that she wanted to keep him from getting involved with someone so incompatible. She was sure there was someone who was just perfect for him—although she couldn't think of anyone at the moment—but not Laurel. Definitely not Laurel.

"I'm blessed with wisdom today," she reminded herself, drumming her fingertips on the newspaper. And then she sighed. "But what counts is convincing Michael. And that isn't going to be easy."

CHAPTER TWO

KEELY FAXED MICHAEL his horoscope an hour after he arrived at his office. Finding the transmission among the other faxes and messages his secretary had piled on his desk, he grimaced. "She never gives up."

From her chair on the other side of his desk, Sandra Jones, his beautiful, efficient and happily married secretary, peered at him over the top of her reading glasses. "Who doesn't give up?"

"Keely." He didn't have to clarify, since Sandra knew he shared a house with co-worker Jonah Parker and Jonah's younger sister, Keely. He turned the fax so Sandra could see the neatly typed prediction and the scrawled message beneath it. "She's determined to make me pay attention to my horoscope."

Sandra scanned the horoscope, then read Keely's message out loud. "'Just keep what this says in mind today, okay?' You're right. She *is* determined."

Torn between amusement and exasperation, Michael pulled the page in front of him again. "I can never tell if she really believes this stuff or if she's putting me on with it. She reads them every day—she and Jonah get a kick out of it—but lately she's been more insistent about them, especially with me. She's decided that it's written in the stars that I should stay away from Laurel.''

Sandra's face darkened slightly in response to the name. She tossed her shoulder-length black braids in a gesture he recognized; it meant she was holding back something she wanted to say.

He sighed. ''What is it with you and Keely? Every time I mention Laurel, both of you practically make the sign of the cross.''

''None of my business who you date.'' Avoiding his eyes, Sandra gathered papers in preparation to return to her own desk. ''If that's the sort of woman who appeals to you, you certainly don't need *my* approval. I'm just your secretary.''

''And don't give me that I-know-my-place routine, either. We both know that's a crock.'' Sandra had been Michael's secretary since he'd signed on with the firm nearly three years ago. The bond that had formed between them had been immediate and strong; they fully intended to rise together in the ranks. Michael valued her competence, her loyalty—and her honesty.

''Look,'' he said. ''Laurel's not all that bad. I know she's…well, socially ambitious. A little materialistic. But,'' he added when Sandra gave an indelicate snort, ''she's got a good heart. All of the volunteer work she does—maybe she likes the applause and social connections she makes, but she does a lot of good.''

''I'm not saying Laurel's a bad person,'' Sandra admitted grudgingly. ''I'm just not sure she's right for *you*.''

Because that sounded exactly like something Keely would say, Michael set the horoscope aside and deliberately turned to his computer. ''I'll keep your advice in mind. Now, about those calls you were going to make...''

''I'm on my way. Boss,'' she added impudently.

He growled at her and sent her off laughing.

A few minutes later he found the fax in his hands again. His attention wasn't focused on the horoscope, but on the note Keely had scribbled across the bottom of the page. Again, he wondered just how serious she was about these things. Did she really think disaster would hit if he ignored the messages supposedly written in his stars, or was she only teasing him? With Keely, it was always hard to tell.

Michael and Jonah had met in law school. Both struggling to make ends meet, they and a third financially strapped law student, Rick Cooper, had rented a three-bedroom house in an old but respectable outskirts-of-Memphis neighborhood. They'd shared expenses all through law school. The arrangement had worked out so well that they'd maintained it even after they were all gainfully employed—Michael and Jonah for the same prestigious firm, Rick in the district attorney's office.

Eight months ago Rick moved out and married after a whirlwind courtship. It had been Keely who approached Jonah and Michael with the suggestion that she take Rick's place. Her art career still at the fledgling stage, she'd supported herself with temporary office jobs after graduating from college two years earlier. Her proposal to her brother and his housemate had been that she would serve as their housekeeper—cleaning, laundry, shopping, cooking—in exchange for a place to live while she took a shot at becoming a self-supporting artist. Though Michael had been hesitant, Jonah had convinced him to give it a try, promising to not cause problems if Michael later decided the arrangement wasn't working out.

On the whole, it had worked out better than Michael had expected. Keely had taken her responsibilities seriously. The house all but sparkled, the laundry was always clean and neatly folded, and the meals she prepared were excellent. There were only a few formal ground rules—each cleaned his own room, they didn't bring home unannounced guests, and they called if they were going to be late or absent overnight—just to keep their housemates from worrying.

Michael had added a few unspoken rules of his own. In deference to Keely's presence, he kept his clothes on, his language clean, and his dirty underwear in the hamper rather than on the floor. He didn't bring his dates home. And he made a concerted effort to treat her much the same way Jonah did—even during those moments when it was impossible to not notice that there was a beautiful, vibrant, fascinating and sexy woman living in his house.

Jonah's little sister, he reminded himself now as he had on those other occasions. Nearly five years younger than he was, she thought of him as an older brother—at least, that was the way she'd always behaved toward him.

Ironically, he wasn't nearly as interested in Laurel as Keely and Sandra assumed he was. Their relationship, at least on his part, was casual at best. They hadn't even slept together. The only reason he hadn't made that clear was that he didn't like being guided "for his own good." And he sure as hell wasn't going to let his actions be dictated by a kooky astrologer in a tabloid paper.

"Michael?" Sandra's disembodied voice came through a speaker on his telephone. "Call for you on line one. It's Keely," she added.

He winced, then felt guilty about it. This could be important, he reminded himself. It probably had nothing at all to do with the horoscope—which he was sure she'd faxed him only as a joke. He lifted the receiver. "Hi, Keely. What's up?"

"Have you heard the latest weather reports? The winter weather system is moving through southern Missouri and northern Arkansas and is headed straight for us. I've already been to the grocery store and stocked up for the weekend. The shelves in the store are emptying fast. Everyone's getting ready for a major storm."

"Yeah, I heard. Jonah's booked an earlier flight out. He's getting ready to leave the office now."

"I know. I just talked to him. Um, what about you, Michael? Are you going to try to get away early? I'd hate to think you'd be caught out on the streets in an ice storm."

"Thanks for your concern, but I've got a couple dozen things I have to handle here before I can leave. Don't worry, I'll keep an eye on the weather."

"Maybe you'd better cancel your dinner plans for the evening," she suggested, her tone much too casual. "Just in case it gets nasty and you get trapped, er, someplace you'd rather not spend the weekend."

He knew she'd used the word "trapped" deliberately, a warning as subtle as her fax. Though he was tempted to growl at her, he restrained himself to a cool, "I'll keep your advice in mind."

The same words he'd used with Sandra. And he knew that Keely was no more likely to be appeased by them than his sweetly interfering secretary had been.

"Michael, remember what the horoscope said—about making a fool of yourself? Driving on ice would definitely qualify as a foolish thing to do. Not to mention being stuck with Laurel for who knows how long," Keely added in a mutter.

"Keely?"

After only a momentary hesitation, she responded, "Yes?"

"Butt out."

An indignant huff carried clearly through the phone lines. "Fine. Ignore the stars. Ignore *me*. But don't say you weren't warned!"

She hung up with a crash that made his ear ring. Exactly the way his own younger sister had done on numerous occasions, he thought with a reluctantly indulgent smile. His sister probably wouldn't like Laurel, either, he had to admit. And she would be just as vocal about her opinion.

The smile faded when he pictured Keely with sparks in her big green eyes and a flush of temper on her soft pink cheeks. So maybe he didn't think of her exactly like a sister. But he'd be damned if he'd let her run his social life based on a newspaper horoscope.

Another call came for him barely ten minutes later. Sandra's voice wasn't as warm when she announced that it was Laurel on the line this time. Mentally consigning all the females in his life to another universe, Michael turned away from his work again and tried to speak cordially. "What can I do for you, Laurel?"

"I've been listening to the weather reports." Her voice was a husky purr that had probably taken years to perfect. "I'm still at my office, but I'm thinking about heading home soon. Since my place is closer to your office than yours is, maybe we should meet there as soon as you can get away. Instead of going out, as we'd planned, we can fix something at my house. That way if you happen to get iced in—well, we'll find something to do to entertain ourselves, don't you think?"

He tried to keep his sudden frown out of his voice. "I, uh, I'm not sure when I'll be able to get away from here, Laurel. I'm swamped with things I need to finish before the weekend."

"You certainly don't want to get stuck *there* overnight."

"I won't let that happen. Maybe we'll get lucky and the storm will pass us by. You know how often the forecasters cry wolf when it comes to this sort of thing."

"I think they're pretty confident this time."

"Then I'd better get busy. I'll let you know when to expect me, okay?" Or *if* to expect him, he thought when he disconnected shortly afterward. He wasn't at all sure he wanted to risk being—okay, *trapped*—at Laurel's apartment for a couple of days.

He'd just gotten back to work when a sound from his doorway broke his concentration again.

"Jeez, Sandra, what is it *now?*" he asked without looking around. "I'm never going to finish this with all these interruptions."

"Sorry, Mike. I just stopped in to tell you I'm out of here."

Glancing over his shoulder, Michael grimaced apologetically. "Sorry, Jonah. I didn't mean to snap. It's been a long, strange morning."

Bundled into a heavy overcoat and an Outback-style oiled leather hat he'd cherished since his college days, Jonah nodded toward the window behind Michael's desk. "It's starting to look ugly out there."

"So I hear. I hope your flight goes smoothly."

"Yeah. Do me a favor, will you? Keep an eye on Keely if the weather really does take a turn for the worse. You know how impulsive she is. She might decide to make a run for the art supply store, even if there's a foot of snow piled on another foot of ice."

"Give her some credit. Keely's not stupid."

"It's just an old habit to take care of her, I guess." Jonah's expression was sheepish. "So, will you look out for her—even if she *doesn't* need it?"

Michael shrugged. "Sure, if it makes you feel better. Now take off. You don't want to miss your flight."

Jonah tugged his hat more snugly onto his head, preparing to go out into the bitter cold. "See ya' next week, Mike."

"See ya', Joe."

Running a hand through his hair, Michael turned determinedly to the computer again. He managed to work for almost an hour this time before the next interruption.

"Michael?" Sandra stood in the doorway, a concerned look on her face. "My sister just called. She lives in West Memphis, Arkansas—just across the river from here. They're getting hammered with sleet and freezing rain, and it's only supposed to get worse. It's going to start here anytime now."

A glance outside showed him the heavy gray clouds had dipped low enough in the sky that he could almost reach out and touch them from his third-floor window. They looked ready to burst at any minute. "Head home, Sandra. Now."

"What about you? Just about everyone else in the building is leaving."

"I'll go as soon as I wrap this up. I'll take the rest of my work home with me."

"Good." She looked relieved. "Don't take long. I have a bad feeling about this storm."

He smiled faintly. "Something you read in your horoscope?"

"Something I heard on a weather report," she retorted. "Take care, Michael."

"You, too. See you next week."

It took him almost another forty-five minutes to finish his task and to pack his attaché case with files, reports, briefs and other research materials.

By that time, sleet and freezing rain were playing a percussion number against the window, and he could see that the parking lot was nearly empty, though it was just before two in the afternoon. Shrugging into his overcoat, he grabbed his case and headed out, nodding to the few diehards he passed on the way.

There was only one other person on the elevator when he stepped in, a uniformed police officer who touched his hat in greeting. "How's it going, Mr. Gordon?"

"Not bad. How are you, Officer Kendall? Been giving a deposition?"

"Yeah. We wanted to get it over with before all hell breaks loose on the streets. I'll probably be pulling a long shift tonight. You know how drivers get stupid when the weather turns bad."

"I don't envy you the next few hours."

The officer shrugged. "It's a living. I suggest you head straight home. The roads are slicker than goose spit already, and I hear we're starting to have some power outages around the city. That'll only get worse when tree limbs ice over and start falling on the power lines."

Everyone was trying to send him home, it seemed. Michael assured the officer he was on his way, then buttoned into his coat and half trotted, half slid to his car. Maybe he should've bought an SUV last summer instead of a sports car, he thought wryly.

Starting the engine, he debated for a moment

about where to go. Laurel's suggestion that he head straight to her apartment didn't really appeal to him. It was too early for dinner, and spending the rest of the day there—in addition to the night if the roads were bad enough to close—wasn't something he was prepared to do. Sleeping over at her place was no way to keep their relationship casual and friendly. Yet he was stubbornly reluctant to let Keely think her fanciful admonitions had caused him to change his plans. Maybe he should just...

He muttered a curse beneath his breath. Now he really *was* in danger of making a fool of himself. Getting tangled up with Laurel just to prove a point to Keely was ridiculous—not to mention terribly unfair to Laurel. Besides, Jonah had asked him to watch out for Keely. That seemed like a pretty good excuse to turn the wheel and accelerate carefully out of the parking lot, toward his own house.

The roads, already slick with a film of ice that was growing thicker by the minute, were crowded with commuters trying to beat the worst of the storm home. What should have been a twenty-minute drive took him more than an hour, and a nerve-racking hour at that. Other drivers, unfamiliar with winter weather in this usually warm southern climate, made stupid mistakes, causing delays and traffic mishaps. It was a relief to turn off the main highway and onto the now-deserted lane that led into his old, quiet neighborhood.

He almost made it. He was less than a mile from home, passing the undeveloped, wooded area that separated his neighborhood from the highway, when a flash of movement at the side of the road caught his attention. Before he could brace himself, two startled deer bounded in front of his car, inches from the front grill. Instinct had him slamming on the brake and jerking the wheel before he was even consciously aware of doing so.

The car bucked and spun on the sheet of ice, skidding toward the deep ditch at the side of the road. Fortunately, there were no cars around him to worry about, so he was able to concentrate on controlling his own vehicle—as much as was possible in a wild spin.

The little car crashed into the ditch. Michael's seat belt slammed him against the seat and the airbag inflated with a force that took away what little breath the impact had left him. There would be bruises, he thought when his mind cleared a bit. But at least he was all in one piece.

He wished he could say the same for his car.

Wearily wondering if this day could get any worse, he reached for his mobile phone.

CHAPTER THREE

KEELY WAS JUST GETTING ready for a midafternoon break from work when the doorbell rang, taking her by surprise. She wasn't expecting anyone, especially in this weather. Michael and Jonah had keys to the house and wouldn't need to ring the bell. Curious, she peered through the security viewer, then gasped and jerked open the door.

"Michael! Oh, my gosh, what happened?"

His hair was wet and icy around his ruddy face. His clothes were soaked and his lips were almost blue. The suspicious bulge beneath his overcoat told her he was carrying something large inside it in an apparent attempt to keep whatever it was dry—probably the reason he hadn't used his key.

She could hear his teeth chattering from where she stood.

When he seemed incapable of answering her question, she reached out and tugged him inside, ignoring the puddle of water that formed at his feet on the floor of the wooden entryway. "You're freezing. And you're bleeding! You've cut your face. We've got to get you warm and dry.''

She started peeling off his wet coat. He was shivering too hard to help her much. "Towel," he managed to blurt.

"Hang on, I'll get you one. Here, give me your attaché case." It was the case he'd been protecting from the weather; she knew he carried his computer inside it, along with important case files.

"I think my fingers are frozen to the handle." He tried to smile as he spoke, but the result was pathetic. A drop of cold water ran from his hair down his nose, falling off the end to splash on the floor with the rest of the water he'd tracked in. A trickle of blood oozed from a bruised cut on his right jaw, just above the chin.

He was so cold. Her first thought was getting him warm and dry, and then she would find out what had happened to him.

Telling him to stay put, she made a dash for towels, stopping in Michael's bedroom on the way back. She found him still standing where she'd left him, though he'd shed his suit jacket and tie. Having been protected by his overcoat and suit jacket, his shirt was dry, but his pants were wet from the knees down, and his leather shoes were soaked and likely ruined. His legs and feet had to be freezing.

"Strip," she ordered, draping one of the towels over his dripping head. "You've got to get dry. Here's your robe and a pair of dry socks. I'll go make a pot of coffee while you change.''

"Coffee?" he repeated faintly. "Sounds good…"

"Just dump your wet clothes on the floor and join me in the kitchen. I'll take care of the puddles later.''

Giving him privacy to undress, she turned and hurried into the kitchen, where she quickly assembled a pot of coffee and opened a can of chicken noodle soup. She suspected he'd skipped lunch, as he often did.

It wasn't long before he limped through the doorway. His toweled dark hair was wildly disarrayed, and he had on his thick, black flannel robe that was belted tightly at his waist. His lips weren't as blue now. He'd wiped at the cut on his face, smearing blood across his jaw.

Setting a cup of coffee and a bowl of soup on the table, Keely motioned him into a chair. "I'll go clean up the mess in the foyer,'' she said. "You get those hot liquids into yourself while I'm gone.''

She didn't have to urge him again. He was already inhaling the hot coffee when she left the room. By the time she returned a few minutes later, carrying a first-aid kit, he'd finished half his soup. She was relieved to see that he'd completely stopped shivering.

"Better?" she asked.

"Much," he answered fervently. "The soup is good."

"Right out of a can." She stopped beside him and reached out to tilt his head so she could see his bruised and cut jaw. "I'm going to clean this with an alcohol pad and spray some antiseptic on it, okay?"

"It's fine. Don't worry about it."

"It's dirty. It will get infected if it isn't treated."

"Can't it wait?"

"It will just take me a minute if you'll hush and be still." Ignoring his winces and mutters, she swiftly and efficiently tended to his wound. By concentrating on the task, she was able to ignore the sensation of standing so close to him, her face inches from his as she bent over him. She wasn't accustomed to touching him so freely. Their relationship had always been friendly and casual, but they'd always kept a bit of physical distance between them.

That, of course, had been before she'd found him half-frozen on the doorstep.

With one last, rather self-indulgent brush of her fingertips against his firm jawline, she made herself step back so he could finish his soup. Setting the first-aid kit aside, she refilled his coffee, poured a cup for herself, then sat across from him. "Can I get you anything else?"

He shook his head, finished the soup, then pushed the bowl aside. "I needed that," he said, reaching for his coffee cup. "I can feel my toes again."

"Are you ready to tell me what happened?"

"I wrecked my car."

She felt her eyes widen in response to the unembellished statement. "You wrecked it? How? Where?"

"About half a mile from here—at the edge of the woods. A couple of deer ran in front of me and I hit the ditch."

"That's when you cut your face?"

His expression grim, he shook his head. "I wasn't hurt in the wreck. I did that when I fell on the ice walking home."

"You *walked?*" She set her cup down so abruptly the warm coffee splashed onto her fingers. "Half a mile in an ice storm?" She could still hear the sleet pounding the windows, driven by a fierce wind.

"It was either that or sit in my car until someone happened along to give me a ride. And that was going to be a while. Every cop and wrecker in Memphis is tied up—I called—and apparently our neighbors are all barricaded in their houses already. I sat there for nearly twenty minutes without seeing a sign of life. It seemed like a good idea to just get out and walk."

"On a clear day, sure. Even in a rainstorm. But in *this?*" She motioned toward the window, which rattled with another gust of icy wind even as she spoke.

"Okay, so it wasn't the brightest decision I ever made. But I'm here now, so it worked out okay."

"You're lucky you didn't— Oh, my gosh!"

He lifted an eyebrow. "Now what?"

"The deer that caused you to wreck—that's the animal your horoscope warned you about."

He groaned and shoved a hand through his still-damp hair. "Don't start that again. It's just—"

"Coincidence," she finished with him, but there were still funny little chills running down her spine. "Believe what you want, but *I* think it's spooky."

He muttered something into his coffee cup that she didn't ask him to repeat. Glancing at the microwave clock, she saw that it wasn't even 5:00 p.m. yet. Michael was never home from the office this early, and the two of them rarely faced this many hours alone. At least, she assumed that was what they were facing. "You, um, aren't going out again tonight, are you?"

"Hardly." His tone was a little clipped. Either he was disappointed that his plans for the evening had fallen through—or he resented having them canceled in this manner. "I phoned Laurel from the car and called off our plans for the evening."

She decided it wouldn't be wise to make any comment on that subject. Instead, she merely nodded and said, "I've canceled my plans for tonight, too. I was going to see a movie with

Steve, but we decided—well, *I* decided to call it off. Steve was sure his four-wheel-drive truck could handle any road conditions, but I wasn't so confident.''

"Trust me, I saw plenty of four-wheel-drive vehicles off the road on my way home. No one needs to be driving on ice if they don't have to— take it from someone who just climbed out of a ditch.''

She thought sadly of Michael's pretty little sports car, still new enough that it had that unmistakable new-car smell. "I hope your car isn't too badly damaged.''

"It wasn't totaled, if that's what you mean. But it's going to need some bodywork.''

"Is there anything you should be doing about it now?''

"I've already made arrangements for it to be towed. I'll have to get a rental car, I guess, as soon as I can get out again.''

A forceful blast of wind threw more ice against the windows. The lights flickered for a moment but, to Keely's relief, didn't go out. She glanced out the window, noting that it was almost fully dark outside because of the storm. "The weatherman said the temperature's not supposed to get above freezing until late tomorrow afternoon at the earliest. They're predicting this ice to turn to snow sometime during the night. We could be stuck here for a while.''

Michael's gaze met hers across the table. And

for some reason Keely's toes curled beneath the table. She deliberately uncurled them.

He looked away first. "I brought quite a bit of work home, so you don't have to worry about me getting in your way."

She hadn't been worried about that, actually, but she nodded. "I've got a project going in my studio that should keep me busy."

"There's no problem then, is there?"

"No, of course not," she agreed a bit too heartily. Stranded for a day or two with Michael, in the house they'd shared for eight months—that wasn't such a daunting prospect. It wouldn't even be the first time they'd been alone in the house overnight; Jonah had made a couple of business trips before. Maybe it seemed different to her this time because they *couldn't* leave.

No big deal, she reminded herself. She certainly trusted Michael to be a perfect gentleman. He always had been before. It would be no different than spending the night in the house with her brother.

Right?

So why were her hands not quite steady when she carried her coffee cup to the sink? And why was she suddenly so aware of Michael sitting there watching her, wearing his robe and socks, looking sexier than any platonic roomie had a right to?

Get a grip, Keely. It's only Michael.

For some reason, she didn't find that reminder particularly reassuring.

CHAPTER FOUR

WITH HER BROTHER'S HELP, Keely had turned a
sunroom at the back of the old house into an art
studio. The big windows gave plenty of natural
light—when the sun was shining, she thought
with a rueful glance at the stormy darkness outside. She wasn't self-conscious about being spot-
lighted in the bright, glassed-in room; a high red-
wood fence surrounded their roomy backyard. It
didn't give much of a view, but it certainly pro-
vided privacy. The back wall of the room was
lined with shelves and cabinets for supplies. Jonah had converted a wet bar into a wash-up area
for her, leaving the sink and small refrigerator in
place.

For the past hour, since parting with Michael
in the kitchen, she'd been sitting on the high stool
in the center of the room, staring at a blank canvas and accomplishing nothing. A rolling table
covered with photographs she had taken was
within her reach, but she didn't turn to it for inspiration.

Despite the peace and solitude, she was finding
it very difficult to concentrate on her work.

She tried to tell herself it had something to do with the storm raging outside. The sleet had changed to freezing rain mixed with the first signs of snow, and the wind still howled around the walls like an angry animal. The big, old trees in the backyard, their winter-bare branches plated with silvery ice, whipped back and forth in ferocious gusts. The ground was already littered with small branches that had snapped. They would have some yardwork to do when this was all over, she mused.

But she knew it wasn't the storm interfering with her concentration. She'd worked in storms before. Even the occasional flickering of the lights didn't particularly concern her. They were prepared for an electrical failure.

She was just…restless, she thought, glancing toward the doorway. Unaccountably edgy. Maybe it *was* the storm.

Sighing, she turned away from the canvas and stood. She simply wasn't in the mood to work, she decided. She might as well go watch TV or read. Maybe she'd cook something; she wondered if Michael was hungry again. She didn't expect that chicken noodle soup to hold him very long.

She'd thought he was working at the desk in his room. She didn't expect to find him in the kitchen, sitting in a chair with his right foot propped on another chair, a bag of frozen peas resting on his right knee, bared by the opening of his robe.

"Michael?" She moved toward him slowly, studying his expression, which was a mixture of embarrassment and annoyance at being caught. "Let me see your knee."

He tossed the peas onto the table and swung his foot to the floor, covering his leg with his robe before she could get a glimpse. "It's nothing," he said a bit too shortly, his brows pulling together in a way that told her his abrupt movements had caused him considerable discomfort. "I thought you were working."

"I got hungry. Let me see your knee."

He placed his hands on the table, as though to push himself out of his chair. "Don't worry about it. What are you—"

She didn't give him a chance to finish. Planting both hands on his shoulders, she held him in his chair. "You aren't getting up until I've seen that knee."

There was no doubt in her mind that he was hiding his leg from her for a reason, and she had no intention of letting him get away with it. Michael was the most stubborn male on earth when it came to admitting any weakness. He'd only let her treat the cut on his jaw earlier because she hadn't given him a choice.

She wasn't giving him a choice this time, either.

Michael sighed gustily—apparently deciding it

wasn't worth the quarrel that would ensue if he continued to refuse—and parted the robe just an inch. "See? It's only bruised. Now, do you mind…?"

It was more than bruised. Catching her breath, Keely knelt beside him and reached down to expose more of his badly swollen, discolored knee. It was twice its normal size and already turning an ugly shade of purple. No wonder he'd been limping when he'd joined her in the kitchen earlier. Why hadn't she realized…?

"We've got to get you to a doctor."

He growled. "I knew you'd say that. That's why I didn't want you to see it. I don't need a doctor, Keely. I just need cold packs and pain medication, and I have both of those here."

She couldn't help but reach out to touch his poor knee, her fingertips feathering against the bruised skin as if she could take some of the pain away with nothing more than that light contact. "It must hurt terribly."

He caught her wrist in his hand. "It's fine, really. I've done this before—I've got a bad habit of landing on that knee when I fall. If I thought it needed immediate medical attention, I would see to it. But with the ice on the roads, the only way to get to a doctor right now would be by ambulance—and I'm sure the ambulances are tied up with much more serious injuries right now."

His undoubtedly hard-won patience paid off;

she had to acknowledge that his arguments made sense. But, still, the sight of that knee broke her heart. "You need to keep it elevated. Let me help you to your bed."

His expression turning stubborn again, he shook his head. "I don't want to go to bed."

"Then I'll help you to the couch. You can prop your leg up on pillows and watch TV." When he continued to look mulish about it, she scowled at him. "I gave in on the doctor, Michael, but I'm going to insist that you be reasonable about taking care of it yourself."

With a martyred air that might have been amusing had she not known how much he was hurting, he gave in. "All right, I'll go to the couch. But I don't need help getting there," he added.

"Pigheaded male," she muttered, straightening away from him.

His lips quirked in a reluctant smile. "That's not the first time you've called me that."

"And I'm sure it won't be the last." She stood close by as he rose stiffly from the chair. He bumped the table and knocked the bag of peas to the floor, but she told him to leave it. She'd pick it up later.

She hovered behind him as he made his way carefully to the living room sofa, his limp visibly worse now than it had been before. Either he'd stopped trying to hide the injury or the pain had gotten worse as the leg stiffened—she suspected the latter. "Have you taken anything for the pain?"

"Ibuprofen," he replied. "It's a painkiller *and* an anti-inflammatory."

The slight touch of smugness in his voice made her smile a little. "Okay, I'll admit that you know what you're doing—for the most part."

She waited until he'd stretched out on the long, soft leather sofa, then propped his leg carefully on several of the many colorful throw pillows they'd used to decorate the room. Another couple of pillows went beneath his head, and she set a thick crocheted afghan her grandmother had made nearby in case he got cold.

Though her hands were basically all over him, she tried to keep her touch impersonal. It wasn't easy—she was entirely too aware of the beauty and strength of the masculine body stretched out in front of her.

Keely, you have been too long between dates, she scolded herself. Steve didn't count, of course. A friend from art school days, he had long ago accepted that Keely thought of him as yet another brother figure. Maybe it was time she stopped collecting brothers and started thinking about lovers, she thought wryly.

"Keely?" Michael was looking at her oddly, making her realize that she'd been standing beside the couch staring at him.

She cleared her throat. "I was just wondering

what else we can do for that knee. I'll go get an ice pack. Can I bring you a drink or something when I come back?''

"Not right now, thanks. But you could hand me the TV remote. I'd like to check the latest weather reports.''

Their fingers brushed when she handed him the remote control, and she jumped as if she'd been shocked. No wonder Michael was giving her such curious looks, she admonished herself, hurrying into the kitchen. For some reason, she had been acting like a total idiot ever since he'd gotten home.

Still lecturing herself about her uncharacteristic behavior, she closed herself in the kitchen and opened the freezer to make up an ice pack for Michael's knee. The frozen peas had been a good idea, she acknowledged, but they were thawed and useless now. She had to remember to pick those up off the floor when she came back into the room. She filled a ziploc plastic bag with ice cubes, wrapped it in a dish towel, and carried it back into the living room, assured that she'd gotten herself under control now.

"What would you like for dinner?'' she asked, setting the ice pack carefully on his knee. "Spaghetti?''

Since it was his favorite meal, she wasn't surprised when he nodded. "That sounds good. I'm not really hungry yet, but I probably will be by the time it's ready.''

"It's cold in here." She reached for the afghan and draped it over him, worried that the ice pack on his knee would give him a chill. "Why don't I light a fire before I start dinner?"

"Jonah brought in a load of wood this morning. It's in the bin. Fortunately, there's plenty more outside if the electricity goes off and we have to use the fire for heat."

"Oh, I don't think the electricity will go out now. The ice has almost stopped..."

She'd spoken too soon. As if someone had thrown a master switch, the lights went out, the television going dark and silent.

Keely sighed gustily. It had been bad enough before—but now she and Michael were going to be spending an evening together in the darkness. For some reason, that made her much more nervous than the storm.

CHAPTER FIVE

"WELL, DAMN."

Though he fervently agreed with the sentiment, Michael couldn't help but chuckle at Keely's thoroughly disgusted tone. "This is your fault, you know," he teased lightly, deciding they might as well make the best of it. "You jinxed us by daring the electricity to go out."

"I wasn't daring it. I was trying to be optimistic. Sorry, but it looks as though spaghetti's out since I have no way to cook it."

"The only downside to having an all-electric home." He wrapped the afghan more snugly around him, feeling the cold from the ice pack soaking through his battered knee and spreading through the rest of him. It was pitch-black in the room, and eerily quiet without the usual hum of electrical appliances. No light seeped in through the windows, since the security pole lamps outside had apparently gone out, as well.

He heard Keely stumbling through the room to the window. "It looks like the whole neighborhood's dark," she said. "I wonder how long it will take to get the power restored."

"I wouldn't count on it being anytime soon. I just heard on the news that there are lines down all over the city, and tree limbs are still falling as the ice and snow pile up. Last time we lost power during a storm like this—back when Jonah and Rick and I were in law school—our lights were out for twenty-eight hours."

She groaned. "I hope it doesn't take that long this time. It's so cold out."

"We'll be okay as long as we keep the fire going." He started to rise. "I'll take care of that. You find candles and flashlights."

"You stay where you are," she ordered sharply. "I want you to stay off that knee. I can start a fire."

Michael hated being treated like an invalid. He was perfectly capable of helping out if he was careful—but he knew Keely would never believe him. She could be just a bit bossy when she was concerned about someone, as he knew she was about him. He didn't take it too personally; she'd have hovered over Jonah the same way.

Laurel, he knew, would be throwing a fit about now, demanding to be immediately transported to the closest luxury hotel with heat, lights and room service. But Keely had already found the flashlight they kept in a cabinet by the door and was making her way to the fireplace, where it wouldn't take her long to have a fire going. There had never been any doubt that she did her share around here—probably more, if truth were told. He'd always admired that about her.

Among other things that he tried not to think about too often.

In less than fifteen minutes she had the fire started and candles glowing in strategic spots around the room. Using the flashlight to guide her, she left the room for a few minutes, returning with a battery-operated radio and a fresh supply of batteries. "I thought we'd want to check the weather reports occasionally," she explained.

Efficient, he thought again, in her own, sometimes offbeat, way. "Good idea."

"So—how about sandwiches for dinner? You have a choice of peanut butter and jelly or bologna."

"Yum. Unless you're really hungry now, why don't we wait awhile?"

"Sure. I'm not starving yet, either." She motioned toward the faded T-shirt and paint-splattered jeans she'd worn for working. "I'm going to go put on something warmer. Is there anything I can get you?"

He'd thought about donning a pair of jeans earlier, but couldn't bear to have anything touching his knee. He decided to stay in the warm robe and tube socks she'd thrust at him when he'd gotten home. "No, I'm okay."

Almost before his words were out, she was gone. Must be the storm making her so nervous this evening, he decided. She seemed to be having a hard time standing still.

This time when she returned she was wearing a fleece pullover and matching pants and carrying a stack of blankets. "That afghan's not going to be warm enough when the chill starts to soak into the room," she said, dumping the blankets at the far end of the couch. "How's the ice pack doing?"

"It's pretty much melted."

"I'll refill it."

She reached for it, but he beat her to it, tossing the towel-wrapped bundle onto the coffee table. "No," he said. "Don't open the freezer while the power's out or you'll risk letting everything in there thaw. My knee's okay."

She hesitated, then nodded. "I'd forgotten about needing to keep the freezer closed." She reached for the ice pack he'd discarded. "I'll go put this away."

She was gone again before he could respond.

"You sure you don't want anything to eat?" she called from the kitchen.

"No, thanks."

"Something to drink, maybe? We have some..."

A crash cut off whatever she'd intended to say. It was followed by a cry that brought Michael abruptly upright on the couch. "Keely?"

She didn't answer.

Adrenaline pumping, Michael swung his legs

to the floor. Pain shot up his right leg, making him catch his breath, but he forced himself to his feet and limped toward the doorway. The candles Keely had set around the room didn't provide much light, but enough to get him to the doorway. The short hallway leading to the kitchen was pitch dark; he put one hand on the wall to guide him. "Keely?"

"I'm okay." Her voice was weak, but it was a great relief just to hear her speak. "You shouldn't have gotten up."

He found the kitchen door with his hand. The first thing he saw when he entered was the flashlight lying on the floor, pointed toward him. He blinked in the glare, then moved toward it. Keely was lying on the floor behind the light, huddled in the shadows. "What happened?"

She sat up, her movements so slow and careful he could tell something was wrong. "It's so stupid," she said. "I fell."

He moved closer, mentally cursing the darkness that kept him from seeing her clearly. "Where are you hurt?"

"I twisted my ankle pretty badly, but it's not broken or anything. It just took my breath away for a couple of minutes."

"You're sure it's not broken?"

"It's just twisted—sprained, maybe."

He held out a hand to her. "I'll help you up."

"And have us both end up on the floor? I'd better get up on my own."

Her lack of faith in him wasn't flattering. He pulled his hand back to his side. "How did you fall?"

Sounding thoroughly disgusted with herself, she replied. "I forgot about the bag of peas on the floor. Put my foot right down on top of it and it slid out from under me. Really stupid of me."

But Michael was the one feeling guilty. He'd knocked the peas to the floor and now Keely was hurt. "Damn. I'm sorry, I should have picked them up myself."

"It's not your fault. I just forgot about them." She rose slowly, using a chair to steady herself.

She was trying so hard to make light of her accident, even though he could tell by the note of strain in her voice that she was hurting. It reminded him of the way he'd tried to mask his discomfort from her earlier. "Two of a kind, aren't we?"

"I, uh—" She didn't seem to know how to respond, as if the concept of them having anything in common was startling to her.

"Sit down. I'll get you some ibuprofen," he said, bending at the waist to pick up the flashlight so he didn't risk twisting his knee.

Her sense of humor slowly began to reassert itself. She laughed softly. "We *are* a pair, aren't we?"

Though he knew she was simply agreeing with the similar sentiment he'd just expressed, her comment made him pause momentarily. He'd never actually thought of them as any sort of pair. It was an interesting picture. One he'd never allowed himself to consider before.

Aiming the flashlight into the pantry, he found the painkillers, then hobbled to the sink and filled a glass of water. Keely accepted the tablets from him with barely concealed eagerness. He held the flashlight at an angle that allowed her to see what she was doing without blinding her. "You should probably put ice on that ankle."

"And risk ruining those beautiful steaks Jonah bought yesterday? I'm not that brave."

"But—"

She reached out to rest her hand on his arm. "I'm fine, Michael. I've twisted my ankle before."

She'd touched him more this evening than she had in the eight months they'd lived together. And, damn—he liked it.

He cleared his throat. "As soon as you can walk comfortably, we should go back to the living room. It's warmer in there."

Since neither of them was particularly hungry, Michael filled a small basket with snacks—a couple of apples, two bananas, several packages of peanut butter crackers, and a handful of Snickers bars. Tucking two room-temperature canned colas and a couple of bottles of water into the basket, he handed Keely the flashlight. "You can make it on your own?"

"Of course. As long as we walk slowly," she added.

He laughed without much humor. "As if either of us has any choice about that."

It was a long walk down the short hallway. Michael shuffled stiff-legged, trying to not bend his injured knee, and Keely sort of hopped, attempting to keep her weight off her sprained ankle. Michael winced at the thought of what Jonah would say if he could see them; they would never hear the end of his teasing.

Adjusting his eyes from the darkness of the hallway to the soft glow of the living room, he set the snacks on the end of the coffee table. "Sit on the couch. I want to look at that ankle."

She sighed a little, but didn't resist. He lowered himself to sit beside her. The firelight and candlelight weren't bright enough for him to see her ankle clearly. He had her turn sideways and rest her foot on his thigh so he could aim the flashlight at her ankle. Trying to keep his touch as impersonal as hers had been when she'd treated his injuries earlier, he removed her warm, fuzzy house slipper and gently probed the area. It was swelling, but not drastically. He suspected she'd been right. The ankle was more likely sprained than broken.

He'd never noticed before how tiny her feet were. Her arch was high, her toes delicately shaped and tipped with small nails that gleamed intriguingly with red polish in the glow of the flashlight. He'd never thought of himself as a foot guy, but Keely's pretty little foot was making him reconsider.

He heard her catch her breath when he absently stroked a fingertip from her toes to her ankle. "I'm sorry. Did I hurt you?"

"No." Her voice sounded just a bit higher than normal. "Have you seen all you want?"

Awareness surged through him as their eyes met. Hers glimmered like dark liquid, flickering flames reflected in their depths. Even her glossy brown hair seemed to glow, as if the soft light came from inside rather than around her. Her face looked pale, either from pain or because of the lack of light in the room, but there were darker spots of color on her cheeks.

He'd always thought of Keely as pretty—he now revised that adjective. She was beautiful. And he was male enough to react to sitting this close to a beautiful woman with her bare foot resting on his almost-bare thigh.

Deciding it was best to leave her question unanswered, he scooted too quickly out from beneath her, causing her to grimace and his knee to clench in protest. Setting her foot on a pillow, he stood.

"You were right," he said gruffly, automatically tightening the belt of his robe. "Your ankle doesn't look too bad. Just keep your weight off of it for a while and I'm sure it will be fine."

"That's what I said," she pointed out, her

quizzical expression telling him she'd noticed his odd behavior.

"Uh—right. I'll just put another log on the fire now." Feeling like an idiot—again—he turned to tend the fire, though it seemed to him that the room had just gotten several degrees warmer.

CHAPTER SIX

MICHAEL HAD JUST SETTLED into the recliner by the fire when a shrill ring sliced into the oddly awkward silence that had fallen in the room. Because the phone was on the end of the table next to the couch—closer to Keely than Michael—she motioned for him to stay seated and stretched to answer the call herself. "Hello?"

"Hi, sis. How's it going?" Jonah asked.

"Everything outside is covered with ice and now it's starting to snow. And our power's gone out."

"Oh, damn, I was afraid of that. You aren't there alone, are you?"

"No, Michael's here. He canceled his date."

"Well, that should make you happy—the way you feel about Laurel and all."

She wondered if her brother understood that her main objection to Laurel was the fact that she didn't think Laurel would make Michael happy. Laurel was demanding and self-absorbed, and Michael was so nice and easygoing—it was practically a recipe for disaster. And friends tried to help friends from making mistakes like that, right?

"Michael wrecked the Mazda," she blurted, a bit too anxious to change the subject.

From the recliner, Michael winced and glared at her, but she merely shrugged. Jonah would have to find out, anyway. Might as well be now.

All teasing abruptly fled from Jonah's voice. "He wrecked it? What happened? Is he okay?"

"He's fine." She understood her brother's concern for his longtime best friend, so she spoke reassuringly. "He slid off the road when some deer ran in front of him on the ice. He's got a shallow cut on his jaw and a bruised knee, but other than that, everything's okay."

Michael seemed to grudgingly approve of the way she downplayed his injuries.

Jonah sounded relieved. "I'm glad he wasn't badly hurt. You said a deer ran in front of him?"

"Yeah. Eerie, isn't it? Remember what his horoscope said this morning about being careful around animals?"

Once again, Michael groaned, this time in exasperation at her insistence in mentioning the horoscope again.

Through the phone lines, Jonah laughed. "That *is* weird."

"Michael says it's only another coincidence."

Michael nodded fervently.

"He's probably right," Jonah commented, "but I bet you're giving him a hard time about it, anyway. I can just hear you telling him that he'll have to pay more attention to his horoscopes from now on.''

"He's too stubborn. He wouldn't accept the possibility even if his name was spelled out in the column, followed by an exact prediction of everything that happens to him for a week.''

Michael nodded again. She wrinkled her nose at him.

Jonah's attention had already moved on. ''Seriously, sis, you two are going to be okay there? The electricity could be out for hours—our neighborhood's never on the high-priority list for the power company.''

"We're fine. Really. We've got a fire going, a good supply of wood, candles and batteries, and a pantry full of snack foods that don't have to be cooked.''

"Watch those candles, okay? Make sure they aren't close to anything flammable. And keep the screen closed on the fireplace, even if it isn't quite as warm that way.''

"We aren't going to burn the house down while you're gone,'' she assured him with hard-won patience. ''I think Michael and I can take care of ourselves for a few hours.''

"You could always go to a motel.''

"I'd rather stay here. Please don't worry, Jonah.''

Though he didn't sound entirely convinced, Jonah eventually disconnected, telling Keely he, for one, was going to obey his horoscope and spend the evening with a good book. She shook her head as she replaced the receiver in its cradle. "I swear, Jonah gets more like our mother every day. Always worrying about something. Like the whole world would go to hell in a handbasket if he doesn't personally take steps to prevent it."

"I noticed you didn't mention your fall in the kitchen," Michael accused her.

"Are you kidding? He'd have called an ambulance, all the way from Birmingham."

"So how come you had to tell him about my car accident?"

Because I didn't want him questioning me too closely about my reasons for wanting you to stay away from Laurel, she could have told him. Instead she said only, "I thought he might get mad if we kept it from him. He won't have to find out about my fall—I'm sure my ankle will be completely recovered by the time he gets home next week."

"I see." Michael glanced at the illuminated dial on his watch. "It's just a little after seven. Seems later, doesn't it?"

"Yes, it does." She cleared her throat and reached for the basket of snacks he'd brought in. "I think I'll have an apple. Do you want anything?"

"An apple sounds good."

She tossed him one, which he caught easily with his right hand. For the next few minutes the only sounds in the room were the two of them

STAR CROSSED

munching their apples and the wood popping in the fireplace. The neighborhood outside was so quiet Keely could almost have sworn she and Michael were the only people in it.

Because that thought made her self-conscious again, she tried to think of something to say. "How's your knee?"

"Fine."

So much for that topic. "Um, have you talked to your mom lately? I guess she's excited about being a grandmother in a few months."

"I talked to her last night, and yes, she's very excited. She's been hinting about grandchildren for a couple of years. Robert and I are glad our sister's stepped up to the plate to take the pressure off us."

Keely smiled, as she knew he'd intended. "So, Robert feels the same way you do about settling down, hmm?"

"My brother and I aren't opposed to settling down—we're just both concentrating on getting our careers established first."

"I know Robert's still in medical school, but your career's pretty well established already, isn't it? I mean, you're on a partnership track with a very reputable law firm and you've already made quite a name for yourself in legal circles around here."

"Yeah, well, I haven't made partner yet. I don't count my chickens until they've hatched."

She shook her head in fond exasperation.

"You're always so cautious and skeptical. Don't you ever just want to cut loose and go with your impulses?"

There was a short pause, and then Michael answered with an odd note in his voice. "Occasionally."

She plucked at the afghan on her legs. "Do you ever? Act on impulse, I mean."

"Not often. My life tends to get...complicated when I'm not careful."

"Better be careful, or you'll end up one of those old bachelors following the same precise routine every day—like Mr. Haley down the street."

"I don't intend to end up like Mr. Haley," he retorted, sounding a little irritated about the warning. "Besides, you're one to criticize my reluctance to get involved in a serious relationship. You've hated everyone I've gone out with for the past six months."

She felt her cheeks warm. "That's not true. I liked Cathy very much."

"Right. So you introduced her to one of your friends—and now they're engaged."

She cleared her throat and spoke with dignity. "Make fun all you like, but their horoscopes led me to put them together. According to the stars, they're perfectly matched—and you have to admit they hit it off instantly. Besides, it isn't as if you were going to marry her yourself."

"That's immaterial," he said with a wave of

his hand. "I'm sure as hell not letting you pick my future mate out of a tabloid horoscope column."

"Did I say I want to pick your mate?" she asked indignantly. "All I do is read the horoscopes to you—it's not as if I write them to manipulate you."

"No, you just interpret them that way."

She glowered at him. "*I* caused those deer to run in front of you today just to make your horoscope come true, right?"

"I didn't say that. You're just—" He stopped, then shook his head. "Why are we arguing? This is silly."

She took a deep breath. "We always argue when we start talking about your horoscope. Maybe it would be better if I stop reading yours in the mornings."

He frowned again. "I don't mind. As long as you don't take it too seriously."

Now he sounded as if he *wanted* her to keep reading them. She sighed, wondering if she would ever fully understand this man. "I don't take them all that seriously," she felt compelled to argue. "I just think they're sort of fun. And even you have to admit that sometimes—even if it's just by coincidence," she stressed, "they're right on target."

"Okay, the thing with the animals was pretty weird," he conceded.

She knew when she was being humored, but she nodded, anyway. "Yes, it was."

"And I'll admit Cathy and Mark seem to make a good couple—even though I believe that has more to do with their personalities than their birthdates."

"Well, of course."

"So, according to your star charts, who do you think *I* should be going out with?"

Even though she suspected he was mocking her, she answered candidly. "A Capricorn is most compatible with Aquarius and, uh, Taurus. And to a lesser extent, Pisces and Scorpio. I know a nice Scorpio—but she's really too young for you," she added thoughtfully, deciding on the spot that Lisa was wrong for him, too.

She was sure there was someone, she told herself again. She just couldn't think of anyone off the top of her head that she felt good about picturing him with.

"Taurus, hmm? Aren't *you* a Taurus?"

Now she knew he was teasing her. She tossed her head. "If you're implying..."

"What am I implying, Keely?"

Oh, that lawyer's voice of his was so carefully neutral—and it made her want to punch him. "Never mind."

"I'm curious. What did you mean?"

"If you're thinking what I *think* you're thinking, then you're totally, completely wrong," she answered haughtily.

He laughed, a rich, genuinely amused sound that made something warm inside her even though she was annoyed with him. Surely he wasn't vain enough to think she wanted him for herself.

Not once in the eight months they'd lived together had she given him any reason to come to that conclusion. She'd been very careful to hide the occasional tug of attraction she felt for him— after all, he was ridiculously good-looking and she was only human. And, sure, she liked him— quite a bit, actually—but only as a friend.

Well, mostly as a friend.

Okay, so it was a little more than that. But she'd been very careful to keep that to herself. She knew better than to start weaving foolish fantasies about a man who treated her with the same casual affection as her big brother did. A man who never dated anyone for more than a few weeks before carefully extricating himself from any developing relationship. A man who was more skittish about commitment and involvement than the most dedicated bachelor she'd ever met.

Not to mention a man who was her brother's best friend and her own housemate—how stupid would she be to ignore any of those obstacles?

This conversation was getting entirely out of hand. Must be the weather, she decided, making no attempt to rationalize that conclusion. "I'm thirsty," she announced, reaching again for the basket. "I'm going to have one of these bottles of water. Do you want anything?"

"I think so," he murmured. "I just hadn't realized it before."

Because she had no idea what that meant, she didn't reply, simply tossing him the extra bottle of water instead.

CHAPTER SEVEN

THE HOUSE WAS OLD, and not particularly well insulated. The relentless wind squeezed through leaks around windows and doorways, which gradually lowered the temperature inside.

Though the fire was still burning steadily, Michael could tell that its warmth wasn't reaching Keely. The couch was too far away and there were no blowers in the old-fashioned brick fireplace to distribute the heat. She'd said very little during the past half hour, but he could tell by the way she huddled into the afghan that she was getting cold.

He pushed himself carefully out of the recliner.

His movement caught Keely's attention. "Where are you going?"

"To put another log on the fire."

She shifted, as if to rise. "Let me do that."

"Stay put. I've got it." He still couldn't bend his knee without having pain shoot all the way from his leg to his teeth, but he'd be damned if he'd sit in that chair and let her take care of them.

"But your—"

"I said, I've got it." His tone must have let

her know it wasn't up for debate, because she settled back onto the couch. He could feel her watching him as he slowly made his way to the fireplace. Though he couldn't walk with his usual easy, rolling gait, he forced himself to not lurch. He had his pride, after all.

After throwing a log on the fire, he gathered the blankets Keely had brought in earlier and spread them on the floor close to the hearth. Piling throw pillows on the blankets, he turned to Keely. "Can you walk, or do you need help?"

"Walk where?"

"You need to move closer to the fire. You're starting to shiver."

"I'm okay."

"Keely, c'mon. It's cold in here, and it's going to get colder during the night. Staying close to the fire is our only option."

He placed his hands on his hips and looked at her. After a moment she sighed and pushed herself upright. "Okay, I'll move to the blankets. But it won't be as comfortable as the couch."

"It'll be warmer. That's what counts."

He noticed that she wasn't limping too badly when she crossed the room. Either her ankle was feeling better, or she was making as big an effort as he had to mask the discomfort. Because he knew her, he suspected the latter. He put out a hand to steady her as she lowered herself carefully to the blankets.

"What about you?" she asked. "You're only wearing that robe. You can't be warm enough."

"I'd put on a pair of pants, but I can't stand the thought of having anything rub against my knee right now," he admitted.

"I don't blame you." She scooted to one side of the big blanket. "We can share. There's plenty of room."

Though her tone had been studiously casual, he thought he saw a blush darken her cheeks in the firelight. He stifled a smile, deciding to not tell her he'd planned to join her all along.

He gathered up a few more pillows, along with the basket of snacks. "Ready for some more munchies?" he asked, speaking lightly to set her at ease. "We've got peanut butter crackers and Snickers bars. And lukewarm cola to wash them down."

"Yum." She pulled a blanket around her and slid her feet closer to the fire. "Sounds delicious."

"Here, take the basket." He lowered himself by bending his good leg and stretching the injured one in front of him. It was awkward, but effective. It got him next to Keely.

A moment later they were both cocooned in blankets and pillows, a snack-food picnic scattered around them. Michael set out to put Keely at ease, talking and teasing as easily with her as he would have with his sister under similar circumstances. His strategy worked; Keely began to relax and chat comfortably with him again.

She wouldn't have been nearly as relaxed, of course, had she known that he'd finally stopped even trying to think of her as a sister.

When had this happened? Was it only the firelight that made him so aware of the perfection of her skin? Only the soft glow of candlelight that brought out the beauty of her intelligent eyes?

No. He'd noticed those things before. On a physical level, he'd always been aware of her.

Now he found himself contemplating the other things he'd grown to admire about Keely in the past months. Her clever sense of humor. Her brisk competence in running this bachelor household. Her rare talent.

He glanced up past the wall above the mantel, where one of Keely's paintings hung—*Child in Flight*. He knew she'd been inspired by a snapshot she'd taken of a little girl on a trampoline, but the end result bore little resemblance to the photograph.

Keely liked to say she didn't paint people, but embodied emotions. The figures in her paintings didn't have discernable features, and the colors she used for skin bore little resemblance to reality. It wasn't even possible to tell gender, unless the emotion she was trying to portray was in some way gender-based, such as the two works she'd done entitled *Mother Worry* and *Father Pride*. But the emotions—it took only a glance at the bold body-shaped blocks of color to be inundated with the feelings Keely had portrayed. Joy. Fear. Insecurity. Jealousy.

Depicted in crayon-box colors, the child in the portrait over the mantel seemed to have broken the bonds of gravity—arms outstretched, back arched, legs akimbo—and Michael never looked at it without remembering how much fun he'd had as a kid playing on a friend's trampoline. Keely said it reminded her of being tossed high in the air by a favorite uncle. And Jonah spoke of boyhood dives from the high board at the neighborhood pool, when they talked about the painting.

That was Keely's particular talent, Michael mused. Plugging into the emotions everyone felt and somehow matching them to half-buried memories. But he'd always admired her talent—so that couldn't be what had caused a change inside him tonight.

The horoscope thing—well, he admitted that had been a bit irritating in the past. But even her enthusiasm for that showed how much she enjoyed studying what made people tick—whether background or genes or the stars—and making herself a part of their lives in some way, even if just by reading them their horoscopes.

Even now she was sitting beside him eating candy and chattering happily about a friend she'd been encouraging in a writing career. The friend had recently been offered a first book contract, and Keely seemed almost as proud and delighted as her friend must have been.

"I *told* her she would get published soon. I just had a hunch. She's talented and clever, and her characters are so realistic and sympathetic. She was discouraged when she got those early rejection slips, but I knew if she'd just hang in there, she'd succeed."

"I suppose success was written in her stars?" Michael teased, lying propped on his left elbow as he watched Keely's face in the firelight.

"Well, actually, her sign is more typical of accountants and engineers than writers," Keely admitted with a wry smile. "I didn't say *everyone* fit the profile. Just a bunch of people."

"Like me."

She shrugged. "You're a classic Capricorn—not that I expect you to believe that, of course."

"Do *you?* Really believe, I mean?" It was a question that had been bugging him lately. Something he thought they needed to get out of the way once and for all. Did she believe that stuff, or was it just fun for her? And did it really make any difference to him one way or the other?

She hesitated only a moment before giving her answer. "It's sort of like psychics, mediums, ghosts and UFOs—and the Easter bunny and Santa Claus, for that matter. I don't know if any of them are real, but it's fun to pretend there are strange and magical things around us. It makes me smile."

As foreign as it was to his see-it-to-believe-it nature, he almost wanted to believe in those strange and magical things—just to make Keely smile. Had he been so resistant to her fanciful morning ramblings because he suspected that she was the only person in the world who could make him believe?

He still didn't know what had happened tonight to make him suddenly open his eyes to things he'd been deliberately avoiding since Keely moved in. He didn't know what had changed between them to make the air around them seem suddenly charged, filled with questions and possibilities. But he was falling in love with her.

He wasn't proud of the fact that he'd been using Laurel as a buffer between himself and Keely—but he knew for certain now that he'd been doing just that. He'd convinced himself that he and Keely were even more wrong for each other than he and Laurel. Keely was too young. Too impulsive. Too easily hurt. What could a fanciful, proudly quirky artist have in common with a staid, tediously predictable corporate attorney? Even if something did happen between them, how quickly would she grow bored with him—and how long would it take him to recover if she did?

And yet...she'd said they made a good match. It was written in the stars. Right?

He tried to remember the horoscope she'd

been so insistent that he read that morning. The part about being careful around animals—okay, that was creepy. What else had there been? Something about a hat. And an unexpected opportunity, he remembered suddenly. One that could pass him by if he didn't act on it.

He stared into the fire, wondering half-seriously if he'd hit his head in that accident. He had to be crazy to even contemplate the possibilities that were in his mind right now.

"Michael? You're being awfully quiet. Are you okay?"

He turned his head to smile at her, noting the look of concern on her face. "I'm fine. Just thinking."

"Your leg isn't hurting you?"

"No more than it already was. It's my head I'm worried about right now."

"Your head?" She reached out quickly to touch his hair, running her fingers carefully through it as if looking for lumps. "You hit your head? Why didn't you tell me? Are you seeing double?"

Damn. It seemed he was falling harder for her by the minute.

Definitely crazy, he told himself, reaching up to take her hand. But right now he desperately wanted to believe in strange and magical things. Such as the possibility that he wasn't the only one who'd been trying to hide an attraction that seemed equally tempting and terrifying.

Because he wasn't sure how to put that incredible possibility in the form of a question, he decided to take this very slowly. Careful, deliberate, methodical—that was the way he'd always operated. As he'd told Keely earlier, acting on impulse had always gotten him into trouble. He had the whole night to find out how Keely felt about him. There was no need to rush it.

"I was only teasing," he said, hoping his smile was more convincing than it felt. He cradled her hand between both of his. "Your fingers are cold."

"Are they?" She looked at her hand as if she'd never seen it before. She didn't try to remove it from his, but he thought he felt a fine tremor go through her fingers when he tightened his grasp. "I, er, hadn't noticed."

This could definitely be mutual, he thought with a wave of nerves and satisfaction. Maybe it had just taken an ice storm and a power outage to bring it out in the open. Almost.

Despite his wariness when it came to following impulses, he tugged her suddenly into his arms, pushing her head gently into his shoulder. He pulled the blankets around them—making a cozy nest to shelter them from the cold air—adding to the warmth of the crackling fire.

Apparently he'd caught Keely so off guard that she didn't even think to resist until they settled. Only then did she attempt to raise her head. "Er, Michael?"

"Don't you know that sharing body warmth is the most practical plan of action during a winter storm?"

"It isn't exactly as if we're stuck in a snow-drift trying to keep ourselves from freezing to death," she said, her voice somehow breathless and sardonic at the same time.

He smiled and tucked her head back into his shoulder. "True. But we'll stay much warmer like this. I'm getting warmer already. How about you?"

"Oh, yes," Keely muttered. "In fact, we could get a bit *too* warm this way."

He smiled again and cradled her closer, enjoying the feel of her slender curves in his arms. "It's a definite possibility," he agreed.

CHAPTER EIGHT

MAYBE MICHAEL *was* suffering from a head injury. He was certainly acting strangely enough. Or maybe Keely was the one who'd had some sort of breakdown, because she wasn't making any effort to scoot away from him.

His thick flannel robe was soft beneath her cheek, though the body beneath it was anything *but* soft. Funny. She'd never realized quite how firm and solid he was. But then she'd never had his strong arms around her before.

She could feel his heart beneath the robe, steady, if a bit fast. Her own was racing—could he feel it? Did he know her skin was tingling with a warmth that had nothing to do with the fire or the blankets he'd wrapped around them?

It was so quiet in the room, the only sounds were of the wood crackling in the fireplace and the wind still gusting outside. Michael lay with his left arm around her, his cheek resting against her hair and his right hand slowly stroking her left arm. She felt her eyelids growing heavy—but she wasn't at all sleepy.

Oh, damn, but it felt good. And if something

didn't happen soon, she was going to totally humiliate herself by doing something really stupid—such as throwing herself all over him.

"Um, how are things going at work?" she asked, latching on to the first conversational gambit that came to mind.

"Okay. Paul's still a world-class jerk, but that seems to be a genetic condition with him."

Resting her hand on his chest, she smiled faintly. "You're actually nicer about him than Jonah is."

"Yeah, well, Jonah has a lower jerk-tolerance level than I do. Besides, Paul's a partner. Which means I'd damned well better get along with him if I want to advance in the firm."

"Jonah's never been as politically savvy as you."

Michael went still for a moment. "Was that a dig?"

"No—just an observation. Why?"

"I know how you feel about politics of any sort."

"I'm aware that they're necessary, occasionally. But some people are better at it than others. It just so happens," she added, tongue-in-cheek, "that Capricorns are typically more suited for that sort of thing than Cancers."

He made a rumbly sound of derision that vibrated pleasantly against her cheek. "Whatever you say."

Her fingers seemed to have gone on a little trek of their own without asking for his permission. They inched across his chest, savoring the contrasts between soft fabric and hard muscle.

Hard and soft. Something about the connotation almost made her gulp—and she would have been naive to not understand the imagery the words evoked.

She wasn't naive.

"Does, um, does Sandra get along with Paul?" she asked, exasperated by the breathiness of her voice.

He chuckled, causing that vibrating sensation beneath her cheek again. Instinctively she nestled her cheek more snugly into his shoulder. "Sandra treats Paul the same way she does everyone she doesn't like—with unfailing professional courtesy."

Keely smiled. "Have I ever mentioned how much I like her?"

"So do I." He must have shifted his head a bit because his lips moved very lightly against her forehead. His breath was warm on her skin—which, oddly enough, made her shiver as if with a chill.

He could hardly have missed that reaction. "Are you cold?"

"No." Her voice sounded positively strangled this time, even to her. Her face flaming, she called herself several choice names and cleared her throat. "I'm quite warm, actually. Maybe we should—"

He took her voice completely away by nuzzling her forehead. "Maybe we should...?"

"Should what?" She tilted her head toward him, trying to understand exactly what was happening here. And Michael's mouth was suddenly on hers.

Surprise held Keely utterly motionless. Her eyes were wide open, locked with his. Her lips were parted—more from shock than invitation. The sounds of the fire and the wind receded in her consciousness, almost drowned out by the pounding of her heart.

He had never kissed her before. Not even a friendly, brotherly kiss on the cheek—which this definitely was not. Now that he had...she wasn't sure they could ever go back to the way things had been before.

Because that thought made a renewed sense of panic shoot through her, she jerked away from him, her heart leaping in her throat. "What—" She stopped to clear her voice. "What are you doing?"

Michael's eyes were a bit glazed, but he managed a fairly credible imitation of his wry smile. "You can't figure that out for yourself?"

She would have scooted away from him, but his arm held her in place. "I, uh, I think I'll go see if it's still snowing."

"It is." He lifted a hand to brush her hair away from her flushed face. "Was kissing me really so terrible that you want to bolt?"

Kissing him had been anything but terrible. Which was exactly why she felt the urge to bolt. The thought of putting their comfortable friendship at risk terrified her.

Play it lightly, she advised herself, deciding that Michael must be indulging in some rather odd teasing. She was taking him too seriously, that was all.

"Terrible?" She pasted on a bright smile and gave him a friendly little pat on the shoulder. "No, of course not. It was quite nice."

"'Nice'?" he repeated, and she could tell he didn't care for the word. "Just 'nice'?"

She chuckled, then congratulated herself because it sounded quite natural—mostly. "What were you hoping for, applause?"

This time she managed to sit up, maybe because she'd distracted him enough to make him loosen his grasp. "Where'd you put the flashlight?"

"Where are you going?"

Rising carefully, she tested her ankle—still sore, but bearable. "To make sure I locked the kitchen door. You need anything from the kitchen?"

It seemed he was still analyzing her response to his kiss. "Uh, no. Not right now. Keely?"

She'd already made it to the doorway. "Hmm?"

"We need to talk."

"Yeah, sure. Later, okay?"

"Fine. After all, we've got all night," he added.

All night. Keely gulped and hurried into the dark hallway.

Once she reached the kitchen, she took a few moments to hyperventilate in private, fanning her face with both hands. Her knees had gone weaker than her twisted ankle; she sagged against the counter for support. At least she'd managed to wait until she was alone to fall apart. Somehow she'd retained her composure in front of Michael.

What was he *thinking,* kissing her like that? Using that sexy, rumbly voice when he talked to her. Acting as if he'd suddenly noticed her as someone other than his buddy's little sister.

How stupid would she be to take any of that seriously?

Oh, *wow,* could that man kiss!

The most terrifying aspect of this entire situation, she decided with a low groan, was that she so very much wanted to believe something real had just happened between them.

It was entirely possible that she'd fallen for Michael within days of moving in with him, though she'd tried her best to hide it—even from herself. But it was a great deal easier to believe in horoscopes, Santa Claus, UFOs and the Easter bunny than it was to accept that Michael had fallen for her, too.

CHAPTER NINE

KEELY WAS STANDING in the dark. She'd laid the flashlight on the counter, its beam just barely illuminating her as she gazed out the window over the sink—as if she could see anything in the pitch darkness outside. Michael knew what she was doing, of course—avoiding him. She'd all but bolted from him after he'd kissed her.

That kiss...

It had been an impulsive move on his part—and, granted, impulsive actions weren't his usual style—but he didn't regret it now. Kissing Keely had answered a lot of questions for him—questions he was only now admitting had been hovering in the back of his mind for weeks.

The most obvious conclusion he had drawn was that he wanted her. Maybe he couldn't pinpoint the exact moment it had happened, but he had no doubt it was true. He wanted Keely with an intensity that made his chest ache.

Now he understood why it had been so easy to resist Laurel's undeniable attractions. Why he'd been avoiding involvement with her—or with any other woman for the past few months.

Now it made sense to him why he'd been spending more evenings and weekends at home, even though he and Keely had usually been in different rooms. Now he knew why he made it a point to have breakfast every morning—though he'd rarely eaten breakfast before she had moved in with her morning-run glow and her cheery horoscope readings.

He wondered why it had taken him so damned long to figure it out. He was usually a bit quicker on the uptake than that.

He hoped Keely's breathless, half-panicked reaction to his kiss was a good thing. With Keely, it was always hard to tell.

He reminded himself that she *had* kissed him back—if only for a moment—and that her heart had been racing as hard as his. And then he pictured the dazed look in her firelit eyes when she'd pulled away. It hadn't been indifference, he assured himself. Whatever she felt for him, it wasn't that.

He hoped it was a good thing.

"You see anything interesting out there?" he asked, deciding it was time to make his presence known.

She jumped and whirled, one hand on her heart. "You startled me," she informed him unnecessarily.

"Sorry. I came to see if you got lost in the dark. You've been gone awhile."

"No, I was just..." Her voice faded away, as if she couldn't decide how to finish the sentence. "Um, how's your knee?"

"It's okay, but I think I'll take a couple more ibuprofen to keep the swelling down."

She snatched up the flashlight and moved toward the pantry. "I'll get them for you."

He groped his way to the sink while she shook two pills out of the container. He filled the glass he'd used earlier with water, then accepted the pills from her when she joined him at the sink. Tossing the tablets down his throat, he washed them down with a few sips of water. He then set the glass on the counter and reached out to catch Keely's wrist before she could move away. "Thank you."

"You're welcome." She moved to pull away from him again.

"Wait." He lifted his free hand to touch her cheek, which felt curiously warm in contrast to the chill in the room. "Keely."

She held the flashlight at her side, pointed downward, casting her face in such deep shadows that he couldn't see her expression. But her voice was strangled when she asked, "What is it?"

"I just wanted to say your name," he murmured, aware that her name hadn't been far from his thoughts for quite a while. "Keely."

"You're...acting very strangely tonight," she said in little more than a whisper.

"I know," he admitted. "I'm sorry if I'm un-
nerving you. It's just that…well, this has caught
me off guard. I generally prefer to be fully prepared for every eventuality. But this time I
wasn't."

"What—" She stopped to clear her throat.
"*What* has caught you off guard?"

He was making a mess of this—making a fool
of himself, he thought with a grimace as he remembered that damned horoscope. And then he
thought again of the rest of it. The warning about
animals, which had certainly proven strangely accurate. And—something about someone in a hat
bringing luck.

Two quick images flashed through his mind—
Jonah in his cherished Outback hat and the police
officer touching his hat in the elevator. Both men
had urged Michael to go home. To Keely, he realized with a hard swallow. And then there had
been the admonition that an opportunity would
pass him by if he didn't act on it.

He needed to start over, that was all. Try to
make sense of this—to himself, and to Keely.

It was so dark in the house, as well as the
surrounding neighborhood. And now that the
wind had died down, it was so quiet he could
almost hear his own heartbeat—maybe even hers,
if he listened hard enough. Eerie—that his major
breakthrough had been accompanied by such dramatic external events.

Strange and magical things, he remembered Keely saying. For the first time in his life, he found himself starting to believe...

"Michael?"

He must have been silent for longer than he'd realized. Keely sounded utterly bewildered by his actions—or lack of them. He smiled ruefully, though he doubted she could clearly see his face. "I'm sorry," he said again. "You must think I've lost my mind tonight."

"The thought had occurred to me."

"I haven't, you know. Just the opposite, actually. I've simply acknowledged something I've been denying to myself for a long time."

He felt her muscles tense, almost as if she knew what he was going to say when she asked, "What do you mean?"

"It's the way I feel about *you,* Keely. I've been trying for weeks to ignore the attraction I feel for you. To make myself believe I think of you only as a friend and a roommate. It hasn't been working."

She'd gone very still now. He could hardly hear her breathing.

"I don't want to frighten you," he said quickly. "If this is something you don't want to hear, just say so and I'll shut up. But I had to say it."

"Why—" Again she paused, perhaps to swallow before continuing. "Why now? What has suddenly changed since this morning?"

"The only thing that changed is that I've stopped trying to deceive myself. I'm finally being honest with myself, and with you. As for what, exactly, made me face my feelings—I'm not sure I can answer that. It was just...well, I looked at you this evening—*really* looked at you—and I finally saw the truth."

"Which is?" she asked in a whisper.

He figured he might as well lay all his cards on the table now that he'd started this. "I want you."

The silence that followed his rather blunt announcement stretched on for so long Michael was beginning to wonder if he'd sent her into shock. When she finally spoke, it was a question he should have anticipated. "What about Laurel?"

He chose his words carefully. "There's nothing between me and Laurel except a casual friendship. We've had dinner a few times, attended a couple of social functions, flirted a good bit—but that's it. We aren't, and have never been, lovers."

He wasn't surprised by the skepticism in Keely's reply. "But you've been so adamant about seeing her. Even when—well, you know."

Even when Keely had tried to convince him that he and Laurel were mismatched, he silently finished for her. There'd been a time or two when he'd wondered if her interest had been personally motivated—but he'd always quickly convinced himself that he was probably wrong. He'd seen her nag Jonah the same way. He'd told himself she'd been treating him like another big brother.

But maybe…

"There's nothing between me and Laurel," he repeated firmly. "What about Steve, the guy you go out with sometimes?"

"Steve's a friend. He's never even kissed me."

Michael smiled in satisfaction. "You can't say that about *me,* can you?"

"No. No, I can't."

Because he suddenly wanted very much to kiss her again, he pulled her closer. "Keely…"

She put a hand on his chest to hold him back— the hand holding the flashlight, unfortunately. The beam shone right in his dark-adjusted eyes, nearly blinding him. At the same time, she moved sharply away from him, causing him to lose his balance. He braced himself quickly by stiffening his legs—and his right knee throbbed violently in protest. He couldn't quite swallow a gasp of pain.

Instantly Keely came back to him, propping the flashlight on the counter and gripping his forearms with both hands. "Are you all right? I'm so sorry—I didn't mean to hurt you. I wasn't thinking. I'd forgotten about your leg. Oh, Michael, I'm so sorry. You *know* I'd never hurt you intentionally. Let me help you..."

She might have kept on jabbering that way indefinitely, had he not stopped her by covering her mouth with his. His knee still hurt—but he no longer cared. Not with Keely in his arms again.

This kiss was longer than the first, and there was no question that Keely participated. But he sensed she was still holding back.

Reluctantly he lifted his head. "Keely?" His voice sounded a bit hoarse even to him. "Do you want me to stop? Is this too much, too soon? Because if you aren't interested, just say so now, and I'll back off. We can pretend nothing ever happened. We can blame it on the storm or the pain pills or the power outage. I'd never do anything to make you unhappy or uncomfortable—but I had to be honest with you."

He heard her take a deep breath. "I have to be honest with you, too," she said, her voice so low he could hardly hear her. "I haven't thought of you as a brother or a roommate for a long time—if ever. But, Michael—I'm scared. I'm afraid if we go on with this, something will go wrong. Something that will ruin the wonderful friendship we have, or the relationship between you and Jonah. What if—"

"Keely, calm down." Her admission that he wasn't the only one with these feelings made his heart beat faster, but he understood her fears.

Her fears...

He thought again of the horoscopes she'd read that morning. "Remember your horoscope? Remember what it said?"

She blinked in the yellow glare of the flashlight. "My horoscope?" she repeated as if she wasn't quite sure she'd heard him correctly. "What does my horoscope have to do with anything?"

"I don't know if I'm your heart's desire or not—but your horoscope advised you not to let fear guide your actions. Now, you know how I feel about those things, but..."

"You listened," she interrupted, staring up at him.

He frowned, not quite sure he understood. "What?"

"You listened to my horoscope. And you remembered."

"Well, of course. I didn't necessarily believe, but I always listened. Why the hell do you think I come to breakfast every morning? I don't even *like* breakfast. I enjoy being with you—starting my day with you."

"Michael?" She took a step toward him and placed both hands on his chest.

"Yes?"

"I'm not so afraid anymore."

He wasn't sure what he'd done to reassure

her—but he wasn't complaining. He pulled her eagerly into his arms and lowered his head to hers.

And this time, Keely held nothing back.

CHAPTER TEN

KEELY HAD BEEN AWARE from the start that Michael was an exceptionally beautiful man. It was why her pulse rate had increased every time he walked into a room for the past eight months. But when she saw his bare chest bathed in firelight and candlelight, her heart almost came to a full stop.

They lay on the nest of blankets he'd made for them, Michael on his back and Keely on her elbow beside him. It was almost as if they were getting to know each other all over again—through kisses, touches, and soft little murmurs. She traced her fingers over his face, down his throat, to the strong chest she'd revealed by parting his robe. She felt his heart beating rapidly beneath his skin as she ran her fingertips slowly down the center of his chest to the loosened belt at his waist.

He caught her hand before she could pull the knot free. "Careful," he warned. "You're moving into dangerous territory."

"Bragging, bragging," she murmured, and covered his lips with hers for a kiss that should have short-circuited his brain waves. It certainly did hers.

He locked his fingers in her hair, holding her mouth to his, his tongue plunging deep into territory he'd already explored quite thoroughly. By the time the kiss ended, several long minutes later, they were both panting—and Keely was reaching for Michael's belt again.

Again he caught her hand. "You're—" He cleared his hoarse voice. "You're sure we're not moving too fast? You don't want to take a little more time to think about this?"

"Why, do you?" She touched her lips to his right nipple as she spoke, making him arch upward in reflex.

"I want you so badly I'm half-crazy with it." His voice grated. "But—well, you haven't had much time to get used to this idea."

She inched down his body, trailing kisses from his nipples to his shallow navel. "I've thought about this longer than you know."

"Have you?" He seemed intrigued.

"Mmm. We have been living together for eight whole months." She toyed with the loose knot, thrilled by the unmistakable hardness she felt beneath it.

He moved restlessly. "And just what have you been thinking?"

"Oh, you know. What it would be like to kiss you." She dropped a kiss on his lips, moving away before he could respond.

"To taste you." She nipped the skin just over his pounding heart, adding a little lick that made him groan.

"To touch you—all over." She ran her hands slowly down his body, sliding under the belt and pushing it—finally—out of the way. And then she touched him more intimately, making him shudder.

"You've...thought about all those things?"

"Mmm-hmm." He wore boxers, she noted with interest. Cotton, in a muted plaid. Very conservative. Sexy enough to make a woman swallow her tongue.

He tugged her on top of him, pulling her mouth to his again. His hands slipped under her fleece top, sliding up her back to her shoulders. And then around to her breasts, his fingers kneading her gently through her thin front-clasp bra. And now it was Keely who shuddered, all teasing evaporating as she fell under the same spell she'd hoped to cast over him.

A moment later it was Keely whose bare skin glowed in the firelight. She had to admire Michael's skill. Even flat on his back with one leg out of commission, he'd gotten her out of her shirt in one smooth move.

Funny. She wasn't at all self-conscious. After all, this was Michael. And she'd been dreaming about this for eight months—dreams she no longer had to deny.

Being very careful to not jostle his injured leg,

she pushed his robe out of the way and straddled his hips, leaning over to kiss him slowly, savoringly. Her breasts filled his hands, and the way his thumbs circled her nipples made her gasp into his mouth. "Michael."

His eyes glittered in the firelight, radiating a heat of their own. His hands moved over her body, making her squirm against him—which only aroused him more.

He caught her hips, holding her still for a moment. "Keely—wait. We can't—"

"Am I hurting your leg?"

"No. It's just…well, I'm not exactly prepared…"

"Oh, that." She smiled and reached into the pocket of her comfortably loose fleece slacks. A handful of plastic packets rained onto his stomach. "Remember that visit I made to the back a few minutes ago? I didn't return empty-handed. Well, empty-pocketed, anyway."

His smile held both surprise and admiration. "It seems you *are* prepared."

She leaned over him, cupping his face in her hands. "You know how I am once I decide I want something—I go after it. I've decided I want *you*, Michael Gordon. Does that worry you?"

"Terrifies me," he murmured, and pulled her into his arms, squashing a half-dozen little packets between them. "But, as it happens, I want you, too."

She kissed a smile against his lips. "So don't you think we've waited long enough?"

Apparently he agreed. He didn't make her wait any longer.

Their few remaining clothes fell aside. Perhaps the air in the room was still chilly, but Keely wouldn't have noticed. All her attention was focused on Michael and the heat they generated between them.

They had to make a few adjustments for his injured knee, but Keely had no complaints. Michael more than compensated for his lack of mobility. Keely's twisted ankle caused them no problems at all.

When they finally came together, it was with a joyous sense of rightness and familiarity. A certainty that the events of this night had been written in their stars all along. At least, that was the way Keely felt. As she collapsed against Michael's chest, sated and exhausted, she decided she'd do well to keep that thought to herself for now.

MICHAEL WOKE ALONE the next morning. He was still lying on the floor in front of the fireplace, covered to the chin by several thick blankets. Keely must have pulled them over him when she'd gotten up. The fire was still burning, so she'd apparently added a couple of logs to it. He was surprised he hadn't awakened when she did. He was usually a lighter sleeper than that.

Shoving a hand through his hair, he sat up slowly. A grayish light came through the windows, indicating the skies were still cloudy, but a glance at the battery-powered clock on the mantel let him know it was late morning—just after ten. He didn't usually sleep so late, either.

Remembering the night that had passed, he told himself he shouldn't be surprised he'd slept so long or so hard. Twice during the night he'd gotten up to limp to the bathroom and into the kitchen for more painkillers for his throbbing leg. Both times, Keely had taken his mind off his discomfort in a most deliciously efficient way.

All in all, it was a miracle he could still move.

Reaching for his robe, he belted it around him as he rose stiffly from the floor. His knee was still swollen and bruised, and he wasn't able to bend it without pain. He'd probably be forced to see a doctor, but he didn't think there was any urgency in doing so. It could wait until the roads were clear and it was safe to drive.

"Keely?" He wondered if she was in the kitchen. The bathroom, maybe. The power was still out, which explained why there was no smell of coffee in the house, but he would have expected to hear her moving around. Yet, the house was quiet, as if he was the only one in it.

"Keely?" Moving very slowly, he made his way to the kitchen. Through the window over the sink, he could see that a good four inches of snow had fallen on top of the ice that had started the storm. Snow was such a novelty in this area that he took a few minutes to marvel at its wintry beauty before returning to his search for Keely.

She wasn't anywhere in the house. A glance out the front door showed him a line of footprints leading off the stoop and down the snow-buried sidewalk.

He scowled and shoved his hand through his hair again. Damn it, what was she thinking, going out like this? Didn't she remember that there was a treacherous film of ice beneath all that pretty snow? He had no way of knowing how long she'd been gone—what if she'd fallen? What if she were lying out there somewhere hurt?

Her brother had been right to worry that her impulsive actions would put her at risk.

And then Michael winced as he wondered exactly what Jonah would say about what *else* Keely had done during the winter storm.

Half an hour later he'd donned a white, long-sleeved shirt and a black wind suit, the pants loose enough to fit over his knee without too much discomfort. Zipping the jacket over his shirt, he thought about putting on his boots and going after Keely, following her tracks in the snow. It might take a while, considering how slowly he had to move with that damned swollen knee, but he *would* find her.

It was a relief when he heard the front door open and her voice call out, "Michael? I'm back."

He felt relief loosen the tensed muscles at the back of his neck. She was home. Unharmed, from the sound of her voice.

Now his only concern was finding out if she had any regrets about what had happened between them last night. If that was the reason she'd felt the need to escape without telling him.

He found her in the kitchen. A thermos he recognized as Jonah's sat on the table beside a brown paper bag and a folded newspaper. Keely was peeling out of several layers of outerwear—a hooded parka, a knit cap, a muffler and gloves—to reveal a thick blue sweater and jeans beneath. Apparently she'd left her snow-covered boots at the door.

Her cheeks and the tip of her nose were bright pink, and her hair was tumbled all around her face, floating with static electricity. There was a warm glow in her eyes when she smiled at him as he entered the room. Searching her seemingly open expression, Michael decided that if there was regret, she hid it well.

She waved toward the thermos. "I brought coffee. And muffins. I got them at that little convenience store a couple of blocks over."

"A couple of blocks? That store's a good half mile from here."

She shrugged. "It was a pleasant walk. It's been a while since we've seen snow, hasn't it?"

"Keely, I was worried about you. You could

have fallen on the ice. And what about your ankle?"

She seemed surprised by his concern. "My ankle's fine. I told you, I just twisted it. As for falling, I was careful. I slipped and slid a bit, but my boots have good soles for gripping, and I watched for icy patches. I enjoyed the walk, and I plan to enjoy the coffee and the newspaper."

Michael was feeling oddly unsure of himself, uncharacteristically hesitant. Because he'd always had some difficulty reading Keely, he wanted to make certain he found out exactly what she was thinking this morning. What she was feeling. But he couldn't quite decide how to ask.

His gaze fell on the newspaper she'd dropped on the table. "Have you read your horoscope yet?"

She pulled two coffee cups out of a cabinet. "Of course not. I always read them aloud, you know that."

He pushed his hands into the front pockets of his wind suit jacket. "You, uh, think there will be anything interesting in there today? More animal warnings? Advice about your love life?" He cleared his throat. "Predictions for your future?"

She laughed and set a steaming coffee cup on the table in front of him. "I don't need to read my horoscope to know about my love life *or* my future."

Studying her face through his lashes, he asked, "You don't?"

"No." She placed a hand on his arm and rose on tiptoes to brush a kiss across his mouth. "I already know that you're in both of them."

"And if your horoscope warns you away from me?"

She only laughed and patted his cheek. "Don't be silly. Our stars are perfectly aligned. I don't need to read an astrology column to know I love you. Or that you and I are going to live happily ever after."

"You, uh—" His heart seemed to be doing some sort of crazy tap dance. He took a deep breath in a futile attempt to calm it. "You don't?"

"Certainly not." Stepping away from him, she pulled fragrant muffins out of the paper bag and arranged them on the table. "Actually, there's something else I want to check in the horoscope column today. When's Laurel's birthday?"

His head was still reeling from her cheerfully casual admission of love for him. Maybe that was why he must have misunderstood what she'd just asked him. "What?"

"Laurel's birthday," she repeated patiently. "It occurred to me this morning that she and Steve could be a great pair. They both like all those charity things and flashy stuff. He's a Gemini. So if she's an Aquarius or a Libra, we should figure out a way to introduce them, don't you think?"

"Keely?"

Taking a sip of her coffee, she glanced at him over the rim, obviously still thinking about her matchmaking plans. "Mmm?"

"I love you."

Something in his voice made her set the cup slowly on the table and look at him searchingly. "You've just figured this out?"

He felt a smile spread slowly across his face. "No. I just thought I should say it."

She looked momentarily sheepish. "I didn't give you much chance to speak, did I?"

"No. But I'm getting resigned to that. After all, when you decide what you want, you go after it," he mused, reminding her of what she'd said last night.

"I'm sorry. I guess Jonah's right that I can be just a teensy bit pushy. But I'll tell you what— you can decide when to propose to me," she offered magnanimously. "Take all the time you need."

"You're so certain that I *will* get around to it?" he asked, his smile deepening.

Utterly confident, she looped her arms around his neck. "Michael, darling, you have no choice," she murmured, lifting her face to his. "It's written in your stars."

Strange and magical things. He wondered why it had taken him so long to understand their attraction.

"Well, then," he said, pulling her closer, his

mouth hovering only a breath above hers. "Who am I to argue with the stars?"

She seemed perfectly satisfied with that response—and with the kisses that warmed them long after their coffee had cooled.

EPILOGUE

The quietly crackling fire spread warmth and soft light through the room as Keely sat in Michael's lap late Monday evening, both of them snuggled into the big, cozy recliner. The power had been back on since noon the day before, and the house was pleasantly toasty again, but they hadn't bothered with lights when they'd moved in here after dinner. Keely thought it was much more romantic this way and Michael was still in a mood to indulge her.

They both wore robes, Keely's short and silky, Michael's thick and warm. Michael's hand rested on Keely's bare leg. As they kissed, his hand crept slowly upward, his fingertips sliding beneath the hem of her robe. Her entire body tingled in anticipation of the culmination of his tactile journey. She wrapped her arms around his neck and let the kiss deepen, knowing exactly where this was headed.

The one thing she hadn't predicted was her brother walking in the front door.

Having been so absorbed in the kiss that she hadn't heard the door opening, Keely was taken totally by surprise when Jonah spoke from somewhere behind her. "What the hell... ?"

They broke off the kiss with a gasp. Michael instinctively tried to rise to his feet, nearly tumbling Keely to the floor with the movement. She managed to save herself just in time. Standing beside Michael, she stared at her stunned-looking brother. "Jonah? What are you doing here? You're not supposed to be home until tomorrow."

"I got an early flight. You want to tell me why you were sitting in Michael's lap with his hand on your thigh?"

"This isn't what it looks like," Michael said, his voice a bit strangled.

Both Keely and Jonah looked at him in question. Simultaneously, they asked, "It isn't?"

"Well, okay, it is," he corrected himself, giving Keely a wry look. "But... "

"What it looked like," Jonah said slowly, his narrowed eyes still focused unblinkingly on his friend's face, "is that you've been making moves on my sister while I was away."

Keely had to bite her lip against a sudden, completely inappropriate smile.

Michael cleared his throat. "Well, yeah, but..."

Taking pity on him, Keely broke in, "Does it make you feel better to know that Michael and I are engaged?"

The overnight bag Jonah had been holding fell

to the floor with a thud. He reached up to remove his hat, lowering it very slowly to his side. "Engaged," he repeated. "To be married?"

"That's what the word generally means," his sister retorted. "Now stop looking as if you're going to call Michael out to a duel and congratulate us."

"You can't blame me for needing a minute to catch up." Jonah shook his head. "When I left here, the two of you were squabbling like cats and dogs—over the woman Michael was dating, I believe. Now I come home and find out you're engaged. It's... disorienting, to say the least."

"So how do you feel about it?" Michael asked, sounding a bit worried. Keely was sure he was concerned about damaging his long-time friendship with Jonah; this certainly wasn't the way they had meant to break the news to him.

While she and Michael held their breath, Jonah gave the question a moment of serious thought. And then his face creased with a broad smile. "I think it's great. My best friend is about to become my brother."

Relieved, Keely stepped into Jonah's open arms for a fervent hug. The next ten minutes or so passed in a blur of hugs, grins, chatter, and a few happy tears on Keely's part.

"I just can't believe you two have come together like this," Jonah said several times, though he seemed to be adjusting rapidly to the news.

Keely laughed and looped her arms around Michael's waist. "We didn't have any choice, really. Our fate was written in the stars."

Both men groaned, but she noticed that both of them were smiling. Maybe they were finally starting to believe in magic.

Love's Journey

Your astrological love guide for 2002

by Susan Kelly

Love's Journey...

To paraphrase an old saying: "Love is a journey, not a destination."

The path to true love never seems to take the shortest route. Sometimes there are rocky roads, sometimes the way lies smooth and easy. And at times it seems lost in fog, others straight and clear.

These twists and turns are what keep it exciting. And though your favorite story may end with the hero and heroine walking into the sunset, in real life that's just the beginning.

How do you get on the right path? And how do you stick to the straight and narrow? Astrology can provide road signs. And advice for navigating the greatest adventure of all: finding your heart's desire.

In Part I, we'll look into the role adventure plays

in your love life as revealed through your astrological element. All twelve zodiac signs come under one of four groupings, which are called elements: fire, earth, air and water. Signs of like elements share certain qualities, including an approach to romance.

Part II is devoted to a sign-by-sign rundown on "Traveling Companions." What does your guy's sign say about him? Look him up and find out.

Want to know the road conditions for the coming year? In Part III we'll take a look at what lies ahead. Turn to your own sign and get a romantic overview of 2002.

Climb the Highest Mountain—FIRE

ARIES (March 21–April 19)
LEO (July 23–August 22)
SAGITTARIUS (November 22–December 21)

"Out of the way!" you cry. A volunteer fire-fighter, you're carrying an unconscious child out of a three-alarm inferno. The tall, handsome paramedic appears before you, offering help. Your eyes lock. In that instant you know you've found the one you'll spend the rest of your life with....

Fire signs are the most dynamic romantics. While you may not necessarily picture yourself as a fire-fighting heroine, you do possess a passion for life. Love without adventure? Unthinkable! No quiet meeting of minds and spirits for you. You want a blaze of passion, a romance that lights up your existence.

Fire is the purest form of energy, providing heat,

light and warmth. So it is with the fire signs. All three have warm, exciting personalities, the kind that can light up a gathering just by entering the room.

Aries is the first in line to dive into any kind of new experience. Leo takes a slower approach, adding some dramatic flair, while Sagittarius maintains unflagging exuberance in romance.

Shared experiences are so important to you, they're often what brings you and your hero together. You may meet him on the job, perhaps while involved in a special project or committee. Or it could be through a group or organization you belong to, especially if it's devoted to a cause you feel passionately about.

Once in a relationship, you may not be able to work side by side with your beloved in an action-filled career. Still, you'll want him to share your interests in some way. You may go white-water rafting or scale mountain peaks on the weekends, if only from your armchair.

You believe that true love can flare up in an instant, literally happening at first sight. But it is exactly this impatience that may quench your chances of long-term happiness. Fire needs solid fuel to keep burning. The most exciting suitor, who sweeps you off your feet on a whirlwind courtship, may not have enough substance for the long haul.

So too, your relationship pattern can be on the short-and-sweet side until you learn to slow down. Once in a relationship, try not to rush any phase, especially the big commitment. Once you master a balance of the tending to the practical while keeping the sense of adventure, you've got it made.

One thing's for sure: love is never boring around you. You can always find inventive ways to keep the love alive. For you can't wait to see what adventures lie ahead to leap into, hand in hand with your best beloved.

For the Long Haul—EARTH

TAURUS (April 20–May 20)
VIRGO (August 23–September 22)
CAPRICORN (December 22–January 19)

*Your heart racing, you notice your hand trembles
slightly. This is it, the "make or break" moment.
He places his hand gently on your shoulder and
at once you feel calmer. Smiling, you begin to
sign the mortgage on the new home you'll share
together....*

The above scenario is certainly not the stuff action movies are made of. But then, earth signs
are the least adventurous by nature. If you're one,
it's very difficult to get you to take a chance on
love. When you do, it will be a very calculated
risk, and you'll insist that the relationship proceed at a slow pace.

"Down to earth" describes you to a tee. Yours
is the element of reality and practicality, of get-

ting the job done. You're uncomfortable with
anything that is too abstract or airy-fairy. Let others walk around with their heads in the clouds.
You insist on keeping your feet solidly on the
ground.

Taurus has the most self-control, mixed with gen-
uine concern for the welfare of others. Virgo is
more idealistic, wanting a love that's pure and
lasting. Capricorn women are very concerned
with getting ahead in life and need a partner with
equal ambitions.

Career and achievement are important issues for
the earth signs. Many of you meet your true love
on the job. You also prefer to adhere to time-
honored ways of meeting someone new. Perhaps
your family or a close friend will arrange an introduction. You may even entertain the idea of
employing a traditional matchmaker.

You believe in very long courtships, sometimes
lasting years. Should differences arise along the
way, you make every effort to work it out. You
don't rush into commitments. When you do make
one, you consider it engraved in granite.

Having some sort of order and routine in your
life is very important to you. Frequent changes
of schedule make you nervous. But what if your
partner complains that things are becoming stale?

Sometimes your relationships suffer from the boredom factor.

Romance thrives on the impromptu and unexpected. So loosen up and plan some romantic surprises for your guy. Make him a favorite dinner in the middle of the week. Try an improvised picnic or a last-minute weekend getaway. Breaking the routine now and then makes love's journey more exciting without causing too much insecurity.

And do keep some photos and souvenirs of your life together. For you, such keepsakes are important symbols of the many milestones of love's long and lasting journey. A journey that grows deeper and more meaningful with each passing year.

In My Beautiful Balloon—AIR

GEMINI (May 21–June 21)
LIBRA (September 23–October 23)
AQUARIUS (January 20–February 18)

His smile is dazzling as he gallantly leads you into his private jet. The cabin is filled with crimson roses, and in the corner vintage champagne chills in a silver holder. "You look amazing," he whispers in your ear, adding that you'll be the belle of the A-list Hollywood party he's whisking you off to....

For air romantics, love's adventure begins and ends in a social whirl. You may not be an all-out party girl. Still, your friends and associates are important to you. In fact, you may have just met a handsome man whom you believe to be the most romantic hero of all time. But if your friends don't like and accept him, it will never last.

In a relationship, signs of this element make communication a top priority. You need someone you can talk to and share your every thought with. This kind of connection is everything to you—only a true meeting of minds will do.

Gemini has the quickest mind and wit, and can be quite the social butterfly. Marriage and partnership are paramount to Libra, while Aquarius is more concerned with finding a friend for life.

It is through conversation that Prince Charming finds out most about you, as you often prefer chats over the telephone before meeting someone new in person. For this reason, while single, you may consider using an introduction service or placing a single's advertisement. Many of you were the first to sign up for online dating services.

If you do use these services, always follow the recommended safeguards before meeting face-to-face or divulging your home phone number to anyone. This is advisable because you're also very trusting, which means you're sometimes too quick to take people for what they seem to be.

Once in a relationship, this same idealism can throw it offtrack, for sometimes reality has a way of paling beside the scenario that you've built in your imagination. When this happens, you may

become disillusioned and even cut yourself off
from the real-life adventure of love.

All of this can be avoided by remembering your
strong suit: communication. For how can your
hero fulfill your dreams unless you tell him what
they are? Remember, it was his ability to listen
that attracted you to him in the first place. So
keep the channels open at all times.

With just the right amount of sparkling dialogue,
your love story will unfold chapter by chapter,
revealing a fun-filled adventure for life.

Taking the Plunge—WATER

CANCER (June 22–July 22)
SCORPIO (October 24–November 21)
PISCES (February 19–March 20)

You adjust your face mask and check your oxygen supply before heading to deeper water. One look at your hero beside you, handsome even in scuba gear, assures you this was the right decision. Hand in hand, you approach the sunken ship, wondering what treasures await....

In poetry, water is often a metaphor for feelings. And water-sign romantics, true to their element, are the most misty-eyed in the galaxy. For you, the adventure of finding true love involves total immersion in the boundless seas of emotion.

Water is also the element associated with intuition, magic and mystery. You are the most sensitive and attuned of all signs. In fact, you possess the quality of empathy, the ability to feel not only your own feelings, but those of someone you're with.

Cancer tends to gently spread the emotional net over the one nearest and dearest. Scorpio yearns for a complete nuclear fusion of souls, while Pisces prefers some lighter, fairy-tale magic in a romance.

And you know your intuition is your strongest ally in finding your true love. You may even tell your friends, "I'll just know when it's him." You believe love can blossom at first sight, that you'll just flow into each other's arms without saying a word. You're also more likely than other signs to believe in soul mates.

You tend to follow your heart rather than the voice of reason. This is mostly a good thing, because your intuition is so finely tuned. But it can lead you into darker waters. This happens when your heart is saying "yes," and your common sense—and often your friends and relations—are telling you "no."

For once you give your heart to someone, your devotion is total. Then you may be swept away by emotional currents. It's very difficult for you to reverse course and extricate yourself once involved.

But you can turn the tide by remembering one thing: Don't be so quick to plunge in emotionally. Make the real adventure creating lasting love. Take a long time to get to know your hero. Make very sure your heart and your head are sending you the same signal before you make any commitment to him.

Once you learn this, you'll find it easier to find your perfect match. And he'll be someone who loves navigating the depths of feeling with you, with whom you can sail into the sunset, off on an adventure-filled voyage to true happiness.

Part II

Traveling Companions

The journey toward true love may be the ultimate adventure. Looking for a new hero to travel with? Or maybe you just met someone and wondered if he's the one. Perhaps you'd simply like more insight into your current companion.

A man's astrological sign reveals a lot about how he approaches romance. Following is a guide to the zodiac's twelve travelers, Aries through Pisces—what to look for and what to look out for!

Aries (March 21–April 19)
"Like a rolling stone..."

Hurtling down love's highway with an Aries will never be dull. This hero boldly and confidently takes on all life puts in his way. And he inevitably assumes the lead, charming everyone with his animal magnetism that is fused with infectious, boyish charm. He's definitely the one who can whisk you through airport gates and past customs officials with lightning speed. But be aware he's very impatient with slowpokes who impede his progress. When things don't go as he likes, he can rage or sulk, and often rubs up against those in authority. You may then have to play the diplomat to smooth things over. But all in all, you can trust your Aries to keep the sense of adventure very much alive over the long haul.

Taurus (April 20–May 20)
"Can't get there from here..."

Never try to get a Bull to charge headlong into anything. His natural instinct is to resist any kind of movement or change. He insists on having all the facts but can then think of a hundred reasons for not doing anything. This reluctance is due to the fact that he never makes commitments lightly. He needs to get to know you—really know you—first. A Taurus man will also hold back on the expenses, including hearts and flowers. Still, there's a great deal of romance in his gentle soul. He simply prefers moonlight walks and quiet outings to far-flung adventures. If you also love a stroll down romantic byways, growing slowly and steadily closer to the goal of happily ever after, then a Taurus is for you.

Gemini (May 21–June 21)
"I'm here, I'm there..."

A Gemini man makes certain the route holds plenty of surprises. He's restless and mercurial; it's like trying to keep up with a bird. He can flit from one thing to another, easily doing two things at once. Last-minute changes of schedule never throw him; he adapts and moves on. This guy is also a great communicator, who can talk to anyone about just about anything. Add his witty sense of humor, and the package seems perfect. However, just when you need him most, you sometimes find he's flown the coop. Never fear. He will come back; just be prepared to be left on your own occasionally. But if you can put up with this idiosyncrasy, you'll have a traveling companion who constantly challenges your mind and lifts your spirits.

Cancer (June 22–July 22)
"A clinging vine gathers no moss..."

A Cancer man tends to be a homebody who doesn't like to travel much, literally or figuratively. Since security is everything to him, adventure tends to make him nervously retreat into his shell. But you have only to reassure him your feelings will never change, no matter what, and he'll get on board. Just be prepared to take the lead and set the itinerary. He'll revel in your strength, and play a supporting role superlatively. He also loves children and doesn't mind having them along for the ride. Your Crab is also very shrewd with money, and will take budgeting chores off your hands without complaint. You'll find he's at your side when needed most, and always, always there in a pinch.

Leo (July 23–August 22)
"Walk in my shadow..."

Traveling with this hero often feels like making a royal progress. He invariably carries himself with a kingly air, and goes out of his way to treat you like a queen. He'll wine and dine you in regal style, and may put on quite a performance. He needs you to be an appreciative audience for his attempts to dazzle you. And he'll love it if you tactfully never upstage him. Still, behind all the showmanship lies a good heart and a hero who's fond of children. He's also the ultimate romantic. Convinced he's the one you want to travel with? He'll prove a most gallant partner, the one who will carry you across mud puddles and throw rose petals in your path forever.

Virgo (August 23–September 22)
"Are you sure this is the right road...?"

Are you willing to put up with some fusspot ways and a little criticism now and then? Then this guy can turn out to be your true-blue companion for life. Be prepared—he'll never be romantic in the classic sense. In fact, overly dramatic or sentimental scenes make him want to take the next train out. Surprisingly, though, this shy soul is a master of the art of subtle seduction. But you'll see this side only after he's pledged his heart. A Virgo man is very selective and best expresses his love through unselfish giving. If you're the chosen one, your reward is a lifetime commitment with a devoted family man, one who will always be there for you down the road.

Libra (September 23–October 23)
"Waltz me along..."

Libra men have very refined tastes in everything. Romance for him is the highest art form, and he always travels in style. He doesn't like to go solo, either, believing wholeheartedly in long-term partnerships. Add his devastating charm, and no wonder all your girlfriends envy you. But once you buy a ticket to ride along with this man, he'll develop an irritating habit. Where once he was easygoing, he'll contrarily try to rationalize everything. What's really eating him is that he wants everything to be perfect and blames himself when it's not. He just needs a little reassurance that his best efforts are more than enough.

He'll then settle down and become a dashing traveling companion for life.

Scorpio (October 24–November 21)
"The spy who loves you..."

Life with this secretive hero can feel like a ride on the old Orient Express. An air of mystery surrounds him, with undertones of smoldering passion. If you find this combination appealing, he may be the one for you. He possesses a personality that's on the complex, sometimes tortured side. Let him know you've figured him out, and he's hooked. If you can add new twists to the itinerary and keep up a sense of intrigue, he'll totally adore you. He is difficult to get to really know, and until he commits he may make you jump through hoops to prove your love. But once he does decide you're the one, no one has more depth of character or is more devoted to his beloved.

Sagittarius (November 22–December 21)
"My way is the highway..."

This is the sign associated with travel—and so the Sagittarius man may quite literally be your traveling companion. This restless hero takes a long time to settle down, though. Even then, he'll require plenty of freedom. In fact, his desire to take off for distant places often results from a need to prove that point. You may have to learn to put up with his impromptu getaways and agree to separate vacations now and then. He'll love it when you don't place demands on him. But to really win his heart, you must share his dreams. His are very big, wide-screen and full color. You'll be in the picture for life if you can also suggest practical ways to help make them come true.

Capricorn (December 22–January 19) "Ever upward..."

Men of this sign come with stone walls surrounding them—not the most portable of structures. But behind the stern and often forbidding exterior lies a secret romantic. He longs to be free, but doesn't know how, being so hemmed in by his obligations. Words of encouragement and even compliments, providing they're not too flowery, go far with this hero. With time and patience you can lure him out of his craggy lair and unleash the inner man who longs for adventure and excitement. And if you prefer to travel for business, then this is the guy for you. A Capricorn man can easily combine business with pleasure, and many have relationships with their mates that span both home and workplace.

Aquarius (January 20–February 18)
"Space traveller..."

Eccentric and prone to taking the path less traveled—that's the Aquarian way. But if you dream of strolling along, just the two of you, pass on this hero. He tends to view any kind of outing as a group event. In fact, you may get the feeling his wide circle of oddball acquaintances means more to him than you do. Relax—he really is more devoted than most give him credit for. There's a great deal of romance in his soul, but it's his own quirky variety. So accept his friends and be willing to improvise a lot. Plan a few surprises of your own to keep him off balance. Then your life together will be a constant and exciting voyage of discovery.

Pisces (February 19–March 20)
"Touring other realms..."

Do you dream of a fairy-tale life full of wonderful adventures, such as slaying dragons to win your favor? Then a Pisces could be the guy for you. He'll also build you a castle in the air, custom-made to your order with hundreds of rooms. Trouble arises, though, when you try to bring him down to earth. Traveling in the stratosphere is more his style than dealing with life's day-to-day trials and tribulations. He also hates real-life confrontations, and so you may have to fight some of his battles for him. If you don't mind keeping one foot on the ground for both of you, you can live an enchanted voyage snug in the arms of a compassionate and dreamy soul.

Part III—Your Romance Outlook for 2002

Is this the year you get on the fast track to romance? Or do you prefer the slow, winding route? Look up your own sign and see what 2002 holds in store.

If you were born on the cusp of two signs, or around the time they change, some horoscopes might tell you you're one sign, another that you're the following sign. For instance, if your birthday is August 22, this horoscope indicates you are a Leo, while another might say Virgo. Because no year is exactly 365 days long, the calendar date a sign changes varies slightly from year to year. Sometimes the only way to know for sure is to have your chart calculated by an astrologer.

**Your 2002 Romance Outlook
Aries (March 21–April 19)**

Overview: You're able to dance around your emotions, dazzling those around you with your energy and ideas. Lately, others just aren't impressed with your fancy footwork. Slow down the pace this year. Try some plain speaking, stating your feelings clearly. Once you do, you'll increase your chances of meeting a hero who gets right in step and waltzes you away without missing a romantic beat.

Timeline: If attached, your other half supports your loftiest ideals in early January, though Valentine's Day may find him a bit distracted. The romantic urge may make a fool out of you in April, a month full of flirtations and invitations. May sweeps in, bringing rough winds, and an ultimatum around the twenty-sixth that proves to be more than hot air. Home is where your heart is until July. Whether married or single, romance is best found around your base of operations. From August on, though, your romance potential soars no matter where you are. Late September through October, your other half challenges your every move. You can sidestep any argument. Just assert yourself with ingenuity and firmness. Open up to new possibilities for growth with your partner, perhaps by enrolling in a course together during November. December brings a light and generous trend, with several candidates lining up under the mistletoe.

Times when love comes easily your way: March 9-21, June 6-25, November 27-December 1
Take the romantic initiative: January 19-February 1, October 23-25 and November 12-15

Your 2002 Romance Outlook
Taurus (April 20–May 20)

Overview: Being in harmony with a special someone hits the top of the charts for you. Recently, themes of love and loss tend to prevail. But this is your year to write lyrics more to your liking. Aspects favor finding the one who teaches you a different, happier tune. The only sour note: finances. Just be honest and clear and you'll forestall any difficulties.

Timeline: A past association comes back to haunt you as the year begins. You easily lay the ghost to rest by Valentine's Day. March looks most promising for a lively, new rapport to begin. You feel surges of power off and on all year, especially in May and September. Don't act on them too strongly, or you could short-circuit a new romantic prospect. Your sweet and gentle nature shines through most in mid-June. You could easily attract someone new to stop and smell the roses with. The summer months pass in a blissfully romantic haze, whether you're in a new or existing relationship. You're still a bit distracted heading into fall, but in October it's back to business. By November, prospects are excellent for meeting a partner in life and love. Just don't let your rose-colored glasses blind you to some glaring faults. The holiday season revolves around more than one gift-shopping excursion on the arm of your hero.

Times when love comes easily your way: April 2-25, July 16-22, November 17-24
Take the romantic initiative: March 2-21, May 14-19 and October 20-27

Your 2002 Romance Outlook
Gemini (May 21–June 21)

Overview: Yours is a butterfly nature that loves to flit from feeling to feeling. The current phase finds you more subdued, even withdrawn. It's just your time to cocoon and form a new personality. You're set to emerge soon, more sure of yourself and what you want in a relationship. You may have to spell this out clearly this year— and more than once. But once you do, your romantic heart takes flight.

Timeline: January heralds a bright new romance to lighten your heart, though your beloved gets a wire crossed around the eighteenth. Someone new could declare his intentions in early March. Resist giving a firm answer, but rather, begin negotiations. In May, a volatile situation triggers some indecision and a little anger. This is one time you should follow your heart and not your head. July ushers in a balmy trend, with whispers of love to caress your ear. You could warm up to the advances of someone you once gave the cold shoulder to. A mood of disenchantment strikes you mid-September. By the end of October, though, the frog you kissed displays princelike qualities. November puts a budding relationship in the deep freeze. Use the pause to reevaluate your true desires. By December, you're very sure of your heart and purpose.

Times when love comes easily your way: January 30-February 2, April 26-May 21, November 25-30
Take the romantic initiative: March 9-18, July 24-27 and November 5-16

Your 2002 Romance Outlook
Cancer (June 22–July 22)

Overview: Most Crabs now feel sidetracked on the path to true love. Just steer clear of clinging types who play on your good nature. Set a course straight toward those who can stand on their own feet and are willing to give you a hand in return. Through August, self-confidence is your best asset in romance. Overcome your natural shyness and speak first. You might like the reply.

Timeline: January's chill finds you in your hero's snug embrace. Any plans for making it a permanent berth will hit a snag or two, though. By Valentine's Day, all is cozy once more. In May, concerns with work consume most of your time. Your other half may resent the change, which makes you feel caught between obligations. But by mid-June you strike upon a mutually suitable arrangement over shared time and space. You gather your rosebuds into the summer months. Single Cancers find being impetuous in an *affaire de coeur* quite thrilling in August. Go ahead, tumble headlong into a new rapport, if you're eligible. You regain your footing in the fall, amidst some turbulent trends. You may find your hero blowing hot and cold, though you're decidedly tepid. By December, stability returns to your life, and with it the warm and comforting glow of romance.

Times when love comes easily your way: February 21-March 7, May 21-June 1, December 4-11
Take the romantic initiative: January 14-19, August 16-21 and November 28-December 6

Your 2002 Romance Outlook
Leo (July 23–August 22)

Overview: Sighing over loves lost? Soon the good things you've been seeing go out with the tide begin to return. Your natural warmth and radiant romanticism are the beacons that draw true love your way. By year's end you realize your romantic ship has come in at last. Some tender reassurances provide a safe mooring for your intended and speeds the process.

Timeline: The year dawns on a dull and uninspired romantic scene. By February, a creative burst helps you paint a new picture, which piques the interest of someone new. April's breezes brush the cobwebs off a relationship you thought was shelved. If the old flame is rekindled, by late May it will be a full blaze. Still, time may prove this person is far too controlling for your emotional health. If you're eligible, someone from out of town could whisk you off on a romantic interlude in June. You then stall in the summer doldrums, but by August you're back in your element. You're ready to roar, and someone close listens and adores. Mid-October brings a slowing trend in an existing relationship. It's a great time to revise and reevaluate any plans. December's exciting social calendar fill up quickly, though the whirl proves a bit stressful. Best delay any moves toward cohabitation with your intended until the new year.

Times when love comes easily your way: January 21-February 1, June 15-July 6, December 8-15
Take the romantic initiative: May 3-14, July 14-17 and October 29-November 4

Your 2002 Romance Outlook
Virgo (August 23–September 22)

Overview: Clarity of intention is your greatest asset in romance. You leave the petty games to others, and always play it straight from the heart. Unfortunately you have a tendency to hide this sterling quality under a bushel. This is your year to emerge and let it shine. You'll feel uncomfortable at first, it's true. But a little boldness helps you attract a new hero, one with a heart of purest gold.

Timeline: You revel in a quiet flirtation in January. It may not come to anything, but a little frivolity helps brighten the winter. Early March brings a trend in which friendship and passion combine easily. By May, though, the urge to bluntly speak your mind is overwhelming. Someone will be wounded by your words unless you choose them carefully. A conflict over career versus family concerns preoccupies you in June. You may have to make some major adjustments to your schedule. The summer seems peaceful, with your other half willing to play your game. Set some new ground rules while you have the chance. By mid-October you'll need them, as your partner in love and life proves fractious. December's trends promise plenty of opportunity for romance, but only if you make the effort. Romance doesn't arrive gift-wrapped now; *cherchez l'amour*.

Times when love comes easily your way: February 21-March 2, July 10-21, October 30-November 7
Take the romantic initiative: March 3-14, October 11-20 and December 8-14

Your 2002 Romance Outlook
Libra (September 23–October 23)

Overview: Your heart's desire has seemed a distant dream for far too long. But planetary alignments suggest setting sights on new romantic horizons. And when a likely new hero comes into view, don't try to hurry him along. It will take time to bring this relationship into full focus. The latter half of the year expands your social sphere exponentially—a nice bonus.

Timeline: Winds of change buffet you through January. Somehow you have the feeling you're being pushed toward Mr. Right. By mid-February you're more sure of your direction and may make your feelings known to someone new. Attached Libras should use April's trends to spring-clean their relationship. Toss out any aspect you don't need. Whether single or married, you'll be ready to turn over a new leaf on togetherness in May. Just don't expect commitment to blossom around the twenty-sixth. The summer unfolds fair and sociable—just the way you like it. An air of nostalgia pervades throughout, and an old flame tries to light a new spark at a family gathering. Mark mid-October as a time for reassessing romantic goals and aspirations. Money may be a sticking point then, so do whatever it takes to smooth the way. By December you're back on track, enjoying a whirlwind holiday season full of romantic promise.

Times when love comes easily your way: February 21-March17, June 6-12, August 7-21
Take the romantic initiative: June 3-14, September 19-23 and December 6-8

Your 2002 Romance Outlook
Scorpio (October 24–November 21)

Overview: You're writing the book of love now—a study in contrasts with a very complicated plot. Your story builds to a romantic peak late in the year. You'll savor more sweetness than you ever imagined existed. But you may be the target of someone's possessiveness. Since this is a page from your book, you'll recognize the plot. You can set some limits and rules, without spoiling the story line altogether.

Timeline: Love is in the air as the new year begins. But distant concerns, many of which involve travel, keep you away from your beloved more than you would wish. Communications hit a snag in February, but ease enough to let a Valentine's Day card or two through. April bids fair and a good time to hit the road as a twosome, or to meet someone new along the way. In May, home or family concerns demand a lot of your energy. But your devotion pays off when a relation introduces you to someone new. The summer period brings ample opportunity for sweet togetherness. You're willing to let many old bygones go. A spiritual breakthrough in September leaves you pondering the subject of soul mates. By mid-October, though, you're dealing with more mundane matters, such as shared space and time together. Over the holiday period, invitations flow, making space on your agenda at a premium.

Times when love comes easily your way: January 6-9, May 17, July 24-30, November 20-27
Take the romantic initiative: April 2-8, September 11-12 and December 1-8

Your 2002 Romance Outlook
Sagittarius (November 22–December 21)

Overview: Your romantic ideal—a hero who shares your sense of fun and is as good a sport as you are. A reliable contender awaits just around the corner. He's a little stodgy and keeps challenging you, which makes you impatient. It could open new channels of communication, though. If you can listen to reason and not reject the situation out of hand, a long-term commitment could be yours this year.

Timeline: Early in January you may feel as if the fleet sailed without you. By the end of the month you're out of dry dock, but Valentine's Day may not be as fun as expected. Someone wants to speak his heart, but is too shy to do so. If you're attached, issues over shared space are resolved during March. You're more willing to compromise then, which helps. May's tense atmosphere stifles a budding romance. By late in the month, your partner may throw down a gauntlet you're only too willing to pick up. Summer brings a calming trend; as the weather heats up, tensions cool. You burn up the lines in August, prime time for creative communications, or possibly a courtship by correspondence. As autumn leaves start to fall, so do your expectations regarding love. But your unfailing optimism rebounds by November's end, when a getaway holds romantic promise. December provides ample opportunity to show loved ones your true feelings.

Times when love comes easily your way: February 6-11, April 26-May 1, November 14-17
Take the romantic initiative: June 6-12, October 7-9 and December 16-21

Your 2002 Romance Outlook
Capricorn (December 22–January 19)

Overview: You begin the year counting the romantic rainy days, wondering how to spend them. But don't just wait for sunnier times—get out and mingle. You could meet someone new who will prove to be much more than a fair-weather friend. This new hero will help you sail above the dark clouds, into a new romantic slipstream.

Timeline: Your romance potential hits a new low early in the year, but it's merely a case of the best is yet to come. During February, single Capricorns find ample dating prospects around office coffeepots and watercoolers. The passion quotient soars in March. Whether single or attached, you find the one you're with more romantically spontaneous than usual. In May, the health of someone close troubles you, and you rely on your other half to bolster your morale. You shift gears easily in June, getting into a romantic mode. You devote much time over the summer months to finding new avenues to explore à deux. Avoid long trips in August; love is more inviting closer to home and September looks promising for impromptu getaways. During October you need more time to yourself. Try negotiating this rather than just withdrawing. You may have to weather one or two dark days in November. The holiday period is full of light, mostly dancing in your eyes.

Times when love comes easily your way: January 3-9, May 21-29, September 5-15
Take the romantic initiative: February 14-22, June 23-July 1 and November 14-16

Your 2002 Romance Outlook
Aquarius (January 20–February 18)

Overview: You're tempted to give up on romance. No wonder—patterns have been highly erratic for so long. But take heart; the sensation that you have one skin too few is easing. You're able to solidly stand your ground by late in the year. With your new strength comes a whole new outlook on love. Then you can negotiate the kind of relationship that uplifts and supports your freedom-loving ways.

Timeline: Tumbling head over heels late in January, you're left quite breathless. February's patterns help you regain solid footing with time for sober reflection. The sticking point: what you really need versus what you can get. A spring fling seems just the thing in May, though the passion factor quickly cools. By the end of the month, you'll tire of this person's possessive ways. June finds you in the mood for lighthearted flirtation. Consider it a dress rehearsal for the summer months, when you'll play out many long, languid love scenes. By mid-September you'll know if your summer romance will last through the winter. The fall is wonderfully stable, and you can pretty well write any kind of love scenario you please. Flag the end of November as a time when relationships become too entangled for comfort. But by the time the holiday period kicks off, the way to your heart's desire lies straight and clear.

Times when love comes easily your way: February 21-March 4, June 16-27, October 14-19
Take the romantic initiative: March 6-14, August 5-14 and December 16-19

Your 2002 Romance Outlook
Pisces (February 19–March 20)

Overview: Beautiful dreamer, more than ever your soul longs for romance. Yet you've tried to stifle that tendency of late, which is a shame. Release your hidden longings and let them take wing. You could very well meet someone whose spirit is on the same flight path. The latter half of the year especially, you may come blissfully down to earth with him. But as ever, at all costs avoid opportunist types, who now come disguised as underdogs.

Timeline: January brings a thaw to an old antipathy. You may finally bury the hatchet with an ex for good. Having cleared the decks, by March you're in an excellent position to meet someone new at a vacation spot, whether near or far. May is a turbulent month, so batten the hatches. Ignore any ultimatums around the twenty-sixth. The relationship climate turns far milder during June, and is downright balmy by July. August, though, sizzles with romantic potential. Get out and mingle at a favorite sunspot if you're single and looking. Disillusionment clouds the romantic atmosphere around mid-September. But if you can ride it out until October, you'll be able to work out a lot through slow but steady negotiating. November offers many opportunities for snuggling by the fire. By the holiday season, though, you may very well make a dramatic appearannce on the arm of someone new.

Times when love comes easily your way: January 6-14, June 15-23, November 4-11
Take the romantic initiative: May 29-June 3, October 23-27 and December 22-3

*Together for the first time
in one Collector's Edition!*

New York Times bestselling authors

Barbara Delinsky

Catherine Coulter

Linda Howard

Forever Yours

**A special trade-size volume containing three
complete novels that showcase the passion,
imagination and stunning power that these
talented authors are famous for.**

Coming to your favorite retail outlet in December 2001.

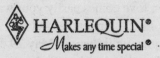